Tiffa

cripes.

hat if she got a hard-on?

r what if she didn't?

he women were gorgeous, spinning around the s in the centre of the stage. Tiffany couldn't stare t any one too long. Making eye-contact was the worst. ach time she found herself captivated by the rotations one of the dancers, the girl would inevitably come over to her, offer a lap dance, and the guys would hoot d howl their encouragement.

'Which one do you like?' Axel wanted to know.

'They're all lovely,' Tiffany said. No, that sounded lame. Nothing like Kurt would say. Ever. 'I mean, sexy,' she amended quickly.

'Yeah, but which one's your favourite?'

She squinted up at the stage. Which girl would Kurt like best? She didn't know. But these guys probably did. 'I like the girl in the nurse's outfit best. She could take my temperature any time she wanted.'

The other men seemed drunk enough to accept this, and Tiffany let loose a sigh of relief. One that died on her lips as Rick waved the girl over and motioned to Tiffany's lap.

12107133

By the same author:

RUMOURS

SWEET THING

STICKY FINGERS

WITH OR WITHOUT YOU

Tiffany Twisted

Alison Tyler

In real life, always practise safe sex.

This edition published in 2006 by
Cheek
Thames Wharf Studios
Rainville Road
London W6 9HA

Copyright © Alison Tyler 2006

The right of Alison Tyler to be identified as the Author of
the Work has been asserted by her in accordance with the Copyright,
Designs and Patents Act 1988.

Design by Smith & Gilmour, London
Printed and bound by Mackays of Chatham PLC

ISBN 0 352 34039 8
ISBN 9 780352 34039 9

*All characters in this publication are fictitious and any resemblance
to real persons, living or dead, is purely coincidental.*

This book is sold subject to the condition that it shall not, by way
of trade or otherwise, be lent, resold, hired out or otherwise
circulated without the publisher's prior written consent in any form
of binding or cover other than that in which it is published and
without a similar condition including this condition being imposed
on the subsequent purchaser.

For Sam

SANDWELL LIBRARY & INFORMATION SERVICE	
I2107133	
Bertrams	19.08.06
GEN	£8.99

'*Girls will be boys and boys will be girls –*'
Lola, The Kinks

'*Her mind is Tiffany-twisted –*'
Hotel California, The Eagles

Prologue

'Rowdy, aren't they?'

Melissa spoke as if she thought the multitude of tourists crowding the main avenue in New Orleans' French Quarter were cute. But 'cute' wasn't the word Tiffany would have used. Being jostled by the swarm of unruly party-goers did nothing to help her mood. The more she was rushed along, the more she wanted to stand entirely still.

Tiffany had never seen so many brightly colored outfits in one place. All were the type found in department store 'cruise wear' sections – sweaters adorned with sequinned palm trees or multicolored dancing cocktail shakers, bowling shirts with animated hot-sauce bottles cavorting on the back. Even though Christmas was only three weeks away, you wouldn't catch Tiffany dressed in a reindeer sweatshirt that actually lit up. She'd chosen her outfits for the trip with extreme care, excited about the opportunity to journey away from the Bay Area and delve into a city known for a twenty-four-hour nightlife. Not that San Francisco could ever be considered boring, but it was *home*, and Tiffany ached for a change.

In S.F., she tended to choose all black, like most Northern California natives, relying on an adult version of Garanimals, the matchy-matchy outfits created for toddlers. Black goes with everything – that was the philosophy, but Tiffany wasn't an adventurous dresser even within the confines of her stark color scheme. She strove to emulate the sleek sophistication of her style icons, Lauren Bacall and Audrey Hepburn, and was the type to carefully decide between earrings *or* a necklace, never both. Her favorite piece of jewelry was an antique wristwatch left to her by her grandfather, featuring a mother-of-pearl face and a thick black leather band. It wasn't that she didn't like clothes or adornments, only that she had her own personal uniform.

Here, in the much more tropical south, she'd decided to take more risks. Today, she had on stovepipe jeans and a form-fitting cashmere turtleneck in dove gray that emphasized her sleek physique. Her long birch-blonde hair flowed loosely past her shoulders, and she'd actually tucked a fragrant white flower behind her ear before leaving the hotel. Melissa had muffled her laughter at Tiffany's 'branching out'. Gray was simply black with a lot of white mixed in it; but she'd known Tiffany too long to point out her observation.

'I can't stand this!' Tiffany hollered to Melissa. 'I feel as if we're caught in rush hour traffic on the Golden Gate Bridge ... minus the cars.'

'For someone wearing a flower behind her ear, you sure don't act as if you're on vacation,' Melissa grinned, not nearly as testy as Tiffany felt. Melissa enjoyed the chaos, bobbing and weaving through the crowd as if moving to the beat at a Grateful Dead show, and Tiffany was jealous of how laid-back her friend was. The duo were in the Big Easy for a four-day getaway, a last girls'-only fling before Melissa got married. If anyone should have been showing a sign of nervousness, it was Melissa. But Tiffany had always been the more uptight partner in their friendship.

Without a thought, Tiffany plucked the flower from her hair and started to violently pull off the waxy white petals. Melissa shook her head at her, and then moved in close. 'Relax, Tiff. This is just one big street party. You have to remember that. We don't have any schedule. There's no place we have to be.'

Tiffany took a deep breath and nodded. She'd try. That's what her look told Melissa. But she liked schedules. Knowing what was next on the agenda was *how* she relaxed. 'He loves me,' she said as she tossed the last petal onto the litter-strewn ground.

'Well, that's good news at least,' Melissa said, smiling.

The women did their best to make their way through the drunken throng. Instead, they became swept up in the joyous sea, until Melissa got smart and pulled Tiffany around a corner and off the main thoroughfare. And that's when they spotted the Witches' Shoppe.

'Let's go,' Melissa urged, her dark brown eyes lighting up.

This was the type of entertainment she adored. Melissa had an old ouija board hidden away in her bedroom closet at home and she routinely checked her horoscope in the *SF Weekly*.

Unsure, Tiffany hung back.

'I've been dying to get my tarot read ever since we got off the plane,' Melissa insisted. 'This is the city for it. You can practically feel the power in the air. Mysticism. Voodoo. *Magic.*' She tried to make the words sound inviting, adding intricate hand gestures to accompany her ardent sales pitch, but Tiffany was having none of it. 'You can find out how Kurt really feels about you,' Melissa offered, trying another tactic.

'I know that already. The flower told me.'

'Then I can find out what Rick really thinks –'

'You're wearing an engagement ring the size of a gum ball. If you don't know by now, then you're in serious trouble.'

'All right,' Melissa said, but she wasn't willing to give up. 'Then I can ask whether I'm going to be made partner this year.' Melissa was a lawyer for a nonprofit agency. She liked to say she was a lawyer, but not a *'lawyer*-lawyer'. Still, she possessed a fierce competitive streak.

'After –' Tiffany told her. Melissa raised her dark eyebrows, as Tiffany pointed to the Magnolia Jazz Bar two storefronts down. 'Let's get a Hurricane first. I'm not ready to face my future sober.'

'What do *you* have to worry about?' Melissa teased. '*I'm* the one about to get married!'

'I can tell your fortune for free – you and Rick will drive off in his convertible Porsche and live happily ever after ... It's what's going to happen to me and Kurt that concerns me. In spite of what that flower had to say.'

Melissa laughed and the two women entered the small dark jazz bar together, instantly enveloped by the mellow sound of New Orleans rhythm.

If they'd had only the one drink, it would have been late afternoon when they left the bar. But Hurricanes are addictive, and the sun had already started to set before the duo was back out on the street.

'Too bad,' Tiffany murmured in feigned disappointment. 'The store will definitely be closed by now.'

'No, look –' Melissa pointed. 'The open sign's out. Let's go, Tiff.'

Tiffany could barely walk in a straight line, so arguing was out of the question. Especially arguing with Melissa, who tended to win even the mildest disagreements. Resigning herself to spending at least a few minutes in the store, Tiffany followed her best friend up three rickety wooden stairs and into the tiny shop.

She had to squint in the dim light as Melissa forged ahead. The place was nearly as dark as the jazz bar had been, but instead of encountering the scents of old beer and spilled wine, the women were greeted with fragrant incense, wisps of silvery smoke curling up to the ceiling. Tiffany's nose wrinkled. If she'd been on her own, she would have turned around right then. Unfortunately, Melissa was already busy poking through the multitude of objects filling the store, items Tiffany wouldn't have touched for money. The twosome had shopped at various touristy locations on their trip so far, but this store didn't offer any of those slogan-emblazoned T-shirts or water-filled 'N'Awlin's' globes. At this moment, Tiffany would have happily spent time in a well-lit storefront, perusing beer steins and shot glasses, key chains and 'gator postcards.

'Isn't this amazing?' Melissa insisted. Apparently, what was creepy to Tiffany equalled authentic to Melissa. 'Look at all this –'

Tiffany looked. She couldn't believe how crammed the place was. Polished bones crowded a basket right next to the door, and the floor was made uneven with handwoven rugs, embroidered with various dark designs. Tiffany liked sunny rooms. White walls. Large windows. This place was dank and dusky, and what little light there was simply shifted the shadows from one wall to the next. Politely, she fingered one of the bones in the basket, surprised when a point of it poked her finger. She dropped the bone quickly and brought her wounded finger to her mouth, liking the store even less.

In spite of the 'open' sign, the place appeared to be entirely empty. She looked over at Melissa, wanting desperately to leave, but Melissa continued to be enthralled with everything she saw. Tiffany watched as her friend fingered a few brightly feathered Mardis Gras masks, then hurried over to the multi-colored bottles of essential oils, before slipping several strands of glittery beads over her head.

'Just look,' Melissa kept saying over and over again, oohing delightedly at her various finds. 'Oh, Tiffany, look at this!'

The entire store wasn't much larger than Tiffany's small bedroom back in San Francisco, yet every part was crowded to overflowing. Rows upon rows of candles stood along one wall, and the glass cases by the front were filled with petrified claws, delicate jewelry made from tiny animal bones, and a slew of feathered trinkets. Assorted hand-crafted objects dangled from the ceiling, and Voodoo Dolls nestled in baskets on the counter.

'I love those,' Melissa whispered as she pointed to the burlap dolls decorated with assorted shiny silver pins. 'I should get one of my boss!'

'Why are you whispering?' Tiffany asked, her own voice hushed. 'We're the only ones here.'

Melissa hushed her anyway, pulling Tiffany's wrist toward the back of the store, where an empty round table stood draped in velvet of liquid crimson. 'Tarot Readings, $50' read a sign above the table.

'Fifty dollars!' Tiffany exclaimed.

'It'll be fun,' Melissa promised.

'No way.'

'*Are you sure?*'

This query wasn't spoken by Melissa, and Tiffany wheeled around, surprised. A man stood behind the counter – but he hadn't been there before, had he? He was tall and lean-figured with gingery red hair and a pointed goatee. His eyes were almost startlingly green, like a cat's eyes, and they glinted mesmerizingly even in the dim light. Tiffany realized that he was extremely good-looking. Devilish, maybe, but dangerously handsome. She had a feeling that if she stared at him too hard, he might disappear, like the smoke curling up to the ceiling.

'Fifty dollars doesn't sound so bad now, does it?' Melissa whispered. And then out loud, added, 'I'll go first.'

5

The man gave her an interested look, clearly appraising her midnight-black bob, large liquid brown eyes, and even larger brown pocket book with the expensive logo embossed tastefully beneath the handle. Then he followed her to the table and pulled the dark violet draperies down in front, giving the duo privacy. Tiffany, buzzed from the early evening drinks, made her way unsteadily to look at the scented candles standing in rows. Unlike those at a bed-and-bath store, where she would have found such banal titles as 'sandalwood', 'tuberose', and 'bergamot', these candles were labeled with the names of various desires: *wealth, joy, peace, happiness, success, comfort, balance, fame, revenge* . . .

She toyed with several of the different twisted wax tapers, lifting them to her nose and inhaling the scents, acting almost as if she might buy one. But she didn't believe in this sort of nonsense. Not the way Melissa did. Melissa was forever calling up psychic hot lines, or journeying to one of the dingy storefronts in San Francisco's Sunset District to have her palm read. For a lawyer, she definitely had her own unexpected ideas about things, which Tiffany, as her best friend, could appreciate. The twosome made a good team, because Tiffany was much more level-headed. She never read her horoscope. Didn't believe in numerology. And was completely miffed whenever her boyfriend insisted that she was a true Gemini. 'Split personality,' Kurt liked to tease her, '*especially* in the bedroom.'

Now, as she gazed over the candles, she thought about him.

Kurt was the closest to marriage-material of any man she'd ever dated, but he had his medley of flaws. He seemed drawn to disorder, a magnet for clutter. His apartment was crazy-messy, filled with the type of chaos that looked almost intentional. Who actually had clothes dangling from light fixtures? Occasionally, Kurt did. He found the effect amusing. 'Don't people drape scarves over lamps and call it romantic?' he'd asked her once.

'Sure they do,' Tiffany had responded. 'But silk scarves create a slightly different ambiance than socks.'

Tiffany hated spending the night there, trying to locate the items she needed in order to feel at ease. She'd taken to bringing over her own little heart-shaped toiletry bag, rather than hope he might have the toothpaste she liked or the brand of mouthwash she favored. And even that wasn't enough. Kurt never kept coffee in the house, preferring to buy it fresh each morning – or so he claimed. He couldn't be bothered to prepare for the future, like for the fact that Tiffany might be sleeping over, that she might crave a cup of java before leaving the building. Worse than that, there was no way they could ever entertain in his apartment, in its constant state of disarray. Tiffany was a party planner who owned her own business: entertaining was more than her job – it was her life.

Melissa said she was insane, that Kurt's pros far outweighed his cons, and that the things that did disturb her about Kurt were all easily mendable, like a hole in an old sock. ('One of the socks hanging from the chandelier in his living room?' Tiffany had asked caustically, but Melissa found the whole situation hysterical; she had gleefully once shown Tiffany a magazine spread featuring a starlet who dangled expensive red leather shoes from *her* chandelier, which Tiffany insisted was a different look entirely.)

When Tiffany talked about Kurt, she ticked off his bad habits. He swore too much. He smoked even though he was always promising to quit. He constantly complained about his relationships at work and the fact that he hadn't gotten a raise in two years. His truck was a disaster area that needed a detail job, or perhaps a proper fumigation. He would rather buy a new shirt than iron the ones he had.

All fixable issues, Melissa assured her. In fact, that's what Melissa called him: a fixer-upper. 'He's funny and handsome and kind,' Melissa spoke in Kurt's defense. 'He brings you unexpected gifts on a Tuesday rather than wait for Valentine's Day, and he's the first man in a long time who's known how to make you smile.' Some of Tiffany's other friends disagreed, advising her to leave him and start fresh with someone more suitable, a man who cared about his appearance, *and* his future –

'What's your wish, darlin'?' The shopkeeper asked, yet again appearing unexpectedly at her side. Was the tarot reading already over? And why was he asking her about her wishes?

'What do you mean?'

'Burn a candle, get a wish –'

'How much?' Melissa asked, striding over to Tiffany's side.

'Five dollars each, or three for ten.'

'That sounds fair,' Melissa said. She seemed to want Tiffany to join in on the exotic experience.

'Different candles, different wishes,' the man continued, his focus on Tiffany. 'What do you truly want, hon? Money? Fame? Love?'

She hesitated. What did she wish for? That was simple:

To have one month – that's all – just one month in Kurt's life. He was a good guy at the heart of things. Melissa was right. He had a decent soul and a considerate nature, and he was as relaxed as she was tightly wound. Whenever she was having a bad day, or needed extra help at an important event, he was right at her side, rubbing her shoulders, folding linen napkins with her, doing whatever was required. Their tastes overlapped in music, movies and literature, and they never lacked for subjects to talk about. Even more important, they were exquisite together in bed. Just the thought of Kurt with his hands around her waist, lifting her up for a mammoth embrace, was enough to turn her on.

But he was a fuck-up.

One more in the ever-growing list of fuck-ups she tended to date. Starving artists. Indie rockers. Unappreciated actors. Yes, Kurt was a photographer, but at least he had a decent job, working at a photo service bureau in the city. He wasn't so wishful as to depend on his art work to pay his rent. Yet he possessed an undeniable rebellious streak in him, the very thing that had attracted her to him at the start. But the rebel in him made for a difficult path through life. Tiffany thought about his turquoise Harley Sportster, his inability to arrive anywhere on time, his closet filled with the same outfits he'd worn – and treasured – since college.

Somewhere in her heart, Tiffany knew that Melissa was right; she could change all that. She could bevel out Kurt's rough edges if he gave her the chance – ultimately it was why she stayed with him. He had potential.

'The candles really do work, you know,' the shopkeeper continued in his soothing drawl. That New Orleans accent was so sexy, and Tiffany found herself almost hypnotized by the lyrical sounds of his words. 'You simply light the wick and concentrate on what you most want in this world. The thing you desire above all else. And I promise you, your wish will come true.'

'I don't really believe in this –' Tiffany stopped herself before she added 'garbage' '– stuff,' she finished lamely.

The man didn't seem to hear her. 'They're powerfully magical,' he said as he began lighting different tester candles, as if trying to woo her to choose at least one. 'Hand-dipped wax made at midnight on a full moon. Some other stores sell you the fakes, the phony ones. But these candles are the real deal. Only the most expert sorceress can create a candle that makes your wish come true.'

The fragrances intermingled with the incense, and Tiffany felt suddenly dizzy. It was the Hurricanes, she reassured herself. Too many drinks on an empty stomach. She ought to know better.

'Close your eyes and make your wish,' the man insisted, his voice unrelenting. Tiffany wouldn't. She didn't have any one wish, did she? Only that she could straighten out her boyfriend's life. But that was ridiculous.

Melissa was at her side, touching the different candles delicately as if handling precious jewels. Tiffany watched her as if looking through a silvery cloud. 'I'll take one of each,' Melissa told the man, who beamed at her and began to gather the pretty tapers and wrap them up in colored tissue paper. The rustle of the tissue sounded loud in Tiffany's ears. Her senses felt electrified. The scents of the candles rushed over her. 'I can always give them out as gifts to the girls at the office,' Melissa told to Tiffany, her voice coming in as if from a great distance.

Tiffany found herself mesmerized by a fat blue candle on the nearest shelf. The flame flickered and danced in her eyes, turning orange, then yellow, then a pure heated gold. Like liquid. Like foil. She peered through the smoke to read the hand-written word on the label below, then reached to pick up the candle and bring it even closer to her face. She didn't notice the tiny drop of blood from her hurt finger that fell into the flame. Her eyes were focused on the word written in the wax: LOVE.

She had love. There was no question that she and Kurt

adored each other. She only wished she could have one month as Kurt to shake everything back into order. That's all she needed: a month.

Tiffany left the store with Melissa, not buying a thing.

Chapter One

Morning wood. No problem with that. A quick tug. A firm jerk. What a way to start the day. Awakening with a hard-on is standard in the a.m. At least, it is if you're a guy.

But Tiffany was a girl. So the sturdy pup tent rising up under the shimmering black satin sheets sent a shudder of fear through her. Slowly, she ran her hands over the length of her body, as if she might be able to smooth the alien form away, to turn it back into the womanly frame she knew so well: 5′ 8″ height, slender hips, nice ass, teacup-sized breasts. It was a body she'd grown accustomed to, even if she struggled with an occasional love/hate relationship with herself. *Were her breasts too small? Was her chin too sharp?*

Now that her figure had morphed into something new and strange, she missed every inch, ever curve of her former self. Knowing somehow that this wouldn't work, she shut her eyes tightly and then quickly opened them again hoping that the previous vision of herself trapped in a boy's body had been a dream.

No such luck.

Her hands – *man's* hands, she realized now – roamed over a firm muscular chest, then slid down an admirably flat stomach before disappearing under the shiny rumpled sheets. Tentatively, those hands moved lower, until they cupped questioningly around the hard-on waiting there. A forceful pulse of pleasure – unlike anything she'd ever felt before – beat through her immediately. Tiffany pulled her hand away fast, as if from something hot.

Without a doubt, she knew that chest.

That stomach.

That cock.

She was in her boyfriend Kurt's body. And this was a dream. It *had* to be a dream. She'd imbibed one too many Hurricanes the night before with Melissa, and Hurricanes were hangovers waiting to happen. That's what Melissa always said. But did the infamous drinks cause more than headaches? Could they be responsible for hallucinations as well? Because she appeared to be in Kurt's bedroom, and she was supposed to have one more morning in New Orleans before heading home to San Francisco.

She shut her eyes halfway. The world was blurry. She *had* drunk too much the night before. No, that wasn't it. Squinting harder, she looked to the top of the bed frame and found Kurt's tortoiseshell glasses. Putting these on made a massive difference. Instantly, her vision returned to normal.

Turning her head from side to side in the dimly lit room, she took in her environment. Yes, this was unmistakably Kurt's bedroom, with the three large round clock faces on the wall over the bed, each labeled with one of Kurt's favorite places: Amsterdam, New York, Honolulu. The times on the clocks reflected the locations, but there was no clock set for San Francisco in the room. Her boyfriend, always late, might be able to tell you when breakfast was ready in the Netherlands, but he had no real concept of time.

Two bold Liechtenstein prints were mounted on the opposite wall above the antique oak dresser, every single drawer of which was open and spilling over with colored T-shirts and frayed oxfords. She knew from experience that Kurt never put anything in its proper place. If he could have gotten away with it, he'd have lived his life with no dresser at all – simply a clean clothes pile and a dirty clothes pile, the heaps ever changing like sands in an hourglass until laundry time arrived again. That's how he had spent his college years, and he often talked about that period in his life with nostalgia. Just one more of the things Tiffany couldn't understand about him – one of the things she couldn't stand, if she were to be perfectly honest.

Come on, how difficult was it to use a hamper?

Yet his aversion to folding his T-shirts with Gap-like precision didn't seem like such a big deal now. Not in comparison to what she was currently going through. If she ever got back into her own body, she would never complain about Kurt's laundry habits again. She'd look at his messy state as an adorable character tic. One that made Kurt who he was.

She promised!

Closing her eyes again, she tried to re-create the previous evening in minute detail. They'd started at the Magnolia Jazz Bar and wound up in the Witches' Shoppe next door. She remembered the sound of the tarot cards being shuffled and the eerie look of the hanging painted masks, the Voodoo Dolls and the rows upon rows of candles ... The multitude of scents seemed to still be on her skin – she put her face to the tender skin on her wrist and breathed in deeply, the heady fragrance tickling her nose – but that was impossible.

Melissa had been the one who wanted to go to the store. That much she remembered. So this was all Melissa's fault. A bubble of insane laughter threatened to escape her lips, but she quickly bit down on the sound, afraid that if she started to laugh she might never stop. She could imagine calling up Melissa and railing against her. 'How could you let me into that store? This cock between my legs is here because of you!' Now, she did laugh, and the familiar sound of Kurt's deep baritone, made her jump.

Had she gone crazy? Was this what going crazy was like? Was the next step a trip in a padded van to a white-walled institution where people wore velveteen bathrobes all day and were never allowed to use sharp objects.

The phone rang, startling her from her worries. Automatically, Tiffany rolled onto her side and reached toward the red lacquered bedside table. She had to shift her hips so as not to crush the new and unexpected protrusion between her legs. How did men deal with this sort of thing? It took her a moment to locate the phone under a rumpled kelly-green T-shirt. *Classic* Kurt.

'Hello?' Her voice was *his* voice, deep and gruff with sleep. She cleared her throat and tried again. 'Hello?' A little clearer, perhaps, yet unmistakably male.

The voice on the other end was speaking so quickly and in such a high-pitched manner that Tiffany couldn't immediately discern the words. 'Slow down, I can't understand you –'

'Who the fuck is this?'

Tiffany thought for a moment. Her whole body quivered with a powerful shudder as she said, 'Kurt Fielding.'

'Well, Kurt Fielding, this is Tiffany Fucking Mitchell –'

Oh, Jesus.

'And I want to know what the f –'

Tiffany suddenly heard Melissa's voice in the background and then the sound of a door closing. She easily pictured the scene, as she'd been in that hotel room only several hours before, had crawled between the crisply ironed hotel sheets and settled her head gratefully on the cool, down-filled pillow. She and Melissa had been given a second-floor room with two queen-sized beds. The windows were covered with white-painted shutters and, when you opened them, you could hear jazz playing from one of the clubs down the street. The sweet seductive music had lulled Tiffany to sleep each night of their trip.

What was happening?

Her head throbbed, and she felt a strange craving inside her. She wanted something urgently, but what? Her eyes scanned the room, taking in the two cameras on the desk in the corner – one digital, one an old-fashioned Nikon – the empty rolls of film, the tripod. Finally, she saw the overflowing ashtray next to a crumpled-up pack of Marlboros on the top of the dresser. She shook her head. Kurt had promised her that he was going to quit. Apparently, during her trip, he'd decided not to bother hiding the evidence of his addiction.

'Hey, sleepyhead, are you up finally?' she heard Melissa saying. 'Those Hurricanes knocked you the hell out, huh? You're such a lightweight, Tiff. I've already been out for coffee and beignets. Are you talking to Kurt?'

'Yeah,' came the mildly confused sound of her own voice through the phone. 'Yeah, I'm talking to Kurt.' The words were evenly spaced out, as if the speaker were conversing in another language.

'Well, remind him that he's picking us up at the airport. And tell him not to be late. Last time, we had to wait for over an hour.'

Burn a candle, get a wish –

Different candles. Different wishes.

What do you want? Money? Fame? Love?

What had been *her* wish?

To have one month in Kurt's body. And it looked as if her

wish had come true. But how in the world was she going to explain that to her boyfriend?

'I'll call you back,' her own voice told her. 'I need a cup of fucking coffee. And about seventeen aspirin.'

While she waited for Kurt to ring back, Tiffany looked down at her body again, naked, still half-aroused. Curiously, she put one hand between her legs, softly touching herself, and instantaneously she felt that part of Kurt's body spring forward, almost as if it were expecting her to stroke its powerful length. Almost as if it knew she would.

Down, boy, she thought, remembering waking up next to Kurt in the morning. He was always ready for a dawn lovemaking session, no matter how early the hour, no matter how late they'd gone to bed the previous evening. 'You want to?' was his standard morning greeting. Now, she knew exactly what it felt like to have something so insistent between her legs.

Without thinking, she made a firm fist around Kurt's erection. The corresponding pleasure felt like a low, powerful hum that ran throughout her entire body. Was this thing ever sensitive! She continued her explorations cautiously, moving her hand along the delicate skin, up the shaft to the bulbous head, learning as she went. Of course, she knew what *she* liked in bed, and up until now she'd thought she knew what Kurt liked. Over their four years together, she'd had her way with this part of Kurt's anatomy many times, and he'd always seemed pleased by any attention she gave him. But the experience of being on the inside of his body made things totally different. It was as if a little voice in her head were pushing her forward, telling her exactly what to do next.

Rather quickly she discovered that the slightest bit of pressure went a long way on the road to pleasure. When she squeezed her fist even a tiny bit tighter, she had to lean back against Kurt's pillows, overpowered by the sensations that ran through her. In this more comfortable pose, she continued caressing herself with more determination. She did all of this without any advanced planning. Kurt's body seemed to demand the treatment she was giving it; who was she to deny what it so obviously craved?

As her heart began to race faster, she started to pick up the speed with her fist, holding on tighter, giving herself little intermittent squeezes. Here was something Kurt had tried to explain to her in the past, telling her that she didn't have to be afraid of his cock, or of touching him with more force as their encounters progressed. But he'd never been able to describe how it felt – not that she'd quizzed him that often. Fleetingly, she wondered why she hadn't. Wouldn't he have been charmed by her natural curiosity as to what pleasure felt like from a male point of view?

The excitement continued to build rapidly as she cruised her hand up and down the shaft of his cock. *Oh, yes*, she thought. That was right. That was unbelievable. Her hand seemed to know exactly what to do, and she could feel this body urging her onward. *Don't stop*, that voice told her. *Don't stop –*

Her fingers tightened, her palm slid up and down, faster, faster. She thought of making love to Kurt. She thought of kissing him, of having him kiss her. She thought of the time that they'd had sex in the back of his truck, out by the Marina, the cool air rushing over their bodies, the sound of the surf lapping at the shore. He had spread a blanket beneath them, taking her on the roughness of the fabric, pressing so hard on her that she could feel the cool metal of the truck bed beneath –

Climaxing happened unexpectedly. Tiffany cried out as the wetness met her fingertips, and her entire body was wracked with spasms. She could feel the blissful waves of release work through her, and she felt contentment immediately replace that sensation of impending pleasure.

Oh, God, that was good.

For several seconds, she lay there in a state of post-orgasmic delirium, breathing hard, feeling giddy with what she'd just done. Not so bad for a girl, she thought to herself, mildly puffed up with pride. Who'd have thought she'd be able to master the controls of this body so quickly? Sure, she'd been with a few different guys, but this was different. This was learning to give a hand job from the inside out.

And then it suddenly occurred to her that Kurt might be taking similar liberties with her own body, and she felt her new-found member go totally limp.

Was he playing with her breasts?

Was he fondling her ass?

She knew that Kurt loved to masturbate in the shower. Might he be lathering her up all over right now with the hotel's French-milled soap, as if she had become his own personal plaything? It didn't occur to her that she was being hypocritical. The body had wanted her to do what she just did. *It* had gotten hard without any real help from her. All she'd done was reward her boy self's most basic male needs.

But what was Kurt doing? And what access – if any – did he have to her thoughts, her fantasies, her desires? She wiped her fingertips off on a tissue from a box she found on the floor, half-hidden under the bed. Then she sat up with her back propped against Kurt's headboard and began to massage her temples. Had their entire gray matter been lifted and placed in the shell of the other person, or were there some remnants remaining? If she concentrated hard enough, would she be able to learn more about Kurt, from within his brain?

Oh, this was too crazy. Kurt was right. How could anyone deal with something like this before caffeine? *She* needed coffee, too, which meant that she'd have to go out. And what on earth was she going to wear? Just looking at the multitude of clothing strewn across the floor made her feel exhausted. With a sigh, she climbed out of bed and rummaged through the dresser for clean clothes. After a brief search, she chose red-polka-dot boxers she'd given him the previous Christmas. Then a pair of hideously rumpled jeans. She'd never seen jeans so wrinkled before. Had he rolled them into a ball before shoving them in the dresser? She topped the outfit with a plain gray T-shirt, thinking that she'd have to find an iron somewhere. Did he even own one? She could bring one over from her place. That was if she didn't correct the situation soon.

Dressing was bizarre. She couldn't get used to anything about Kurt's clothing. The buttons were on the wrong side. The shoes were so heavy her feet felt encased in stone. But mostly she really couldn't handle the way it felt to have a –

The phone rang again, and she grabbed the receiver immediately, gearing herself up to hear her own voice talking at her.

'Melissa just went into the shower, so tell me what the fuck is going on.'

She tried her best. In the most matter-of-fact way possible, she described the scene. The shop. The man. The candles. All the while, Kurt made murmuring noises of assent. 'Mmm hmms' and 'yesses' at all the appropriate spots. When she'd finished her story, she told Kurt that he seemed remarkably calm for someone who had woken up more than two thousand miles away from where he'd gone to sleep.

'Yeah, that's only because I'm sure this a dream. One of those super-realistic ones. Like thinking you have a final exam to take, but you didn't study. Or showing up at work totally naked and having everybody point and laugh. You ever have those? Or the flying ones. I *love* the flying ones. I read that they're a really good omen –'

'I don't think that this is –'

He cut her off. 'I'm going to run with it. By the way, exactly how many Hurricanes did you drink last night?'

'I lost count after three.'

'My head is fucking killing me.'

'Sorry –' She started to laugh as she said it, because this was insane. Was she sorry for giving him a hangover, or sorry for magically transporting him into her body? After a moment, he laughed back at her.

'Kurt,' Tiffany said, 'I really don't think this is a dream.'

'It's gotta be, kid. But I'll go down to that store again, just to make fucking sure.'

All day long, Tiffany hoped that Kurt was right. That this *was* a dream and that she'd wake up at any moment, sporting a monster hangover of her own. She knew Melissa would make fun of her, but she could live with that.

'And you jerked him off?' Melissa would say, delighted at the idea.

Sure, Melissa might tease her, but she was Tiffany's best friend in the world. They'd always been there for one another. Happily, Tiffany imagined drinking coffee and dissecting the nightmare of waking up as Kurt. Melissa would get a huge kick out of the whole thing.

Unfortunately, Tiffany didn't wake up.

At first, she paced through Kurt's apartment, just waiting. After several hours, she found herself growing antsy. If this were a dream, it was unlike any she'd ever remembered. It was realistic down to minute details. The sound of the three large clocks ticking. The scent of Kurt's unwashed gym clothes. The drip of the faucet in the bathroom.

Almost without thinking, she started to clean – to do his laundry, to fold his clothes and put them away properly in his dresser and his closet. Just before eight, she called his office and left a voice-mail message, to let them know she – *he* – wasn't feeling himself today. That was true, wasn't it? If this turned out to be a dream, she knew Melissa would have something to say about how she was spending it. Who did laundry in their sleep? Who spent their nightmares covering for their boyfriend at the office? Apparently, Tiffany did.

To keep her hands busy, she organized the bills on his desk and the cutlery in his kitchen drawer. She was midway through throwing out expired medicines in the mirrored cabinet in his bathroom when she understood for a fact that this was real. No dream could be this precise. No dream could conjure up bottles of Tylenol that were more than four years out of date.

Realizing this made her heart race. She tried to get Kurt on her cell phone, but the automated machine picked up, letting her know that the person she was trying to reach was out of range, and would she like to leave a message? She hung up the phone, not having any idea what to say.

After puttering around Kurt's apartment, she ran several errands in the afternoon, her thoughts swimming with different possibilities. What would it take for the spell to be broken? The man at the store had told her that the candles worked, but he hadn't mentioned any antidote.

Perhaps when she and Kurt saw each other at the airport, the magic would reverse itself. A flash of light, a loud gong, and then she'd be herself again. Or maybe the spell had something to do with time, and it would wear off at the final stroke of midnight. Like in Cinderella. She had no clue. What other sorts of magic had she heard of before? You could make a wish on a falling star. On dandelion fluff. On candles decorating a birthday cake. But none of the wishes she'd ever made previously had ever come true.

Her mind on magic, she didn't allow herself to spend much time thinking about how Kurt was doing. So she was unprepared for what she found at the airport: Melissa carefully leading an extremely drunk version of herself through the other travelers and to the baggage-claim area. Melissa was shunting both of their small carry-on suitcases, the straps crisscrossed over her shoulders, and she looked like nothing so much as a very pretty pack mule.

'Over here!' Tiffany called, waving to the two of them.

Tiffany saw that Kurt had dressed her body in an oversized touristy New Orleans T-shirt – the one she'd bought for him as a gag gift. The bright blue shirt said 'Shuck me, suck me, eat me raw', referring to the New Orleans specialty of dining on raw oysters. He'd paired the shirt with a baseball cap worn backwards, Tiffany's favorite pair of jeans and her bright-pink Nikes. It was an outfit she would never have traveled in. The shoes were for gym only; the hotel had boasted a private workout space. The baseball cap was something he'd clearly bought at the airport to hide the fact that he hadn't known what to do with her hair. Tiffany was chagrined. When she traveled on a plane, or went anywhere in public, she liked to look nice. She found herself actually embarrassed by how poorly her ensemble looked, even though she wasn't the one inside of her body.

Oh, Lord. That thought made her head spin.

She looked closer and realized that Kurt had no make-up on either. But maybe this was a good thing. God only knew what he would have done to her with mascara and lipstick. The one time he'd worn cosmetics in the past was for a randy Halloween bash she'd orchestrated, when he'd chosen to play the Tim Curry role in *The Rocky Horror Picture Show*. He had brushed off her offers to help, choosing to do the make-up himself for that event, and he'd used an extremely heavy hand, a look which had worked for the costume, but would not have played out nearly so well in real life.

'Can you get this?' Melissa asked her breathlessly, breaking Tiffany from her reverie.

Quickly, she grabbed one small suitcase from Melissa, and then helped to prop up the sloppy-drunk vision of herself. A version she'd never seen before. When she put her arms around her own body, she felt that Kurt was braless.

'I don't know what got into her,' Melissa tried to explain as they limped together to the baggage-claim carousel. 'She lined up those little vodka bottles from the hotel minibar and went at it. I couldn't stop her. And she continued to drink more once we made it onto the plane. I haven't seen her drunk like that since Ryan –' Melissa stopped speaking. It was obvious she wasn't sure how much Kurt knew about Tiffany's ex. But Kurt, somewhere lost deep inside Tiffany's body, didn't seem to notice. He was slurring, holding onto Tiffany tightly around the waist and repeating something over and over. Tiffany bent in to hear, as her own voice said, 'Noshop. Noshop.'

'What's he – *she* saying?' Tiffany asked Melissa, amending herself mid-sentence. She would have to get used to thinking of Kurt as a *she*. At least, she would until they managed to reverse the spell. Vaguely, she realized that Kurt was drawing some attention. But she noticed that all the looks aimed in his direction were from men – Tiffany's body turned heads even drunk and in slovenly clothes. How odd to see people check her out. Perhaps it was the risqué statement on the T-shirt.

'It's funny. She's hooked on this one silly thing,' Melissa explained. 'That we couldn't find this crazy little place we went to yesterday.'

Tiffany felt a chill run through her. 'What place was that?' she asked, even though she already knew.

'We went to this hole in the wall store last night. It was called the Witches' Shoppe, and I thought I knew exactly where it was, but we couldn't find it today. I wanted to go back again, to get three more candles. I don't think I bought enough to pass out to all of the assistants. But we just couldn't find it. Tiffany had wanted to buy a few, too.'

No shop. That's what Kurt was saying. And he seemed to have realized that this wasn't a dream. That explained the drunken state of him. And the outfit. Gently, Tiffany tightened her grip around Kurt's waist and helped him to walk to a row of black chairs to wait for the luggage to arrive.

'Lightweight,' he hissed in her ear. '*I* could have handled the booze.'

'You know me,' she told him back, 'I'm a cheap date.'

Later, after an interminable wait at the baggage claim, only to find that Melissa's luggage had gone astray, Kurt and Tiffany dropped her off at her apartment. They sat in Kurt's truck and stared at each other. It was so strange to see herself like this – or her body like this. Drunk. Confused. Upset. Generally, Tiffany tried to put on a happy face. When life gave her lemons, she made lemonade. It was her all-time favorite slogan. Kurt's favorite motto was 'It's five o'clock somewhere'. The philosophy went nicely with his standard craving for a martini in the evening after a particularly hard day at the office.

'What the hell happened?' Kurt asked her now. He was drinking a cup of coffee they'd snagged at a fast-food drive-through, and he winced after each sip, not waiting for the java to cool down.

'I can't explain it,' Tiffany told him honestly. 'The guy at the store kept urging me to make a wish. He was very forceful, and I guess I finally did what he was asking. I wasn't even thinking about what I wanted. The concept just came unbidden into my mind.'

'You wished to be me?' Kurt set the coffee in the truck's cup holder, then cradled his head in his hands. He looked as if he were trying to make the world stop spinning. 'To try life out as a guy?'

'Well, sort of –' Embarrassment flooded through Tiffany. She was going to have to tell him. She didn't want to. Not with him sitting right there next to her. It was the moment she'd dreaded all day long. Coming clean. It's why she had spent hours working on his apartment rather than preparing what she was going to say when they finally met in person. 'But not entirely. I mean, that wasn't the whole wish.'

'You'd better explain everything,' Kurt said in a low voice, 'because this is fucking crazy.'

Tiffany winced, but she didn't say anything. He was right. It *was* crazy. Yet hearing herself swear felt bizarre. She tended to watch her X-rated language. This was a leftover habit from attending an all-girls Catholic school. And in her family, when you swore, you had to put a quarter into a communal jelly jar. If Kurt had a rule like that, they'd save up enough money for a trip to Jamaica within a month. She was constantly hounding him to watch his dirty mouth, but now didn't seem the appropriate time for criticisms.

'Go on,' he demanded, 'the more information I have, the better we can deal with this.'

'I wanted a month in your body,' she explained. 'So I could sort of, you know –'

'Fix it?' The concept seemed to sober Kurt up considerably. When he sat up straight, Tiffany saw a cold look glaring from within her own deep blue eyes. What if Kurt was so angry that he decided to break up with her? What would *that* do to the spell? Oh, God, what if she had to stay as him forever? She reached out a hand to touch him, but he slapped it away. She saw that he'd been peeling the ballerina-pink nail polish on her fingernails, and she had to work hard not to make a face. Tiffany hated when girls did that. In her opinion, chipped nail polish looked cheap.

'I'm sorry,' she said, 'I didn't think it would come true. It's just that –'

'I'm a fuck-up and you wanted to make me over.'

She sighed and looked out the window, watching as the traffic light down the street changed from green to yellow to red. Kurt seemed suddenly to have realized something. 'And what the fuck are you wearing, anyway?'

Tiffany stiffened. She had gone out and bought new clothes, and shoes, and an iron, unable to live with the state of his wardrobe, even for a day.

'Just an outfit.' Her cheeks burned.

'I'd never wear that color.'

She knew this to be true. For years, she'd been after Kurt to try something exactly like this outfit, and he'd flat out refused every time. But she also knew that Kurt would look great in pink. The salesman had assured her she was right. Perhaps the clerk at the high-end department store in Union Square had simply been interested in his commission, but he had echoed her own beliefs right back to her. That she looked divine in the brand-new attire. She felt slightly guilty for putting the purchase on Kurt's MasterCard, but she'd had no choice. Her purse was with him. She could pay him back later – call it a gift.

'How about you?' she countered. 'You're not even wearing a bra.'

'I couldn't make the clasp work,' he said through gritted teeth. 'My head was killing me because *you* can't handle *your* liquor, and I've never had the enlightening experience of putting a bra *on* before. I've only taken them off. I thought Melissa might find it strange if I asked her for assistance getting dressed.' With a cruel look on his face, he playacted an imaginary scenario for Tiffany: 'Oh, Melissa,' he cooed in a falsetto, 'can you help me fasten up my frilly little bra? And which way does the floss on the thong go?'

'I don't talk like that,' Tiffany insisted.

'You get the idea, though. And, man, those panties are much sexier-looking than feeling.' He shifted uncomfortably. 'I'd rather go without than try that again.'

The image of Melissa woke something inside Tiffany. 'Did you see her naked?'

'Yeah,' Kurt said, still clearly seething. 'She came out of the shower and dropped her towel. Oh, baby, what a body she's got on her for a lawyer. That Rick's a lucky fucking man. She must work out even more than you do.'

'Come on,' Tiffany said, disappointed. 'You didn't have to look at her. She wouldn't have wanted you to see her like that if she knew who you really were.'

'What are you talking about? The two of you have been friends for decades. What could I do?'

'*Not look.*'

'Like that was an option. Hey, I didn't know she had a tattoo on her –'

'Stop it!' Tiffany snapped.

He was obviously enjoying himself a little bit now, getting back at her. He sat back in the seat and put his feet up on the dash. Tiffany clenched her fists at her sides and took what she hoped was a deep, cleansing breath, something she'd learned in her power yoga class.

'It was pretty sexy, you know? That little red rose on her hip. You know, you'd look good with one, too,' Kurt grinned snarkily at Tiffany's horrified expression. 'Maybe right here.' He lightly touched Tiffany's left breast, and even though she wasn't in her body, she could almost feel the ghostly tracing of his fingertips on her skin. 'A butterfly perhaps. With multicolored wings. I always thought butterfly tattoos were incredibly sexy. That's something to consider. I could take your sweet little body down to the Castro. There are plenty of tattoo parlors down there –'

'We have to fix this.'

'Be my guest,' Kurt told her with a half-sneer. 'You like to fix things. Make this all better.'

He took his feet off the dash and maneuvered around in the seat until he was sitting up on his knees. While Tiffany watched, he reached into the glove compartment and started tossing stuff around. He didn't seem to notice that she'd organized this area for him. His registration was in a neat little white envelope paper-clipped to the top of the truck's user's manual.

'What are you looking for?'

As he glanced up at her, he seemed to finally take in the all-around change in his truck. Tiffany had gotten the Dakota detailed before heading to the airport. She couldn't stand the state of the vehicle. The clutter was gone now. The Big Red gum wrappers on the floor. The crumpled-up fast-food papers. As were the Marlboros that Tiffany knew he was searching for.

'I need a smoke.'

'You're not smoking in my body.' The very thought repelled her.

'Well, how about you? Aren't you going through withdrawal?' He appeared interested in this concept, wondering for the first time how his own body was faring after this unexpected change of events. Up until now, the thought hadn't seemed to occur to him; he'd been too intent on dealing with his new-found female shape.

Tiffany flipped up the sleeve of her pale raspberry Polo shirt, and Kurt stared at the patch there.

'I think it's working. This morning I had this yearning, a strange sort of pull, but I got over it with some of that Nicorette gum I bought for you, and then I picked up the patch at the drugstore. But I don't really know what it's like to want a cigarette, so I can't tell for sure that's what I was feeling.'

'Part of it's physical,' he explained to her in a matter-of-fact tone of voice, 'and part of it's mental. I'm jonesing for one now because I mentally know it would make me feel better, so you better get my mind off it quick, or I'll pollute your pure and perfect body.'

Tiffany didn't know what to do. She'd kept herself busy all day long so that she wouldn't have to think about the reality of the situation. Now that she was face to face with the problem – and quite literally face to face with her own self – she was at a complete loss. 'You said the store wasn't there anymore,' she told him. 'Or that you guys couldn't find it. I have no idea how we're supposed to reverse the situation. The man didn't tell me the rules of the wishes. He only told me to make a wish. What do you want me to do?'

'I don't know. Give me a blow job or something –' He started to laugh at the look she shot him. 'I'm kidding. That's physically impossible anyway. Besides,' he gazed at her in a skeptical way, 'I actually don't think I'm all that attracted to you.'

Tiffany's hurt expression made Kurt laugh harder. He watched as she turned the rear-view mirror so that she could see herself. She thought she looked exceptionally handsome. Kurt had thick dark hair and eyes that could look green or gray, depending on the light, or the clothes he had on, or even his mood. Right now, his eyes shone almost silvery. The glasses were a bit heavy. Perhaps she herself would choose different frames but these weren't bad. She didn't know what Kurt was talking about – he'd never looked better.

'I'm not gay, Tiff. I don't know if I can get it up for a guy. Especially one in a pink shirt. You look like one of those asshole preppies, for God's sake. Is that what you're really into? If it is, I don't have any idea what you've seen in me for the last four years.'

'You don't have to get it up at all,' she reminded him in a dark voice.

'Well, whatever. And why didn't you shave? The Miami Vice look has been out for almost twenty years –' He reached out and ran his hand over the stubble on Tiffany's chin, and Tiffany was surprised at what that gentle stroke did to her.

Was she going to get hard again? How did men deal with that sort of thing. She squirmed in the seat of the pick-up. Adjusting her package wasn't something she'd grown adept at in the half day she'd inhabited Kurt's body, and she hadn't shaved because she was frightened of cutting his face. She'd chosen to think of the look as George-Clooney-scruffy.

'God, I have to pee again,' Kurt muttered. 'You have a bladder the size of a fucking golf ball, you know it? I spent half the flight going to the john. But at least while I was in the lavatory I didn't have to listen to Melissa drone on about her wedding.' He sighed. 'That's all the girl wanted to talk about. Let's head to AJs. I could use another cup of coffee, as well.'

'The ladies' rooms there are disgusting.'

'Then I'll pee outside.'

Tiffany shook her head. 'You're a girl, Kurt, remember?'

'That's right,' he said, lowering the sun visor with a casual flick and then gracefully catching the emergency pack of Marlboros that fell down into his open hand. 'I'm a fucking girl.'

Chapter Two

'So you have a plan, right?' Kurt asked plaintively. 'I mean, tell me now and put my mind at ease. You *always* have a plan. It's why you're a party planner –' Kurt's voice rose in pitch with each word, so Tiffany could definitely hear what he was saying. She drove back to her apartment in total huffy silence, and then sat in the front seat without looking in Kurt's direction once. Her beau appeared to be totally sober now, but his drinking on the plane wasn't what she was upset about.

'What is this? The silent treatment. Christ, I seriously hate when you do that. It's one of my least favorite things about you –'

'Well, if we're making a list –' she hissed, so angry she was shaking. She found it surprising how tightly she could grip hold of the steering wheel. Her knuckles were actually whitening from the force. Kurt's body was much stronger than her own. She actually felt as if she might be able to rip the steering wheel from its stem, and the thought pleased her immensely. It would feel good to break something right now. To punch something – was this testosterone talking?

'You know, *I'm* the one who ought to be pissed,' Kurt insisted, blowing perfectly executed smoke rings out the window. He looked like someone from one of the art-house movies Tiffany was always dragging him to see. A French movie with a heroine who was beautiful but damaged. '*Not* you.'

All right, Tiffany thought. He had a valid point. But she didn't seem to feel as upset as Kurt.

'And I'm the one who had to listen to Melissa blather on for six fucking hours on the plane, talking about her wedding in the most minute detail. How can you stand it? Garter this and canapé that. I thought I was going to go out of my head.'

She would not even look at him.

'Fine.' Kurt ground the cigarette out in the ashtray. Tiffany didn't appreciate the gesture, because the thing was smoked down to the butt by now anyway. Besides, she had paid to have the truck detailed and now it reeked of smoke all over again. 'I'm sorry –' his voice – *her* voice – was a growl, '– but when things are stressful, I like a smoke.'

'I don't want you to mess up my body.'

Now, Kurt gave her an evil laugh. 'Your goal was to fix *me* up. You never really gave a thought to what damage I might do to your own pristine self, did you?'

Tiffany leaned back against the headrest and closed her eyes. He was right. She hadn't considered that at all. What might Kurt do to her body? What if he pierced her nipples or – oh, God – her clit?

'I could wreak havoc, couldn't I?' he insisted, answering her silent question with one of his own. 'Forgo your stringent diet. Eight fruits and vegetables a day. No alcohol until Friday night. Fuck all that. I could eat like a little piglet, buffalo wings every night, extra large pepperoni and olive pizzas. I could gain fifteen pounds in a weekend if I tried hard enough. You never even thought about that, did you?'

He wouldn't really harm her, would he? This was only anger speaking.

'Don't worry, kiddo. I won't. I like your figure –'

Tiffany opened her eyes to watch as he ran his hands along his body – her body – and she shook her head. This was too much. He was treating her body as if it were a playground. Of course, he did that when she was in it, and she enjoyed every sexy moment. But now things were different. She wouldn't tell him that she had played around with his cock – that was her own secret. Anybody would have wanted to try it out at least once.

Kurt slapped his hands together, as if trying to rouse up her energy. 'Look, Tiff. We're here. We don't know how long we're going to be like this. Let's brainstorm.'

She took a deep breath. She couldn't really blame him for being upset. How would she have dealt with the situation if he'd been the one who'd made the wish? 'I've been racking my brain all day,' she told him. 'I called your office early and said you were sick, because I didn't think I could fake out your boss.'

He nodded appreciatively. 'Good thinking, Tiff, But, I hope this –' he hesitated, not sure what to call the crisis they were in, '– this *situation* reverses itself soon. I'm supposed to be leading a big presentation in two weeks. You're supposed to do –' He grimaced. One of the things that annoyed Tiffany the most was the fact that Kurt never paid proper attention to her career. She was a party planner, and she threw some of the most expensive events of each season, working for upscale museums, famous hospitals, and wealthy private clients, the ones who lived in Pacific Heights and had garages bigger than Kurt's entire apartment. Tiffany could multitask with the best of them, Kurt always said proudly when he talked about her, but he couldn't ever seem to keep clear in his head which event she was currently working on.

He seemed to sense that there would be fireworks if he didn't have at least some vague grasp of her itinerary. Still, he searched his mind and came up blank. He had nothing. 'You're supposed to –'

'I'm planning Melissa's wedding,' she reminded him coolly. 'That's the only event I'm working on this month. It's why she wanted to talk to you about the details today on the plane. She probably thought it was strange that you weren't taking notes.'

'God, that's right.' He looked stricken. 'You're the maid of honor, aren't you?'

'You mean *you* are if we don't get this thing fixed before Christmas Eve.'

He blanched. 'No offense, Tiff, but I have zero desire to pour myself into that little purple dress.'

She gave him a look. 'It's not purple. It's called "morning lilac", and it's a beautiful dress. You know that Melissa spent hours settling on that style.'

That wasn't a positive in Kurt's mind. Why would anyone spent hours choosing a dress? Especially a dress they weren't going to wear themselves. The whole point of a bridesmaid, in Kurt's mind, was to make the bride look good. He had come to this determination after attending so many events with Tiffany in which the bridesmaids were draped in the most horrible get-ups, making even the most monstrous of brides look radiant in comparison. He and Tiffany had gone to one wedding the year before that had actually shocked him. The girls had been wearing dresses so hideous they looked as if they were torn from Hefty's bags. Tiffany had assured him that black was a new thing for weddings, but Kurt had thought the girls looked like the walking dead.

He kept his mouth shut on those thoughts now, saying instead, 'Yeah, but you said yourself that the corset part pinched the hell out of you.'

She gazed at him, surprised he'd remembered.

'Although you did look amazing once you were all tied up,' he mused. 'I had visions of doing naughty things to you after the ceremony.'

'Really?' Tiffany asked, intrigued in spite of herself.

'Anyway,' he continued forcefully, 'what are we going to do about *this*?' He motioned first to Tiffany in her pink Polo and then to himself in his disheveled traveling clothes.

'Let's call Melissa. We'll get her to give us the LOVE candle that she was planning on passing out to one of her coworkers. You'll make a wish over that, and hopefully all of this will be back to normal. I mean, the magic took place within hours. Maybe the spell will fade away just as fast.'

Kurt sighed, visibly relaxed. 'All right. That sounds good. I knew you'd have a plan. I don't know why I didn't think of that myself.' Suddenly, he eyed her, and when he spoke, his voice was rich with curiosity. 'What's it like, anyway?'

'What do you mean?'

'Being me.'

She shrugged. 'Not bad. I like the extra leg room.' She arched her back and stretched, taking up space in the truck's cab. 'You really have a lot of power in a body like this. Wearing glasses took some getting used to –'

He interrupted her. 'Seeing clearly for the first time in my life was pretty cool. I kept touching my nose to slide my glasses up to the bridge, and coming away empty handed. I hope Melissa didn't notice.'

'She probably thought you were trying to massage away your hangover.' Tiffany hesitated. She was almost embarrassed to admit this next part. 'You know, I was hungry all day long.' As a girl, she always felt somewhat proud of her rigid meal plan. As a man, she'd been ravenous all day, and the consuming hunger had surprised her. She'd started out with her basic diet, and ended up practically wolfing down a cheeseburger before heading toward the airport, so hungry that her hands were shaking.

'What'd you eat today?'

She described her basic, everyday diet, up to the dinner: The oatmeal. Coffee. Fruit salad. Turkey sandwich. V-8.

'That's not even a single proper meal,' he said.

'It's about what I eat every day.'

'Yeah, but you weigh right around a hundred and ten. I outweigh you by a good seventy pounds. You're not eating enough to fuel me up, kid. You'll lose weight on that diet.'

She patted his stomach. It was flat, but she couldn't help but tease him. 'Not a bad thing,' she said, grinning. 'How about you?'

He was the one to shrug now. 'Too high maintenance,' he said. 'I didn't know how to work any of those damn bras in your suitcase. I hate all of your fucking shoes.' He glowered at her. 'And why did you have to bring so many shoes with you anyway? You were only gone for four days. There were seven pairs of heels in your bag. All black. And only one pair of trainers.'

Tiffany shrugged. She couldn't explain that. No woman would have asked her such a question.

'I was lucky you showed me how to walk last Halloween. I would have looked like a Clydesdale if we hadn't practiced so much. Melissa didn't seem to think it was odd that I tried on several pairs before settling on the sneakers. I guess that's a standard girl trick?'

Tiffany nodded. 'What else?'

'Well, I couldn't figure out the make-up.'

'I did have all those Hurricanes –'

'Sure, I was hungover, which added to the confusion, but what a nightmare. Melissa caught me staring at the case filled with little tubes and she had an absolute giggling fit.'

'There weren't *so* many tubes,' Tiffany said in her defense. 'Just foundation, concealer, mascara, liner, lipstick, blush, eyebrow pencil, eye-shadow . . .' She ticked these off on her nails, surprised herself at how many items that added up to. 'Other women wear much more make-up than I do. Primer and highlighter and eye-shadow base –'

'Sure they do,' Kurt agreed, 'but any make-up is more than I'm used to. What do I know about concealer?'

'You always said I looked better without any make-up.'

'Well, I didn't know what you actually *looked* like without it.'

Tiffany sulked.

'I don't mean it like that,' he said immediately, placing a small hand on her broad shoulder. How strange to be comforted by her own stroking fingertips. The feeling was surreal. 'But I'm guessing that you even wore make-up when you said you were au naturel, didn't you?'

She nodded. 'Sometimes, I've gotten out of bed and put make-up on while you were asleep.' She hadn't meant to tell him that, and she waited for his response without meeting his eyes.

He appeared both fascinated and disturbed by this confession, as if he couldn't believe she'd do something like that for him, and yet he couldn't understand why she'd go to all that trouble. 'See? This is the first time in four years I've ever actually seen the real you.'

'And?'

'You're beautiful, Tiffany. I always said so. Even hungover your skin just glows. But until we straighten this out, I need to know how to work this body better, in order to pass more convincingly as you. I don't know what Melissa thought of me. Thank fuck I had those drinks to blame it on.'

'Stop swearing so much. That's one thing. I really don't ever swear. You ought to know that by now.'

He considered that for a moment, then nodded. 'What else?'

'Sit up straighter. I don't slouch.'

He did as she said, immediately moving his body into an upright position, then admiring the way this made Tiffany's breasts look. The effect was instantaneous and quite perky. He hadn't told Tiffany yet, but just being inside her body was something of a turn-on for him. 'Anything else?'

'I'll have to do your make-up for you. And I'll choose your

wardrobe.' She eyed the casual outfit he had on, wrinkling her nose in distaste.

'You don't like my style?' he asked her.

'I don't think it's the same as mine.'

'And that's a bad thing?'

She sighed, realizing that they were in this whole situation mostly because of thoughts like this. 'Kurt,' she started, showing her first sign of total weakness, 'how are we going to make this work?'

'We just will.' He held her hand, and she closed her eyes, automatically waiting for him to kiss her. This was when he would have normally. Cradled her in his strong arms. Held her tight against his chest so that she could hear the steady rhythm of his heart beating. Soothed away any fears. After a moment, she opened her eyes and saw him staring at her with the most unusual expression on his face – her face – and she shook her head again.

'I can't do it,' Kurt said solemnly.

'Can't –' Tiffany started, not sure what he meant.

'Kiss myself.'

She started to cry. Or, rather, she *thought* about crying. Being Kurt was strange. She couldn't cry on command. Her emotions were there. Right at the surface. But no tears came out. Instead, there was an odd tightness in her chest that made swallowing difficult, and she suddenly felt that she *did* want a cigarette. She really did. Perhaps the power in the patch was starting to wane. She needed to read up on the instructions again. If anything good was going to come out of this bizarre happening, it would be that she'd kick nicotine for him.

'I'm kidding, Tiffany,' Kurt said, gripping onto her hand and making her look at him. 'Really. I was just messing around. I'm a guy. Of course I want to do it. I'm not about to let an opportunity like this go by. This is something every guy imagines his whole life –'

'Being a girl?' she was incredulous. She thought she knew all of Kurt's fantasies. The one about doing it on a touristy cruise around the Bay while wearing a set of headphones that described the sights they were passing. The one about picking her up in a bar, pretending she was a stranger, and taking her off to the back room where there was a pool table and fucking her on the faded green felt. The one involving a blindfold, a bungee cord, and a bottle of sweet almond oil. But being a girl had never come up when they'd been in that private confessing mode.

He shook his head. 'Giving himself a blow job.' And then he started to laugh so hard that *he* was the one who cried.

Thank God he hadn't worn mascara. It would have streaked down his face in black tears.

Chapter Three

Kurt couldn't stop giggling. 'This is crazy,' he said breathlessly. 'Totally fucking crazy.' His eyes were watering and his cheeks were flushed the bright pink of dyed carnations.

'I know it,' Tiffany agreed, watching him.

There they were, on Tiffany's king-sized bed, confined within two bodies that generally seemed to know how to properly fit together. Often when they made love, Tiffany would actually forget where her body ended and Kurt's began. Yet tonight they couldn't seem to make the connection.

'Melissa's going to give us the candle,' Kurt said, as if to calm Tiffany's fears but clearly trying to reassure himself as well. 'Tomorrow morning. You don't have to worry about it.'

'I'm not worrying,' Tiffany assured him. That wasn't the problem. As soon as they'd entered the apartment, she had coached him as he left a message on Melissa's answering machine. Tiffany was certain that upon making the opposite wish over one of Melissa's candles, the two would be back in their own bodies in a flash. There was no longer the anguish she had felt at first. Still, the spark wasn't there. Not like it usually was, and not for lack of trying.

'I'm sorry,' Kurt told her, doubled over on the bed. 'I really am. Stop looking at me like that!'

Sex was something that pleased each of them, and neither had any peculiar hang-ups about doing the deed. In fact, making love was one of the activities they were best at. From the very start of their relationship, their sex life had sizzled. But this new change of events had thrown off their timing.

'I didn't even touch you,' Tiffany said, frustrated.

'I know,' he told her. 'But when I even *think* about you touching me, I start to laugh.' He scooted further away from her on the petal-pink comforter, as if needing to put as much space between them as possible.

Tiffany sighed, disappointed. Back when they'd first started dating, she had been pleased to learn that Kurt was up for a variety of positions: spoon, girl on top, even reverse cowgirl, a particular favorite. Her previous beau had been satisfied with engaging in the missionary style with the lights out. But not Kurt. He encouraged experimentation. Once, Tiffany had bought a book called *Thirty Days of Excellent Sex*, and she and Kurt had spent an eventful month trying out each of the positions, ultimately adding several of the acts into their standard repertoire. Now, things were different.

'Look, we don't *have* to do this,' Tiffany said after a moment. She'd just moved forward and put a hand on Kurt's thigh and he'd squirmed away once more, nearly hyperventilating with laughter. 'I'm sure Melissa will call back first thing in the morning. She's probably out with Rick tonight.' *Doing the exact thing we're not doing*, she thought, but didn't say. 'We'll turn back into ourselves and catch up then. No harm done.'

'But I want to,' Kurt insisted when he caught his breath again. 'When are we ever going to have a chance like this again?'

Tiffany shrugged. Sure, she was excited by the concept of discovering sexual pleasure while in Kurt's skin. Yet engaging in the act appeared to be more confusing than arousing. And even though she'd already fooled around with her new cock once, Tiffany didn't precisely know how to work this new body. Every touch seemed heavy-handed. Every gentle caress came out like a tackle.

'It's really not my fault,' Kurt claimed. 'Your body is simply incredibly ticklish. I mean, I feel like laughing when you're only looking at me as *if* you're going to touch me.'

'I've told you that,' Tiffany said in an accusatory fashion. 'Whenever you touch me too lightly, I laugh. You never believed me before.'

'Well, I do now,' he conceded. 'And I'll remember that for the future.'

The future. They were both silent while each made a

private wish that this would all be sorted out in the morning.

'But that's not all of it,' Kurt continued. 'I can't get used to you looking like that.'

Tiffany stared at him. 'Like what?'

'Like me. I was teasing in the car, but it's really too weird.' He shut his eyes tightly and then opened them again. Tiffany had a feeling she knew what he was doing.

'I tried that already,' she told him. 'You're hoping to wake yourself up, aren't you?'

Sheepishly, Kurt nodded.

'It's not going to work. We're really in this. I mean, pinch yourself. Jump up and down. This is you.'

'I know that. I thought it was all a bad dream at first, but that flight was real. Air travel is desperately, boringly, frighteningly real. Melissa talking nonstop only made it more of a nightmare. A waking nightmare. I couldn't have conjured up that conversation if you'd paid me.'

Tiffany shrugged. 'So where does that leave us?'

Kurt held up a finger and then sprinted from the room. Tiffany couldn't guess where he was going, or why, so she just settled back on her bed, arms crossed behind her head while she waited. Her room, simple and understated in the décor, was strikingly different than Kurt's. There was a white-washed dresser against one wall with an oval mirror suspended over it. Both were thrift-store finds that she'd refurbished herself. On one wall hung a photograph that Kurt had given to her one Valentine's Day. The picture featured the Golden Gate Bridge shrouded in fog. Kurt had used black and white film to take the shot, then shaded the bridge in Tiffany's favorite color: pink.

This color was repeated in various hues around the room: Tiffany's silken bedspread, her 300-thread-count sheets, even her lamp shade. Girly, girly, girly. No wonder she'd chosen a pink shirt for Kurt to wear. The color always lifted her spirits. But aside from color schemes, their tastes weren't so dissimilar. They both appreciated modern art, as reflected in the Warhol print of flowers above her bed. They both admired simple furniture and clean lines. The main difference in her décor from Kurt's apartment was in what *wasn't* around. Unlike Kurt's place, there were no clothes decorating the floor. The princess phone by the bed was in plain sight, not hidden under dirty laundry. The box of tissues stood on the bedside table, rather than turned upside down underneath the bed. There was no loose change dotting the rug, having spilled out of the pockets of various upturned jeans. No magazines lay scattered in stacks around the room. There was no mess.

The room exuded an atmosphere that generally made Tiffany feel calm. She shut her eyes, trying to drink in that feeling. Breathing in a slow and conscious fashion, she relaxed her body, and she was almost asleep by the time she heard Kurt's footsteps on the hardwood floor. With a yawn, Tiffany opened her eyes and stared at Kurt as he struck a pose in the bedroom doorway.

Ingeniously, Kurt had decked himself out in Tiffany's own favorite silver silk robe which usually hung on the back of the bathroom door. He had brushed her long blonde hair so that it shone, and he had even used a bit of her favorite perfume, Coco Chanel. Tiffany could smell the scent from the bed. He was gorgeous – or *she* was. It still hurt Tiffany's head to think like this. Yet Kurt's body responded to the sight of her own, responded as if on autopilot, as if the cock between her legs had eyes. Unfortunately, her mind would not make the leap.

'Not working?'

'Well . . .' Tiffany sighed, motioning to the hard-on shrouded beneath the boxer shorts. 'Yes, and no. I'm ready, I think. I just don't know how to start.'

'We'll start like we always start.'

They stared at each other.

'How do we always start?' Tiffany asked softly.

'You know, we're thinking about it too much. *That's* the problem,' Kurt proclaimed. 'Usually, we fall into bed together. There's not so much discussion or planning, right? We meet somehow, connect, body to body.'

Again, they stared each other. Time seemed to stretch out. This wasn't getting any easier.

'God, Kurt. What are we going to do?' Tiffany murmured as Kurt sat on the edge of the bed. In spite of his pep talk, he appeared to be as nervous as she felt. It was as if they were virgins all over again at age thirty. Who would ever have thought? 'What if we're stuck like this forever?' That was the main problem, she realized. Fear.

'I have another idea.'

She waited, silent, as Kurt stood again and rifled through the contents in her top dresser drawer. What he was looking for, she had no idea. Then suddenly, Kurt brought out a pair of her black silk stockings. A pair they'd played with in the past. A pair that had brought Tiffany a great deal of pleasure.

'Are you game?'

She shook her head immediately. 'No way.' Adding bondage play to the already tumultuous events of the day seemed too much to expect her to handle. What was Kurt thinking?

'Come on, Tiff,' he urged. 'I'm sure it will put you at ease. Because we really can't let something small like this come between us.'

'Small –' Her response was more of a whimper than a shriek, although part of her did feel like screaming right about now.

'Hopefully, the candle thing will work. If it doesn't, we're going to have to deal with this situation on our own. But there's no way that I'm forgoing sex for the rest of my life just because of a technicality, an inconvenience . . .'

Tiffany interrupted, 'An *inconvenience* –'

'You know what I mean.'

She nodded and then meekly held her arms over her head. It was a trained response. She'd always been the one bound. Kurt had never shown any interest in being submissive when they played together. Taking the lead, Kurt immediately began to tie her wrists in place against the bed frame, then removed her glasses and used the second stocking as a blindfold.

'Just imagine that things are what they were.'

Tiffany tried, eyes shut under the silk, fully aware that she could break out of the bindings if she needed to. The strength of this body was something she definitely could get used to. It was empowering – empowering in an entirely different way than the women she knew used the term. Right now, the word meant force, and this body was definitely strong. She felt the subtle weight of Kurt in her own body on top of her and she tilted her head back against the pillows. In a moment, Kurt's lips were pressed to hers, and she responded instantly to the sensation. Kissing was intensely erotic. By keeping her eyes shut tightly, Tiffany could imagine that she was herself again. Pleasure was pleasure, after all. Sexual bliss wasn't compartmentalized, wasn't something that belonged solely to one sex or the other.

As Kurt continued to kiss her, she lifted her hips, raising her boyfriend into the air and unintentionally sending him flying off the bed with the movement. He landed with a soft thump on the floor, and Tiffany would have reached over to help him up, but her hands were still bound.

'Sorry –'

'Forgot my own strength?' he teased as he climbed back onto the mattress.

'Yeah –'

Then they were kissing again, truly kissing with the passion that Tiffany always felt when she and Kurt were making love. With their lips pressed together, she became aware of the changes that went winging through this new body of hers. She was hard again. So hard.

Oh, the hell with it, she chided herself. She was in Kurt's body, she might as well think like he would in the same situation. She was so *fucking* hard. It was interesting what the mere power of a kiss could do to this body. She quite liked the effect. If kissing made her as hard as a tent pole, what would actually making love do? She couldn't wait to find out. She shifted her hips, moving more cautiously this time. Kurt, understanding what she wanted, pulled the boxers off her and tossed them aside. When he put one hand on her cock, she moaned so loudly that he immediately moved away from her, alarmed that he'd somehow hurt her.

'Are you okay?'

'Oh, my God –' Her voice was a whisper, a whimper.

'You like that,' he said, understanding. This wasn't a question. Of course, Kurt knew what his body liked. Without another word, he began to stroke her, handling Tiffany expertly, and she responded before she could help herself, moaning again, even louder this time. When Kurt gripped onto what she now thought of solely as *her* cock, and moved his hand up and down sensuously, she felt so grateful to him she could hardly breathe. Being bound while he treated her to the steady stroking meant that she had to concentrate all of her attention on what was going on between her legs. She couldn't touch him back. She couldn't engage in the action in any way. She was helpless.

They often played little bondage games together, sometimes using these stockings, other times using a pair of leopard-print fur-lined cuffs Kurt had bought her one Valentine's Day. Tiffany enjoyed giving herself over to Kurt, and he never let her down, never frightened her with his fantasies. But this was different from being bound as a woman. She didn't know exactly why. Kurt touched her with a perfect motion, and she shuddered all over. Eyes shut under the blindfold, arms above her head, she surrendered to Kurt's ministrations. He seemed to have gotten past the awkwardness of the situation. Even beneath the stockinged blindfold, Tiffany could feel him watching her, judging her responses. She arched her hips again and groaned as Kurt added something new to the mix. Lubrication. He must have pulled out a bottle of K-Y from the bedside drawer. She felt the smooth, slickness surround her cock – *her* cock! – slipping down to her balls. Yes, the lube was unexpectedly cool, but the temperature somehow didn't matter. The sexy wetness of the added lubrication increased her desire to make love to Kurt. She was astounded by how close she was to coming, and so quickly. Her thoughts were a blur, her mind focused only on the pleasure from Kurt's fingertips around her.

She was selfish. Was that the difference? Greedy. She wanted more. She wanted release. Kurt continued to stroke her, slowly, then gradually with a faster motion. Tiffany could tell that he was completely focused on the expression on her face. She hoped that he could sense how turned on she was. But of course he could. There was no hiding this fact. Not as a boy. Yet, she didn't want to hide it. Surprisingly, she found that she wanted to scream out loud.

'Don't hold back,' Kurt told her, as if reading her mind. 'Be loud for me.'

This was a request she'd heard before. Kurt always wanted her to express herself vocally in bed. She responded as she generally did to his urgings. 'I can't –' Didn't matter that she wasn't in her body anymore. Being loud during sex was something she was far too self-conscious to do. But for the first time, she actually could envision letting loose. Oh, she adored the potency of this sex. The stark, unadorned power that accompanied being a man.

'That's amazing,' she hissed. 'I can't –'

'Wait,' Kurt said. 'Wait –'

And then things got even better. Kurt was astride her, and the wetness changed in an instant from cool to warm. She didn't understand at first, and then she realized as he pushed up on her and then slid back down so that skin met skin that he was naked under the robe, that he'd left his panties in the bathroom, that they were fucking. The thought of it astonished her; they were actually connected at their cores, and before she knew what she was saying, what she was doing, she cried out, 'I'm going to –'

'I know,' he said softly, and his voice seemed curiously resigned. 'I know you are.'

Without another thought. Without an ability to hold off, Tiffany came.

Technically speaking, the first time was sloppy. Pleasure seemed to be something that Kurt's body didn't know how to handle. Or at least, *Tiffany* didn't know how to handle the force of sexual pleasure while trapped within the confines of this six-foot-plus form. She felt as if she were walking a big dog for the first time, having the beast pulling on its leash until she tumbled down and was dragged along after it, a total slave to the potency of the pleasure. That was her explanation, and it sounded fairly poetic to her own ears. Kurt, however, waved her words aside as he undid her blindfold and set her glasses back in place, saying simply, 'You prematurely ejaculated.'

'Sorry,' she murmured, thinking: *Was that all?* What a clinical-sounding name for an experience she would have to describe as earth-shatteringly erotic. She'd felt as if she'd been pulverized. Coming like a guy was totally different from any orgasm she'd ever experienced, and this had been far better than her early morning tryst with her own solitary hand. This had been magnificent, a symphony of sensations. Generally, when she climaxed, the sensual excitement started slowly, built, then spread throughout her body until her very fingertips tingled. There was nothing wrong with coming like a girl, but it was different. The satisfaction lasted longer and spread throughout her slower. But this had been an explosion.

A big bang.

Trying to explain this to Kurt, she likened the feelings of a woman's orgasm to a pebble thrown in the center of a still pond, the ripples radiating outward to lap seductively at the shore. She would have used her hands to show him what she meant, but they were still captured over her head.

'Ripples,' he nodded, nonplussed.

'It's good,' she insisted. 'Just not the same.'

Christ, no wonder he always wanted to roll over and nap afterwards. She felt as if she'd done a full body workout. Even her hair was tired.

When she squirmed one hand free from the bindings, she was able to push herself up on the headboard into a sitting position. Breathing was still more of an aerobic activity than normal. Kurt seemed extremely amused by the situation, if a little bit let down. He had a half smile on his face, and he reached out one hand and stroked the hair off her face. Winded with the effort of simply being, she looked at him, 'I'm sorry. I couldn't help it.' At least, she wasn't squawking out the pathetic 'Was it good for you?' query that bad lovers often used. She knew it hadn't been good for him. He hadn't reached the same heights that she had. God, she hadn't even given him a chance.

'It's going to take more than one time,' he said. 'That's to be expected.'

'What do you mean?' She pushed up against some of the pillows in her bed, and then, unable to get comfortable, threw several of the more girly ones onto the floor. The ones with the little daisies embroidered onto the surface. This was something Kurt did every single time he stayed over at her house. Now, she finally understood why.

Kurt grinned at her. 'See? Those decorative ones are just fucking annoying. There's no way to get comfortable on them when you're tall like me.'

'Okay, but what about the sex?'

He shrugged. 'I started to feel something right at the end. Right before you came. A little flicker of something. But there just wasn't time.'

Why did she feel let down? *He* was the one who hadn't gotten off. But it was her fault. She hadn't pleased him. Hadn't shown him how fantastic it was to be a girl. If she'd been paying attention to his needs, rather than focusing on her own, she could have given him multiple orgasms, could have stretched out the experience for him until he was the one breathless and panting. She could have told *him* to be loud for her. She shook her head. Why hadn't she thought to tie Kurt down, to play with him in a way that would be new and exciting for him? Although he hadn't said anything of the sort, she felt as if she owed him something. For putting him through this. The craziest day of each of their lives.

'We can try again in the morning,' Kurt patted her on the arm in a very Tiffany-esque manner. 'It's fine,' he said as he curled up next to her. When he put one arm over her body, her stomach contracted.

How could he be so understanding? If he had done this to her, there would have been no stopping her rage. Not for coming before she did, but for making the stupid wish in the first place. She would have sulked and yelled and pouted and ranted. She would have shamed him into oblivion. All Kurt did was find a comfortable space against her and close his eyes. 'It's been a long day,' he said, as if feeling her gaze.

'I know.'

'Don't worry so much, Tiff. Get some sleep.'

His kindness made her feel even worse. When she'd been tallying his list of faults, had she put thoughtfulness into his pro column? Kurt never held a grudge. He was infinitely caring. She felt like a heel.

Not tired in the least, she wished she could call Melissa. They could talk about everything; they always had. Wistfully, Tiffany thought about slipping out of the bed and dialing from the cordless phone in the kitchen. A glass of chilled white wine and a long conversation with her best friend would make her feel better. But she didn't want to disturb Kurt. He was right; it had been a long day. He'd started by waking up in her body in a strange hotel room, and ended by being shut out of an orgasm during his first-ever-as-a-woman sex-fest.

Without feeling the slightest bit sleepy, she watched the hands move on the sterling silver clock by her bed, watched Kurt at her side, and waited. Then finally, when she was sure Kurt was sleeping soundly, she decided to risk it. Tiffany actually had begun to extricate herself from his embrace when she realized that Melissa would find a post-midnight phone call from *Kurt* fairly freaky, and that there was no good way to explain her predicament over the phone. The thought of saying, 'It's not Kurt, Melissa, it's me, Tiffany!' wasn't a joyous one. Sadly, she relaxed back on the pillows and stared up at the ceiling.

'You still awake?'

Tiffany turned on her side to look at Kurt.

'Yeah.'

'Me, too.'

'I thought you were sleeping.'

'I know how you sleep. Sometimes I stay up and just watch you.'

'Seriously?' She hadn't known that.

'It makes me feel calm,' Kurt explained. 'I faked you out pretty good, though, didn't I? I thought if I acted like I was asleep, you might unwind and go to bed, too.'

Tiffany looked at him. She was touched by what he'd just said, but her mind was on other thoughts entirely. If she couldn't talk to Melissa, then she might as well talk to Kurt.

'Do you wanna try that again?' she asked, 'and not wait until the morning?' Why was her heart beating so fast? This was just Kurt. He'd never turned her down before. So why was she feeling so insecure? She could answer that question without thinking too hard. She felt out of control and, above all else, Tiffany liked to be in control. Melissa called her 'rigid', but she didn't see herself like that. *Orderly* was more like it. Still, she waited, biting her lip, for Kurt's answer.

He smiled. 'You bet.'

'It's just that it was the first time for me,' she continued in a rush, 'and I didn't really understand how everything works.'

'Of course,' Kurt said, magnanimously. 'It's all new, right? For both of us. You've never been a guy before.'

She nodded in agreement. 'So explain it all to me.'

Kurt looked at her seriously. 'I can't tell you how the whole male libido works in one night, Tiffany. That would be impossible.'

She looked at him skeptically. 'I always thought men were easy.'

'Do you think so now?'

'Not really. I mean, you seem to get excited quickly, but controlling that excitement is much more difficult than I would have expected. It's as if you have to learn to rein in the pleasure if you're a guy, while you have to strive for it if you're a girl.'

'The best thing to do is for us take things slowly. One step at a time.' He gave her a sharp look. 'And don't go getting a pad out to make a list. I know what you're like.'

'Lists are good,' she said defensively. How had he known she was itching for a pad and paper?

'Not in bed, Tiff. Just relax. Let's start with kissing –'

Tiffany was hard already. Jesus, in spite of what she'd just said, this body *was* easy. Easy to arouse, anyway. 'Okay,' she agreed, shifting on the mattress. 'Kissing. I know what you like.' Without thinking, she bent down and started to kiss Kurt's earlobe, because even though he was in her body, she had to think of the delicate earlobe as *his*. Otherwise, her head would spin and they'd be back at that awkward stage of staring at each other without being able to make a move.

Immediately, Kurt started giggling again and pushed her away. 'Naw, that doesn't really work for me right now.'

Without missing a beat, Tiffany started to gently blow into Kurt's ear, but he swatted her away, laughing harder.

Tiffany sat back, frustrated. Generally, Kurt adored it when she nibbled his earlobes or whispered sweet nothings into his ears. The act was definitely working for her. She felt that randy part of her throb against her thigh. She had to move quickly, didn't want another replay of what had already happened.

So what else turned Kurt on? He loved to have his fingers sucked on. Sometimes, she would reach for his right hand while he was driving, and she'd start by very softly licking his fingertips, showing him with her tongue and teeth what she'd do to his cock when they got back home. But when she reached for his hand, he pulled back, seeming to know what she was thinking and vetoing the idea.

What else?

He absolutely swooned when she gently scratched his back with the very tips of her fingernails. She would do this while he lay face-down on the bed and she straddled his body, punctuating the designs she traced with her finger-nails with small kisses placed at the nape of his neck. She looked down at Kurt's nails. They were too short for that sort of thing.

Her mind was filled with X-rated concepts, because truth-fully, when Kurt was in his own body, he seemed to like every erotic activity she could dream up. Foreplay was fine, but he especially loved her adventurous side in bed. He was particularly thrilled whenever she did this one move where she manipulated her body while he stayed inside of her, moving from doggy-style to missionary without pulling off of him by shifting the position of her legs. He said that it was all the yoga she did that allowed her body to be flexible enough to pull off a trick like that.

But she was getting ahead of herself, and her cock was pulsing so fiercely that she was finding it difficult to think. It felt as if all the blood had drained from her body to that one area in her groin.

'Start slow,' Kurt whispered to her, bringing her back around to his needs. 'Really slow. Back to basics, Tiffany. Pretend you've never done this before. 'Cause that's really where we are.'

He was right, and suddenly Tiffany realized the major mistake in her thought processes. She'd been thinking about what *Kurt* liked, when she ought to have been focus-ing on what she liked Kurt to do to her. She took a deep breath. Mentally, she put herself back in her old body, and she considered exactly what turned her on the most. After a moment, she kissed Kurt gently, then a bit more forcefully. She cradled his head in her hands, being the aggressor. Kurt sighed with pleasure, and Tiffany instantly felt that things were looking up, but her new body had a definite mind of its own. They'd only just started and already that cock between her legs was screaming for more. It was as if there were a voice in her head calling out: *Faster. Harder. Now!*

She had to shake off the kiss and pull away.

Why was this body so insistent?

'Slow down,' Kurt reminded her. 'Slow way down.'

Breathing hard, she tried again, stroking Kurt's breasts, kissing his neck. Kurt was making little humming sounds of pleasure, cooing even. Tiffany liked that. She desperately wanted to make him feel good. Still visualizing herself receiving pleasure, she pulled open the robe Kurt was still wearing and sucked on Kurt's nipples – first one, then the other. Yet as soon as she got into a real groove, there was that cock again, as if it had a megaphone, shouting at her, demanding satisfaction. Gratification.

'You okay?' Kurt asked tentatively. 'You look a little as if you're in pain.'

'I'm fine,' Tiffany assured him, wondering if this is what guys meant when they said they had blue balls. 'It's just that –'

Kurt put a hand on her, and it was as if his fingertips were hot. Electricity flickered through her, and she shuddered all over. She wanted to lie down and let him take over as he had before. Being in the driver's seat was such an unusual feeling. 'It's just that –'

'You're so turned on you can't stop it.'

She nodded, feeling like a teenager all over again, rediscovering what pleasure was like, but this time from a boy's point of view. It was crazy, the urges that rose up inside her. She had flashes of images of what she'd like to do to Kurt. But they weren't actually stories or fantasies, mere visions of fucking. Different positions. Different situations. Different people. When she was herself, she often fantasized during sex. She didn't see this as a problem, or as an indication that

Kurt wasn't giving her everything she needed. Playing out make-believe stories was something she'd always done, telling a tale to go with the action. But this body didn't want to hear a sexy little bedtime story. This body wanted action now.

She realized in a flash that Kurt had moved his hands lower, was slowly touching her cock, and she barked out, 'No! Don't.'

He looked offended.

'It's just that I don't want to come so quickly again –'

'But I think I'm ready,' Kurt told her tentatively, and Tiffany had the curious sensation of being the one who really was in power. Kurt was waiting for her. Ready for her. *Needing* her. She took him in a different position this time, moving his body so that the two were in a spoon embrace. Entering from behind allowed her to be drawn inside that wet womanly warmth. Working hard, she kept her head and she used her fingertips to stroke Kurt while she fucked him.

This was a little bit more like normal. Her fingers on herself. She knew the perfect melody required to give Kurt the pleasure he craved. Her fingertips trailed up and down, and then made a series of rapid circles, growing smaller with each rotation as she neared the very center of Kurt on her body. She was gratified to hear Kurt sigh deeply as he arched back against her. She knew exactly what that felt like, to be filled and stroked simultaneously, to have Kurt match his thrusts to the gyrations of his fingertips.

Yes, this was nice. She thrust her hips forward again and again, moving slowly, hitting a steady rhythm. She could do it. She could make love like a man!

Kurt seemed to like this position because he groaned and took one hand and pressed it harder against Tiffany's, urging her on. In an odd flash, she wondered if he would ever want her to fuck him again, once they returned to themselves. Would he let her buy a harness and synthetic strap-on tool and try that out? Would that actually be as arousing for her once she was a woman again?

Tiffany continued to trick her fingers up and over his clit – *his* clit! Two words she never would have thought to put together – timing the cadence of her strokes with the designs she skated up and over, around and around.

'Oh, yes –' Kurt sighed. 'Yes –'

Women in porn films came loudly, their mouths forming delicious Os, their bodies shaking with the fierce force of their pleasure. The women Kurt had been with in the past came a whole variety of ways. Some were silent as old-time screen stars, expressing everything without words, their bodies saying everything necessary. Some lovers were merely quiet, like Tiffany, giving in to the occasional moan or sigh, but never yelling, never crying out. Others had been porn star loud, as if a camera were trained on their every expression.

Aside from being a willing participant in the quest to make his partners come, Kurt had never actually given much thought to what it might be like to climax as a girl. Without a doubt, he'd wanted his lovers to reach the elusive finish line – simultaneously with him, before him, slightly after him. It didn't matter. He only hoped they had the same pleasurable experiences that he did. But what it felt like to be within their bodies, that concept had never occurred to him.

Now, he was draped in a woman's skin, and the sensations were totally unique. Sexy, yes. Sensual as all hell. He liked the silk robe against his body, open in the front, hiked up at the waist. He liked the long hair flowing down his shoulders, sometimes covering part of his face. And he especially liked the way Tiffany was touching him. Yet he could not get used to the feeling that he was missing something. Something more than a cock, that is. He felt a swelling of feeling, and he tried to imagine the ripples that Tiffany had so intricately described. Passion built within him, and that craving grew stronger. Subtly. Gently.

Was this what she meant? Her fingers teased him, the sensation taunting him with a taste of pleasure. Was this it? Was this what it was like to climax like a woman? He didn't think so. Something was missing. And then Tiffany's fingertips brushed over that little magical button, and it was as if the pleasure increased by tenfold, leaving him shaking, momentarily winded.

Yes, this is what she meant. He wasn't there yet, but close. He was almost ... almost ...

'Oh, yes,' Kurt murmured, squeezing down on her tightly, and it was all over in a heartbeat. Tiffany cried out and came, her eyes shut, her body shaking, all thoughts of holding back in order to please Kurt gone in a single breath.

Chapter Four

Sunlight played over the sheets, warm bands of gold-streaked orange that woke Tiffany before the alarm. She opened her eyes slowly, hardly daring to ask herself whether or not the previous day had all been a dream.

Oh, please, God, please –

When she rolled over on the mattress, seeing her own body peacefully asleep on the pillow, she sighed sadly and climbed out of bed. She hadn't actually expected the magic to have worn off overnight – but she couldn't help but hope.

Quietly, she made her way to the kitchen and snatched the bag of French Roast out of the freezer. As she did every morning, she turned the coffee maker to brew extra strong. Then she took a quick shower, got dressed with more ease than she had the day before, and waited for Kurt to wake up. She felt jittery about what the day held in store for her. Until they received the candle from Melissa, Tiffany was going to have to pass as Kurt, and he would have to do the same in her body. And this time, they would be mingling with a multitude of people they knew well – coworkers as well as friends. Kurt wouldn't be able to hide behind too much vodka. Tiffany wouldn't be able to hide out all day in Kurt's apartment.

As she poured herself a cup of coffee, she understood in a flash why she felt so excited. Nothing like this had ever happened to her before. Her life was all about schedules. *Predictable* schedules. Melissa often said that she was far too unyielding in her world. Tiffany laughed out loud as she headed out to get the newspaper.

If Melissa only knew.

'What the hell are you reading?'

Tiffany looked up, startled. She'd been skimming the *Style* section of the *San Francisco Chronicle*, exactly like she did every other Friday. And on Sunday morning, she would read the *New York Times Style Section* to learn all about what was fashionable on the East Coast. She especially liked the photo section, which might display twenty different tiny pictures of people wearing down vests with fur collars, or bright turquoise jewelry, or shrugs, or whatever else was currently the rage. In spite of her preference for all-black attire, Tiffany followed the fashion trends with a fierce loyalty. Anyway, Kurt knew her routine well enough. So why was he asking? When she stared at him, waiting, she saw that he was shaking his head at her. 'You need to read the Sports page.'

'I don't want to read the Sports page.' This went without saying. She'd never read the Sports page in her life.

'Yeah, but Tommy is going to want to shoot the shit with you about sports when you walk in the door. He always does. And you need to respond with something other than "Don't wear white after labor day".'

'That's not what the *Style* section says. It's all about breaking the rules now. You can wear white whenever you want to. In fact, white is the new black.'

'Whatever the fuck that means,' Kurt fumed.

Tiffany opened her mouth to explain, but Kurt didn't give her a chance.

'It's all I could come up with. I don't know anything about what your ladies' guides say.' He was clearly in a foul frame of mind, and Tiffany couldn't figure out why. Well, she could and couldn't. Yes, they were still stranded in each other's bodies, but she thought they'd begun to deal with that fact. At least, as well as could be expected. How many other couples would have been able to handle this awkward a situation without blowing up at each other? It was to be expected that there'd be a little friction, right? But *she* was the one wearing the Nicotine patch. She was the one fighting off his ugly cravings. In fact, she was the one doing all of the hard work, as far as she could tell.

'What's wrong with you?' she finally asked him after watching Kurt stomp around the kitchen. She hoped her voice sounded kindly and concerned rather than pissy. 'It's not as if you have PMS, or anything.'

'I forgot, all right?' he shot back at her.

She had a moment of mental clarity to realize that this was how *she* appeared to others when upset. She was surprised to see how ferocious she looked. Was that energy coming solely from Kurt, or did she project this sort of forceful emotion normally? She was rather impressed by the power emanating from her body. 'Forgot what?'

'I forgot that you'd absconded with my cock –'

Tiffany couldn't conceal her grin. Kurt made it sound as if she'd actually stolen the thing and run away with it, Lorena Bobbitt-style. 'And?' she asked, still smiling.

'And I peed all over the bathroom floor.'

'That's disgusting.' She couldn't help herself, but from the look in Kurt's eyes, it was the wrong thing to say.

'I've been peeing standing up my whole life. I can practically do it in my sleep. So reaching between my legs and coming up empty handed was a rude awakening, let me tell you.' He paused, then added, 'How the fuck do you girls do it anyway? Seriously.'

He slumped heavily on the chair, his legs spread apart in a most unladylike fashion, and Tiffany almost laughed.

'We sit.' She said this very primly, and Kurt looked as if he was going to brain her with the polished chrome toaster. 'What's so great about peeing standing up, anyway?' She was genuinely curious – this was something she'd never thought about in her entire life – but Kurt didn't answer. She had peed standing up now for two days and she could take it or leave it. At least as a girl, you never had to mess with the lid. Although as a boy, she was definitely conscious of making sure to leave the seat down for Kurt. She had no desire for him to experience the awful cold wetness of falling into an open toilet. See that? She was a conscientious boyfriend. The thought made her want to chuckle, but glancing at Kurt killed the desire.

Scowling, he stood up again, stamped his way toward the coffee pot, and poured a cup for himself. Tiffany was enchanted to see that he'd chosen a porcelain mug with little pink roses dancing all over it. She was fairly sure that he'd done so unintentionally, but the effect was sweet nevertheless. After watching him burn his tongue and embark upon a two-minute swearing streak, she decided to continue reading the *Style* section. Ignoring him seemed the best bet at the moment. If he was going to *try* to have a bad day, let him.

'It's great,' he said after a moment.

Well, that was better. Much more positive. 'I know,' Tiffany agreed. 'I love French Roast. See how nice it is to have coffee in the house? You could do that too if you ever planned ahead.'

'Not the coffee. Peeing standing up. It's cool, and it's fun and it never gets old. Not ever. You can go wherever you are, against a tree, behind a building. It's frigging awesome.'

Tiffany didn't look up from the paper. 'Peeing in public is revolting. The world is not your urinal.'

'Well, what's so great about the *Style* section?'

Now, she peered at him over the top of the newspaper. 'I didn't say it was so great.'

'Yeah, but why do women even care? You can buy one outfit, or a few outfits, one for each day of the week, if you like, and be done with it. Why do you always want more? More clothes. More shoes. More earrings. More bras. I really hate your bras, you know.'

'Women like to keep in style –' As soon as Tiffany said the words, she realized she'd fallen into his trap.

'Yeah, but if you just bought a week's worth of clothes, you'd never have to think about it again. Monday, black suit. Tuesday, red dress. Wednesday –'

'Die of fucking boredom,' Tiffany cut him off. Kurt looked pleased with her for remembering to swear.

'Anyway,' he said, 'it's just a rat race. Always wanting to outdo your friends. Showing off, that's what I call it.'

'Feeling good about yourself is different from showing off,' Tiffany corrected him, wondering when he'd notice that she was wearing another new outfit. She'd bought two just in case. Today, she had on a white shirt and a canary yellow tie beneath a gray cashmere sweater. To tone down the formality of the outfit, she'd put on a pair of buttonfly Lucky brand jeans. Kurt always wore zip-ups, but she thought buttonflys were cooler. She wondered if he'd like the effect – when you popped open the buttons, there were the words 'Lucky You' waiting, like a secret, to be revealed. 'I feel better in nice clothes. I like to dress for my moods. For instance,' she continued, biting back a smile, 'if I were you, I'd be in black. To match the cloud over your head –'

'Ooh, call the papers,' Kurt said sarcastically.

'What do you mean?'

'That's no fucking surprise. You *always* wear black. Your entire closet is monotone. It's like you think you're a funeral director, or something. If white is the new black, then, baby, you are mercilessly out of style.'

Tiffany didn't even know how to answer that. 'Why are you so upset this morning? You don't have to be anywhere until two. *I've* got to get to work in less than forty-five minutes.' She was strangely excited about this. 'Why are you even up?'

'Because your bladder is the size of a fucking pea. You could never be a long-distance trucker, you know it?'

'I've never *wanted* to be a long-distance trucker.'

'Well, I've never wanted to be a girl,' Kurt shot back.

Tiffany sighed. 'Now that you *are* up, remind me what I have to do today –'

'You have to call in sick –'

'What do you mean?'

Kurt was eyeing Tiffany in a slightly new manner. Apparently, the coffee was starting to take effect, lifting more than his spirits. He seemed much less grumpy all of a sudden. 'You heard me.'

'But I thought we'd worked this whole thing out.' Tiffany was confused. 'I'm going to play you today and you'll play me. At least, until we get hold of Melissa.' Melissa still hadn't answered her home phone or her cell. Neither had Rick. But Tiffany had a final cake-tasting appointment with the couple this afternoon, and she was certain Melissa wouldn't miss that. Where the wedding was concerned, Melissa was as committed as she could possibly be. As soon as they got the candle from Melissa, they'd be able to solve everything. 'You said you didn't want to miss another day of work,' Tiffany finished.

'Yeah,' Kurt agreed. 'But I changed my mind.'

'You changed your –'

'Mind. Women's prerogative, and all that shit –' He had a Cheshire cat grin on his face, and Tiffany felt her heart sink.

'You think I'm going to mess up at your office, don't you?' she asked, her confidence shaken. Kurt was in charge of a team at the photo service bureau, where he complained bitterly and often about his ineffective boss Carly. Tiffany was ready to go in all shiny and new. To show his coworkers what the real Kurt Fielding was like. To win them over with her charm.

'That's not it at all,' Kurt assured her. 'I just want to try out what we did last night all over again.'

'You want me to call in sick so we can make love –' Tiffany flushed.

'Fuck,' Kurt interrupted. 'I want you to call in sick so that we can fuck all day. Or at least, half a day. Now you say it. It's not that hard.'

'Fuck,' she echoed quietly. Why did she find swearing so difficult? Expletives were only words, after all. At least, that's what Kurt always claimed. He disliked when dirty lyrics were bleeped on the radio, couldn't understand why 'darn' was acceptable but 'damn' was not. 'It's all a sham,' he liked to say. 'If everyone realized that saying "having sex" is the same thing as saying "fucking", the world would be a much more honest place.'

Now, Kurt waited for Tiffany to agree with his new plan. 'We can spend all morning in bed together. Then I'll meet up with Melissa this afternoon, scoop up the candle, light the fucking thing, and make the reverse wish.' His blue eyes were shining brightly as he spoke. 'What if it works, Tiff? What if we're back in our bodies in an instant? Then we'll have wasted the whole day trying to fool other people into believing we are who we aren't when we could be doing so much more fun things together.'

Tiffany's blush deepened. Kurt started to laugh at her. 'You always get that look on your face when you're thinking of doing something wicked – at least, something *you* consider wicked. It's odd to see the same look on *my* face. But you are, aren't you?'

'Are what?'

'Considering it.'

Reluctantly, she nodded. If she only had one more day in Kurt's body, it *would* be kind of silly to spend it trapped in his office. Even if she'd been enjoying the thought of cleaning up his desk, something she hadn't yet told him. That was going to be a surprise. She'd even bought a new leather desk blotter and pen-holder when she'd purchased the new clothes. But perhaps she'd given him enough surprises already. In fact, if she were to look at the situation from Kurt's perspective, the whole switching of bodies thing might have used up her surprise allotment for an entire life time.

'Well –' she said hesitatingly. 'What are you thinking of exactly?'

'I want to try out a few different positions. I want to see how things feel from your point of view.' He had an ulterior motive for this, but he didn't want to share it with Tiffany just yet. During their previous two encounters, he hadn't actually climaxed. At least, he didn't *think* that he had. Being a woman was so strange. There was much more to fucking as a woman than he would have thought. In the past, he would have believed that giving pleasure really was the man's responsibility. That women could sort of lay back and enjoy the show. But after the past twenty-four hours, he felt differently.

'Positions,' Tiffany repeated. From the start, this conversation had been turning her on, which meant she now sported a woody any man would have been proud of. She shifted gently on the wooden kitchen chair, and Kurt glanced at her with obvious interest. 'You're hard, aren't you?'

She nodded.

'Good. That's the first thing we need. But I want you to last a bit longer than last night. So we'll have to take things slow. Even slower, I mean. You're a bit over-zealous – very willing, very ready.'

'I thought you said I was doing well,' Tiffany pouted. What did he expect? Yesterday had been her first time screwing as a man.

'You were fine,' Kurt assured her. 'But let's get even better.' While he spoke, he headed to the phone and dialed a number by heart. 'Tell Mari-Beth that you're still fighting off that bug. You'll tele-commute again today.'

'Can't you call? You know how awful I am at lying.'

'For obvious reasons, I can't.'

Tiffany nodded, taking the phone and clearing her throat. When she'd called in sick the previous day, she'd told herself that she was trapped in a bad dream. But this was reality, and she felt as guilty as she had the one and only time she played hooky from school. Now, when she caught sight of her reflection in the toaster on the counter, it was as if she could actually see her true self within the confines of Kurt's handsome frame. He never appeared nervous like this. His confidence was one of the things she found sexiest about him. Certain that she'd be found out, she squeezed her eyes shut tightly behind Kurt's glasses and said, 'Hey there, Mari-Beth.'

'Hiya Kurt,' the receptionist responded without missing a beat. 'How was your game?'

Kurt, who was standing right next to Tiffany, whispered, 'Great, we won.'

'Great!' Tiffany said as enthusiastically as possible. 'We won.'

'Awesome, I knew you would,' Mari-Beth purred. 'Would have liked to have seen you beat Jarred.'

They were talking about a basketball game at the Y, Tiffany suddenly realized. Kurt must have played with his league while she'd been in New Orleans. She opened her eyes again and looked over at him. But why did Mari-Beth know about this, and why was the girl being so hyper-friendly? Mari-Beth never attended any of the games when she'd been there in the stands. Jealousy coursed through her, and she narrowed her eyes as she stared at Kurt.

'So what's up? You on your cell?'

'No,' Tiffany said coolly. 'I'm still fighting off this sore throat. Thought I'd stay home today and tele-commute. Keep you all from getting sick.'

'We'll miss you –'

'See you Monday,' Tiffany said, her voice dropping another notch on the coldness level to reach Arctic territory. What was *that* all about? She hung up the phone and glared at Kurt, who seemed to have read her mind.

'Mari-Beth is like that with everyone.'

'Like what?' She wouldn't give him an inch.

'Friendly –'

'I'd say that was considerably more than friendly.'

'Flirty, then. Whatever. She wants to work her way up, and this is the way she thinks will make a difference. But you do know she's got a girlfriend, right?'

Tiffany stared at him.

'Really. She's dating this girl in Human Resources. They live in the Castro together in an old Victorian called Knobby Clark's Folly. The rest of it is just an act. So drop the hurt look on your face and meet me in the bedroom. I want you to take me doggy-style –'

As soon as he said the words, Tiffany realized she wanted that, too.

Quickly, she shook off her feelings of mistrust and headed after Kurt to her bedroom. When she arrived, he was already in position on the center of the mattress, long waves of white-blonde hair tossed over his shoulder, looking at her expectantly.

Her hard-on throbbed.

There were definite benefits of being in this body. Apparently, Kurt needed no foreplay at all to get in the mood. The mere whiff of sex in the conversation was all it took to have him raring to go.

Tiffany thought of all the comedians she'd ever seen who had riffed on the differences between men and women. And then there were the self-help books that strived to explain how partners ought to best get along. Melissa had a whole shelf full of titles that claimed men and women came from different planets, and other ones that coached potential lovers through all sorts of problems based on their Zodiac signs. Nothing, however, had ever prepared Tiffany for a situation like this. She stifled a laugh at the thought that she ought to write her own book when this whole mess got straightened out. *If* it got straightened out. *Women Who Are Men Who Love Men Who Are Women.* That might just be an all-time best-seller. She could go on *Oprah . . .*

'How did you ever learn so much about the male psyche?' Oprah would ask her.

'Well, you just have to put yourself in their skin,' she would reply, and no one would understand her own private joke but Kurt.

'Tiffany,' Kurt murmured, bringing her around again.

As she stripped out of her outfit, she began to plan the encounter. Kurt had told her that she was behaving like a teenager raring on hormones. So how would she improve? Just as she had the previous evening, she tried to remember the times when sex had been the very best for her ... Kurt liked to experiment. That was one of her favorite things about him. She felt sad for a minute realizing that when she talked about Kurt with Melissa, she tended to dwell on the things she didn't like. At some point, she ought to make a list of his positive attributes, because there were many. Like the fact that whenever she bought new lingerie, he noticed. And that occasionally he would call her up from work to ask her what color panties she had on. He thought it was sexy to have her peek down and describe the design, the style, the color. For as much as he claimed to hate her bras right now, he had a bit of a fetish when it came to the lingerie she chose, and that suited her just fine. She liked to put on private fashion shows for him, revealing emerald silk peignoirs and candy-pink marabou-trimmed nighties. The only thing sexier than displaying her lingerie for him was to have him take the flirty nothings off her. Or take most off. Sometimes, he was so hot he didn't even have time to take her panties down her slim thighs, making do with simply moving them aside.

She shut her eyes, remembering a recent tryst in the bathroom. He'd faced her toward the mirror and entered her from behind, his hand sliding automatically between her legs, stroking her: *'Is that your clit? You know it is. I can find it without even thinking, can't I...'*

'Yes,' Tiffany had sighed.

'I always can,' Kurt had said, satisfied as he'd touched her.

So yes, he was a talented lover – and thinking like this made her even harder. When her cock was this erect, suddenly she had little thoughts for anything else. Her brain became consumed with a lustful need. Was it like that for Kurt? That rod between her legs became a beacon, pulling her, urging her, demanding that she pay attention to its hungry appetite. Testosterone coursed through her body, and she had instant visions of how she'd like to fuck. Kurt was right. There wasn't anything about this body that wanted to make love. Not right now.

Fuck, she thought with relish. The word made her whole body stand taller, made her heart race even faster. Maybe she could actually get into this. It was difficult to admit even to herself, but she rather enjoyed being in charge, looking down from behind, taking control of her own pleasure as well as Kurt's. As she *did* know what gave her the most pleasure, it was easy to be kind to Kurt in his new feminine form.

For the first time in her life, she could see her body from a distance. With a critical eye, she realized that she was actually quite beautiful. She had pale skin, but healthy and pink-flushed. She'd always thought her hair was plain, too straight, too bland. Now she saw that when Kurt brushed it just so, her long tresses shone even in dim light. The curves of her body were enticing, and she could appreciate parts of herself she'd never been able to really see before – the dainty dimples above her ass, the strength in her calves, the beauty of the muscles in her back.

'Tiff –' Kurt said again, wriggling his hips.

Doggy-style. He'd chosen this position because it was one that they enjoyed all the time. Kurt liked to stand behind Tiffany, to wrap one hand in her long hair, to pull her head back while he thrust inside her. Tiffany worked into the same position more slowly. She held onto Kurt's waist and slipped just the head of her cock inside him, and he immediately contracted on her, sending her thoughts spiraling out of control. Good Lord, that felt amazing. Regaining herself with extreme effort, she slid one hand under Kurt's waist and felt how wet he was. The liquid of his arousal glistened on her fingers when she pulled back her hand. Yes, he was ready. Gently, she touched Kurt the way she'd always liked Kurt to take care of her – and he responded immediately and positively to each caress.

'Oh, God, Tiffany,' he moaned.

A warm rush of pleasure spread through Tiffany's entire body. She was doing it! She was pleasing him. Her fingertips continued on their concentric trip around Kurt's clit. She made small diamonds between his pussy lips, then broadened the designs to ovals and circles within circles.

'Don't stop,' he begged her, his head lowered, hair falling across his face and onto the mattress. 'Please, Tiff, don't stop.'

She continued to treat him sweetly, touching him as she fucked him. Working to retain her sense of balance. She was a master at yoga, knew how to breathe deeply from the diaphragm, to hold a difficult pose for an extraordinary length of time. Stamina. She had it as a woman. She needed it as a man.

With an eye on the finish line, and on keeping herself from arriving there too soon, she continued to use her fingertips to make those decadent circles up and around Kurt's clit. Each time the balls of her fingertips caressed him, he moaned and arched against her, rewarding her with pleasure of her own.

'Please –' he moaned. 'God, Tiff, please –'

She would last longer this time. There was no chance that she would fail him again.

'Don't stop,' Kurt begged. 'That feels unreal,' and Tiffany could tell that he meant the compliment from deep inside of himself. With her cock, she continued to thrust into Kurt, pushing forward with her hips, her fingers still tapping a delicate tune against that softly swollen button between his legs. And then, without a thought, she let her free hand fall down on Kurt's ass. Not too hard, but hard enough. The sound of the spank rang out in the air, a staccato applause-like burst shattering the quiet of the room. Immediately, Kurt pulled away from her and looked over his shoulder, giving her an incredulous stare.

'Why did you do that?'

'I don't know –' she stammered. That wasn't entirely true. She *did* know, but she wasn't sure she could explain the reason to Kurt. Especially not now, while they were enmeshed in such an erotic moment. She'd always wanted him to do something like this to her, and from her perspective, behind him, looking down, the time had seemed right. And perhaps there was the tiniest part of herself that wanted to get him back for the flirtiousness of Mari-Beth on the phone.

'How'd it feel?' she asked cautiously.

He shook his head, and his long blonde hair fell forward into his eyes. He looked sexy like that. All rumpled and sensuous. 'Just startled me, that's all.' And with a little jut of his chin, he said, 'Keep going.'

She did, gripping into his hips, fucking him even harder now. They were in rhythm, in tandem, and as the pleasure swelled within her, Kurt said softly, 'Do that again.'

'Spank you?'

His voice was low. 'Yeah.'

She obeyed immediately, letting her hand smack against Kurt's ass, thrilled by the reverberations that each blow won. Echoes of pleasure. She only stopped when she came, holding onto his hips even harder, knowing that she would be leaving fingermarks against his pale skin, and not caring the slightest.

'I didn't know you liked that,' he said afterward.

She shrugged. 'I didn't either.' Once again, this wasn't the straight truth. She had an idea that she'd wanted to play that way for a long time. She'd had fantasies, after all. Visions that brought her over the top when she was all by herself. But aside from the light bondage games she and Kurt had tried, they'd never pushed this sort of boundary.

'Did you want to spank me, or be spanked?' he asked, curious.

She had to shrug again. 'Well, you're usually the one in charge, so I've envisioned you putting me over your lap before, but I guess I'd have to say that my fantasies run both ways.'

He looked exceptionally thrilled to hear this. 'Cool,' he said simply, laying back on the bed and staring up at the ceiling. 'Totally cool.'

She was excited by his response. She'd never have dared to confess this sort of dirty desire before. Or if she'd thought of it, she'd backed out, afraid of Kurt's reaction. There was a big difference between wearing fur-lined cuffs and being the recipient of an over-the-knee spanking. At least, she'd always thought there was.

But now that she'd told Kurt, they would be able to play this way in the future. Switching roles. Taking turns. How strange that they were reaching these new heights of honesty while encased in one another's bodies. Tiffany felt closer to him than she ever had before. She supposed that made sense in a way. She was in his skin, after all. But there was more to the feeling than that. They were sharing an adventure, one that equally involved them both. It was like embarking on a trip to a strange land, with only one person as your mate. If she'd had to choose someone to venture out with, she definitely would have picked Kurt.

Tiffany realized how lucky she was that it was Kurt who she had switched with. What if she'd unwittingly thought of an old beau at the moment the wish was made. Like Ryan? Or what if something completely different had fluttered through her mind – where or *who* might she be right now? An astronaut? The president? A race-car driver?

'You know what I could really use right now?' Kurt asked, bringing her back down to earth.

'Don't say a cigarette,' she winced, 'I've got the patch on.'

'A shower,' he told her. 'With you. I've got a few fantasies of my own I'd like to try out.'

Chapter Five

'Hey, Melissa.' Kurt's eyebrows were raised at Tiffany, silently asking if he'd nailed her general tone of voice. Even though she thought Kurt was acting a little too effervescent, Tiffany nodded encouragingly. She didn't want to criticize him. Not after all that she'd put him through since the switch had taken place. She was doing her best to learn from the situation, and being less critical was at the pinnacle of her list of things to change about herself.

'What's up, Tiff?' Melissa asked. 'You all recovered from your little binge?'

'Hmm? Oh, yeah, much better. Sorry about that.'

'You got a taste of the Big Easy and just couldn't let go –'

'You know me. I spend so much time worrying about what people will think of me, that I forget to let my hair down.' Tiffany punched Kurt in the shoulder when he said this, but he shrugged her off. He was having a good time ragging her, and she knew that she deserved the teasing and ought to be a good sport. That was also high on her personal list.

'That's why this mini-break was so important for you. You need to unwind more, Tiff. Let up a little bit.'

'Well, as a matter of fact, that's why I'm calling –' Kurt responded, using her comment to segue gracefully into the reason for all the phone messages he had left on Melissa's machine. 'You know those candles – the ones you bought at that Witches' Shoppe?' Kurt drove forward, not even letting Melissa say yes. 'I was wondering if I could have one of them.'

'Of course, Tiffany. But why –'

'One of the LOVE ones. I'd like to try it out. I thought you could bring one with you to the cake-tasting today.'

'But you don't believe in that stuff. You said so yourself.

As I remember, you were quite emphatic about labeling the whole adventure as an overpriced load of rubbish.'

Tiffany, listening in on the cordless extension, felt as if she could actually hear the sound of Melissa's liquid brown eyes widening in disbelief.

'Yeah, well, Kurt and I had a little spat today,' her boyfriend continued, improvising now, 'and I just thought –'

'A candle won't fix your problems with Kurt, Tiff. You know that as well as I do.'

'Really?' Kurt asked, his interest piqued. 'What will?'

'A Valium.' Melissa laughed darkly.

'What do you mean? Drug him?' Kurt looked horrified.

'No, drug *you*. You need to learn to relax, not care so much about Kurt's little idiosyncracies – and that's all they are, Tiff – tiny little character traits. So he has socks hanging from his ceiling fan? So fucking what?'

Why was Melissa going on like this? It hadn't occurred to Tiffany that her friend would want to chat, to talk casually as they usually did. What if she told Kurt something that Tiffany had revealed to her in private? Was there anything truly damning that Melissa might reveal?

'Maybe some of the things that he does *are* annoying,' Melissa blithely continued, 'like his penchant for pranks, or his tendency to be late, but you should focus more on trying to enjoy life rather than working to change everyone to fit your ideal model. Didn't the Katrina hurricane teach you anything? And just look at the way people in New Orleans are pulling together, not letting little nothings bother them.'

Kurt made a face at Tiffany – an 'I told you so face' – smug beyond belief. He even stuck his tongue out at her. Tiffany scowled back at him, still holding the extension to her ear so she could hear every word. Why was Melissa rambling on like this? She'd have given anything to be able to tell Melissa to hush up – or better yet to explain what was really going on, but she couldn't.

'Anyway, I'd still like to try it.'

'No problem. I think I got extras, actually. So when the luggage turns up –'

'The luggage –'

'They lost my bag. Remember?'

'The candles were in your bag?' The thought hadn't occurred to either Kurt or Tiffany. The whole baggage claim had been much of a blur to both of them.

'Yeah. But the airline promises to send the bag over. Just as soon as they find it. I think they mentioned the suitcase was on route to New Zealand right now. And if they don't locate the case within three weeks, they're going to reimburse me. I think the witch on the phone mentioned $420 dollars, or something minuscule like that. Won't even cover the original cost of the suitcase, let alone what was inside of it. Rick was right about that. Why I thought I needed a matching set of Louis Vuitton luggage.' She sighed deeply. 'I really ought to have bought one of those voodoo dolls, Tiff. I could have poked the pins into it and imagined the handlers in baggage claim –'

Tiffany watched Kurt's shoulders sag.

'You still there?' Melissa asked, sounding concerned.

'Yeah,' he said, nodding as he spoke but looking miserable.

'So, I'll see you later, at Jo-Jo's Bakery for the cake-tasting?'

'You bet,' he said, still looking dumbfounded.

'And maybe we can go out afterwards. For a Cosmo.'

'Or a Valium,' Kurt told her before he hung up the phone.

'She suspects something,' Tiffany said as soon as Kurt had replaced the receiver. She began to pace around the kitchen, her heart racing.

'No, she doesn't,' Kurt emphatically disagreed.

'She must. You didn't really sound like me. And at the end there, you really almost blew it.'

All plans of not criticizing Kurt had evaporated once Tiffany had remembered that the luggage was lost. This was her only hope, as far as she was concerned. Now, she had absolutely no idea what to do. And Tiffany was never without a plan. She felt as if she were drowning. Each breath came with great difficulty.

'Are you kidding? I sounded exactly like you. I should get a fucking Oscar.' Kurt was clearly feeling tetchy, as well.

'But she's known me forever. She's sure to pick up on any little difference –'

'She didn't guess. She doesn't know. Nobody in their right mind would think this had happened to us.'

'How can you be so sure?'

'Because it's not one of those explanations that comes up on a daily basis. Someone might be late because of traffic. Or acting nasty because of a wicked headache. But in the history of time nobody has ever sounded strange on the phone because they mistakenly switched bodies with their lover. That's just not something that happens, Tiffany.'

When he put it like that, she realized he was right. Still –

The phone rang before she could respond. Tiffany shot Kurt a look as he answered, saying 'You see?' with her expression.

'Hello?' Kurt said, his voice softer than before, more subdued.

'Hey, Tiff.' It was a man. And Kurt knew exactly which man it was.

'Hiya, Rick.'

'Look, I was wondering if we could get together some-time, to talk about the wedding –'

Tiffany mimed to Kurt to put his hand over the phone, then whispered, 'Remind him about the cake-tasting this afternoon.'

Kurt relayed the information to Rick. There was a brief discussion, and she listened intently as Kurt put Rick off with a casual comment about checking his calendar and getting back to him.

'He says he wants to meet with you privately,' Kurt told her once he'd gotten off the phone.

'I wonder what that was about?' Tiffany mused.

'What do you mean?'

'Why would he want to meet with me without Melissa?'

Kurt shrugged. 'Maybe he wants to plan a surprise for her. Or perhaps he wants to tell you he despises the color scheme. That he wants to start over from scratch.' He said this last part with an evil gleam in his eye.

Tiffany's face whitened. 'Everything's already set. The colors are lovely – that morning lilac and –'

'Murder-me red?'

She shook her head. 'You're not funny. And anyway, it's

far too late to change all of that. But it's strange, isn't it, that he'd be calling me?'

Kurt shook his head. 'You're way too suspicious, Tiffany. I know much more about guys than you do. Trust me. I know Rick. He's fine –'

Tiffany couldn't shake the feeling that something was wrong. But she decided she'd have to listen to Kurt right now. What other options did she have? Still, the fact that they were stuck indefinitely as one another weighed heavily on her.

'Look,' she felt she had to say, 'now that we have to wait a little bit longer than we'd thought, we need to work on some guidelines in order to get through this situation.'

'Guidelines?' Kurt asked hesitantly. He didn't think he was going to like where this conversation was headed.

'If we're not careful, people are going to think we're crazy, or stupid, or on drugs, or something. I'm not going to be by your side all day long, and vice versa.'

'And your recommendation is what, exactly?'

'For the first thing, we should probably plan to live in each other's apartment for the time being.'

'Why?'

'Come on, Kurt. Because that's where all of our stuff is.'

'I know, and I like my stuff.'

'But you can't go around dressing me in your clothes. And I won't fit in mine anymore. Besides, wouldn't you be embarrassed if I started to trick you out in my favorite dresses?'

'All right,' he agreed, nodding. 'What else?'

'We need to make lists.'

Kurt looked less pleased by this idea. Tiffany created 'to do' lists all the time. She had note pads displayed all around the house, in every one of her purses, and by her bed. There was even one suctioned to the wall of her shower, complete with a waterproof marker on a string at its side. Kurt felt that Tiffany's life was run by lists, and he didn't want his own life to follow suit. But Tiffany wasn't looking at his face, so she couldn't see his lack of approval. Instead, she reached for the pad of paper she always kept by the phone and settled down on her sofa. She looked convincingly bookish. Kurt had never seen himself in such a serious pose. Even when he *was* serious, he tended to joke around about things. Not Tiffany.

'But *why* do we need to write lists?' he asked, sounding as if he were afraid he might be bored.

'Because I'm afraid you'll forget everything if we don't.'

'I won't forget.'

'When's my birthday?'

'June third.'

She shook her head.

'Second,' he said next, clearly guessing.

Another head shake, more upset this time.

'First. I knew it was the first. That's the same day as Marilyn Monroe's, right? That's what you always say. Of course, it would be the perfect mnemonic if I gave a fuck about when Marilyn Monroe was born.'

'What year?'

'I don't know. 1926? Somewhere around there. She wasn't that old when she died, was she? Like forty-something.'

'Not Monroe. Me.' Tiffany was losing her patience.

'1970 –' He paused. '1975.'

'1976. Do you really think I look thirty-one?' She was aghast.

'Oh, God, Tiffany. Don't start. You don't look a day over twenty-nine. Is that what you want me to say? Why do I need to know all this again? Do you think someone's going to card me?'

'No, I just don't want to worry about you goofing up. And you're not going to be able to access my accounts if you don't have the code.'

'Which accounts?'

'I use the same code for my email password and my ATM –' When he started to interrupt, she spoke over him. 'Six one seven six, and *no*, you can't use yours when you're out and about. Sometimes, a clerk will want to check your ID, and you can't be Kurt Fielding. You have to be Tiffany Mitchell. My VISA card has my photo on it. So you *have* to be me. When you go to the cake-tasting, you're going to pay with my debit card. That means entering the code. You've got to be able to remember it.'

'You use your birthday for those? You're not supposed to do that!'

'It's year first and then the day. Why? What's yours?'

He hesitated.

'Tell me, Kurt.'

'It's three two three three.'

'What's that stand for?'

'The two jersey numbers of my all-time favorite basketball players.' Now *he* was the one to look suspiciously at her. 'And you ought to be able to name them. You've heard me talk about them enough.'

Tiffany felt herself go pale. 'Um, Michael Jordan and Magic Johnson.'

'One right.'

She took a deep breath. 'Magic Johnson and – and Joe Namath.'

'He was a football player, you ninny.'

'I was kidding. I know that. It's Larry Bird. And I've never understood how you could like someone from the Lakers and someone from the Celtics? Aren't they sworn enemies?'

Kurt gave her a look of deep admiration. 'At least you know the teams.'

'Well, how *can* you?'

'Doesn't matter. They were both excellent, and I got to see them play live.'

'That's awesome –' They looked at each other a minute. Tiffany realized that she'd just learned something new about Kurt after four years of dating. How often did that happen? She wondered what else she might not know about him, and found herself unexpectedly excited at the prospect of uncovering more secrets. It was the same way she'd felt about going into his office, being undercover, like a spy in his private world. She'd never been the type to do any covert searching about her boyfriend's activities, but she couldn't deny the thrill she felt at the thought of her furtive plans.

'Okay,' Kurt pressed on, 'so now we know the codes. What else?'

'Well, there are things you ought to do – and not do – as me.'

'Like?'

'You shouldn't eat too much sugar, because my body can't handle the buzz. I get kind of hyper.'

'You? Hyper?'

'Sarcasm is out,' she said. 'That sounds way too much like you and not like me at all.'

'I'm taking your body to a cake-tasting. How'm I supposed to avoid the sugar?'

'Have little bites,' she told him. 'And you shouldn't drink too much caffeine. Or chew that Dubble-Bubble gum you like. Or eat shellfish, because I'm allergic. Or –'

'Have any fucking fun –'

'Swear!' she nearly shouted it. 'If you're going to be me, you need to act like me. This afternoon, you're going to be out with Melissa all by yourself. You can't behave strangely. I don't care what you say. She might not guess the real cause for your weirdness, but she'll definitely know that something's up. It's not as if you can be drunk all the time when you're with her.'

'Well, how about you?'

'How about me what?'

'You're way too put together. You look like an ad for some men's style magazine. *GQ* or *Esquire*, one of those.'

Tiffany took this as a compliment, even though she knew he didn't mean it as one. 'I'm only enjoying dressing your body.'

'Well, stop it. You should be a little more rumpled. People are going to wonder if you're going after a new job, or something.'

'As a matter of fact, I've been getting tons of compliments.'

'From who? Guys in the Castro?'

'Kurt –'

'The only people who dress like that are guys who like guys, Tiffany. I swear.'

'That's not true,' Tiffany informed him. 'Everyone likes the new you. The clerk at the newsstand this morning. The lady at the flower store yesterday.'

'Why on earth did you go to a flower store?'

'I had to check up on the order for Melissa's wedding.'

'As *me*?'

'I told her that I was doing a favor for you. She didn't

have a problem with that at all. Thought it was sweet. And she said she liked my tie.'

'Well, at least listen to me about this – you don't have to wear ties to work. Not every day. Not on days that there aren't major meetings. You can get by in a button-up shirt, or even a T-shirt under a jacket as long as it's clean.'

'Yeah, well, you look good in a tie.'

'I thought we were making lists, here.'

'We are. What else is on your list?' She didn't really want to hear his list, because she was fairly sure he wouldn't take the concept to heart. But she felt she had to ask any- way, out of politeness if nothing else.

'You're right. Since this is going to take a bit longer to sort out than we originally thought, there are some things you need to do as me. First, you have to go to the Y and practice with the guys. And *without* the guys. You're going to need all the extra help you can get. You have to work out at least three times a week.'

'Do *you* do that?'

'I'm saying what *you* have to do.'

'All right.' She wrote down everything he said.

'You have to learn to play Centipede.'

'Why on earth would I have to do that?'

'Because sometimes I go over to Axel's and play it. He's got a whole slew of classic video games. PacMan. Asteroids. Centipede. That's the one I kill at. And if you don't bone up, you'll crash and burn.'

She wrinkled her nose. She thought video games were a waste of time. But at least he wasn't asking her to learn one of the exceptionally violent ones. Centipede she could handle.

'You have to eat a donut when you get to work, and you have to dunk it in your coffee.'

'Can't I get a carrot muffin or something healthier?'

'Donut. Cake donut. They're the best. They've got some weight to them. Dunk it in the coffee and eat it while you check your email. I do that every morning. Oh, and you have to make plans to go fishing.'

'Fishing –'

'I promised I'd go with Rick at some point after he gets back from his honeymoon. We're working out the schedule now. I'm sure I told you about that.' He gazed around as if trying to remember all the important things that made him who he was. 'Oh, yeah, and you have to jack off in the morning –'

'That's on your list?'

'There's nothing wrong with a little self-pleasure. And my body expects the release. Otherwise, you're going to be getting hard on and off all day long.'

'Are you kidding me?'

'Look, Tiffany, we men are very sexual creatures.'

'You make it sound as if you live in a jungle.'

'I do. The asphalt jungle, baby –'

'You're not taking this seriously at all.' Tiffany pouted.

Kurt started to laugh. 'You're right, Tiff. I'm not. We'll be able to pass convincingly as each other. We've been dating long enough. I know all of the little things that you do that drive me and your friends crazy. I know how you take your coffee. I know how you wear your hair. I know how you write your lists.' He sighed. 'But I still can't believe I'm going to a cake-tasting.'

Better than a flower show, she thought, or that afternoon she'd spent watching a caterer demonstrate for her the seventeen different ways that linen napkins could be folded. Like swans. Like fishes. Like cranes. Like lilies ... He'd have gone out of his head.

'You'll have fun,' she assured him. 'You and Melissa and Rick, tasting icings.'

Kurt shook his head. 'Rick backed out. Said he couldn't tell French Vanilla from Tahitian Vanilla, so he'd leave the final decision up to Melissa –'

'That's not really what he said, was it?'

Kurt shook his head. 'You're right. He said that once you licked one type of frosting, you'd licked them all –'

'And you're still telling me that wasn't a come-on?' Tiffany was concerned.

'If that's his type of an advance, he needs to work on his delivery,' Kurt told her.

Tiffany hesitated. Maybe Kurt was right. He definitely knew more about men than she did. 'But what am I going to do while you're out? I called in sick today. I can't go to work.'

'Weren't you paying attention to your list? You need to go to the gym. Jerk off. And have a jelly donut.'

'You said cake.' She glanced down at her handwriting to make sure.

'I'm messing with you, Tiffany.'

'Well, stop it.'

Kurt sighed. 'Try to have a little fun, Tiff. We don't know how long this is all going to last. You can't get twitchy over every little bump in the road. Go to my apartment. Get some sweats. And head to the gym. You like to work out. It'll be fun for you to try things from a new perspective.'

When Kurt put it like that, Tiffany had to agree. But she was still so wound up in what people might think of her that she couldn't stop herself from asking the next question: 'What are you going to wear today?' Kurt was in one of his own faded T-shirts, which hung well past his thighs.

'Don't you worry so much about me. I'm a big girl. I can handle myself. You're the one who's way overdressed.'

Tiffany wouldn't listen to him. She liked the way his body looked clad in the new style. Rather than defend it anymore, she simply said, 'If we don't work all these things out, Kurt, I know there are going to be problems.'

'Let's just go for it, Tiff, and if there are problems, we'll handle them as they emerge.'

Problems emerged almost instantly. Once Tiffany had left for his apartment, Kurt kicked back on her sofa and paged through the magazines fanned neatly on the antique coffee table. He checked out each title, and grimaced. All Tiffany had to read at the house were ladies' magazines. Kurt rifled through one, reading the article headlines: From Blah to Beautiful Before You Know It, The Twelve-Thousand-Dollar Workout Plan, Thirty-One-To-Die-For Little Black Dresses, A Gold-Digger's Guide to Getting a Man, and then he tossed it onto the floor. He couldn't stand the selection. There was no *Sports Illustrated*. No *Maxim*. No *Playboy*. No *Penthouse*. Nothing worth reading. He stood up and looked at her bookshelves. Maybe there was something here for him.

No such luck.

After glancing along the titles, he had a sudden desire to

knock all the books off the shelf. They were too well organized, to start with, and the bindings were so stiff it was as
if they'd never been read. He looked closer. She'd placed the
books alphabetically by author's last name, as if her home
were a bookstore. Jesus. He'd had no idea she was like this –
for some reason, when he'd come to stay, he hadn't looked
so closely. Now that he might be living here for a while,
well, it was different.

He sighed deeply and settled down in front of the TV,
clicking quickly to the History channel. Kurt always felt the
shows on this station were mesmerizing, and thankfully
this was true whether he was a man or a woman. What a
relief. He'd had a moment when he thought that his tastes
might have switched along with his body. If he'd been
interested in soap operas, or – God help him – *Oprah*, he
wouldn't have been able to live with himself.

As soldiers marched across the screen in black and white,
time got away from him. The phone rang at a crucial part
in World War II, and Kurt pulled himself away from the
action with difficulty before going to answer it.

'What are you still doing there?' Tiffany demanded.

'Are you checking up on me?' He looked at the clock, then
sadly at the show that he wouldn't be able to finish.

'You're watching the History channel, aren't you?'

'So?'

'We won the war, Kurt. Now go meet Melissa!'

'Don't worry so much,' he told her. 'I'm on the way.'

He sprinted to the bedroom to see that Tiffany had laid
out an outfit for him in spite of what he'd told her. Typical
Tiffany. Still, for a second, he was relieved. One less thing
for him to worry about. Then he felt a spark of anger flare
within him. What was he? Five? He could pick his own
damn clothes out, thank you very much.

He slid open Tiffany's closet doors to be greeted by a sea
of black. She dressed chic, he had to give her that. San
Francisco was a city drenched in noir. But Kurt preferred
color. Vibrant reds. Electric blues. As a photographer, he
picked up on hues other people might not even notice. The
silver quality of the mist early in the morning. The neon
lights at night. Even the way that Tiffany's clothes were

made up of shades of black. He wondered if she'd ever noticed that. Black itself could be dissected into a multitude of tones.

But they were still black.

One time the year before, he and Tiffany had vacationed in wine country for four days. Tiffany had kindly offered to pack for him, and Kurt had accepted. He hated packing. Hated folding. Hated the whole process of choosing his clothes. But when they'd arrived at the little B&B, he'd discovered she'd packed only black for him, culling his entire wardrobe down to black jeans, black T-shirts, a black cable-knit sweater. 'I'm not a vampire,' he'd told her, horrified. She hadn't chosen the clothes to be cruel. It simply hadn't occurred to Tiffany to bring anything else along. In retaliation, Kurt had gone out and bought several brightly colored T-shirts, unable to stand wearing black from his head to the tip of his motorcycle boots.

Now, confronted with the black dress spread out on Tiffany's pink satin comforter, or the black suits; black slacks, black sweaters filling her closet, he felt equally rebellious. He tore through her drawers until he found an outfit he considered worthy of wearing and, without a thought, he left her dresser looking a whole lot like his own chest of drawers back home. Clothes were tossed half-in and half-out of the opened drawers, but Kurt didn't even notice.

He glanced back at the bed. She'd even put out a bra and panty set. The bra was a simple one, a tank style that he could pull over his head. Luckily, Tiffany had understood how difficult the clasp in the back thing was for him to finagle. But the fact that she'd set out a matching set made him frown. Tiffany didn't even trust him to choose his own underwear! He returned to her dresser and pawed through her lingerie drawer. She actually kept her panties folded, and she separated bras on one side of the drawer and underwear on the other. Like colors were together, a row of reds, a row of golds, a few leopard-prints. If he'd still been a man, he would have gotten hard simply from touching the silky fabrics. As a woman, he dug through the sweet items until he found a pair of decent bikini-style bottoms. He hadn't enjoyed the six-hour flight wearing a thong. How girls made that style work, he had no fucking idea.

Unfortunately, the whole dressing like a female thing took much longer than he was accustomed to. Generally, he could pull on a pair of jeans, his beloved docs, and a T-shirt in thirty seconds flat. His hair was short enough that he could spike it up with gel if he wanted to, or just run his hands through it and leave it alone, tossing the occasionally wayward strand out of his face with a little flick of his head. Tiffany's hair was unexpectedly difficult to manage. In New Orleans, he'd pulled her hair into a ponytail and thrown on a baseball cap. Today, he knew he couldn't get away with that. He tried a braid, but failed, tried a bun and failed even worse. Finally, he used her hair dryer and blew it out, creating a sexy windblown bed-head style he had seen on the front cover of one of her magazines. He hoped this would pass as acceptable. For an instant, he wished he'd let her continue with her lists. Perhaps she would have given him some tips.

Like for make-up. She'd told him that he had to wear make-up when he went out. And she was supposed to help him apply it. But she'd left. Christ ... He went back to the living room to find one of her magazines. The one that said, 'Five minutes to a fresh-faced you.'

When Melissa called to find out why he wasn't at the bakery, he had to finish up in a rush and sprint out the door. He hoped that he looked okay. Was it possible to wear too much blush? The phone rang again as he clicked the lock, but he left it unanswered, sure that this call was from Tiffany. What was with these girls and their phone calls?

He was in a mood by the time he arrived in the garage at Tiffany's pretty pink VW bug. God, he hated the color of this car. The pink actually hurt his eyes. He wondered why he'd never realized how much he disliked the car before. Because he'd never had to drive it before – *that* was why. Being behind the wheel made him feel as if he were on display at a fucking circus. Yes, he understood why Tiffany got to drive his truck and he was stuck with the beetle. They were each insured only for their own vehicles. If there were an accident and he (in Tiffany's body) was behind the wheel of Kurt's truck, the insurance paperwork would be brutal and their rates would undoubtedly go sky high. Tiffany had explained this to him in a careful manner.

So, yeah, he understood it. But he didn't have to like it.

As soon as he pulled out into traffic, he could feel people's eyes on him. How strange that Tiffany would choose such a noticeable car. She tended to prefer being behind the scenes, which was why she was so good at party planning. She could orchestrate an event from the engraved invitations to the tri-folded thank-you cards, acting like a master puppeteer secreted behind a curtain. But the car was something else. Her VW screamed for people to look at it.

Tiffany had explained this by saying it was her 'calling car', rather than calling card. The name of her company was emblazoned in a tasteful decal on the rear window. Still, as Kurt maneuvered through traffic, he wished she'd chosen something less obvious.

An ambulance screamed by, and he quickly maneuvered to the side of the road. Yes, there were things to be thankful for, he decided. Like the fact that she wasn't a doctor, or an emergency-room nurse. Or a firefighter. God, there were so many things he couldn't do for the life of him. Going to a cake-tasting seemed suddenly less demoralizing.

As he pulled back into traffic, he suddenly heard an unexpected sound. Not ringing. A bit of a song. A Kinks song . . . and then he realized Tiffany's cell phone had gone off. They'd switched phones as well in order to keep things real, as Tiffany had said. Tiffany downloaded new ringtones on her phone so often that it was difficult for Kurt to keep track. But he'd have to change that one. He liked *Lola* just fine, but the lyrics hit too close to home right now.

'Tiffany Mitchell,' he said in his sweetest voice possible.

'Hey, it's Melissa. Rick just told me that he can't make the cake-tasting –' Big surprise there, Kurt thought. No real man would attend if he could help it. 'So we're going to reschedule for next Thursday' – Ah, Melissa hadn't let him off the hook entirely – 'but I thought since I cleared out my afternoon, we might go shopping instead and you can help me pick out my trousseau. Meet me at the Embarcadero, okay?

Kurt told her certainly, and then immediately dialed Tiffany who, he discovered, was still on her way to his gym. She'd stopped at his apartment to suit up in his sweats first, and she'd ended up doing a few more loads of laundry while she was there, and putting fresh sheets on the bed, airing out some of his cupboards, taking advantage of the situation while she could –

'What's it mean, Tiff?'

'Trousseau. It's an old-fashioned word to describe the various items a bride brings with her on her honeymoon.'

'In English, Tiffany. What's going on? Why does she want me to meet her at the mall?'

'You're going lingerie shopping.' Tiffany had a difficult time saying this without bursting into hysterical laughter. The thought of Kurt in a girly store clearly made her afternoon.

Lingerie shopping. Jesus.

Kurt was generally an excellent driver. But that didn't stop him from nearly hitting the Muni bus on his left.

Chapter Six

Being a man wasn't all bad. Tiffany hadn't shared this fact with Kurt, especially as she could barely admit the concept to herself. But the truth was that she liked quite a lot of what went with owning a cock. There was an unexpected confidence that accompanied standing over six feet tall, having broad shoulders, and being more than a little bit handsome. *Much* more.

She'd always known that Kurt was exceptional looking, yet being inside of his body drove this point home. Women on the street turned to stare at her as she got into Kurt's truck, and she felt a serious thrill from the attention. Kurt never let on that women flirted with him. Was it possible that he didn't notice, as he always claimed when she told him that some waitress wouldn't stop talking with him or that the bartender couldn't take her eyes off him? How could he *not* notice? Girls were everywhere.

Now that she was in his body, she felt as if she were always accidentally making eye contact with some woman who would then bat her eyelashes at her. Or give her a little sexy smile. Or stare pointedly at her package. Women could be just as randy as men, she quickly learned. She'd *never* stare at a guy's crotch. Especially a stranger's! But she knew girls who would. Melissa, prior to her engagement, had been one of them. It was a bizarre feeling to have other girls size her up. The first time it had happened, she'd become terri-torial – *like, stop looking. He's my man.* And then she'd realize that she *was* her man, and she'd begin to feel dizzy with the transformation.

She would have loved to discuss the whole situation with Melissa. Her best friend would undoubtedly have been able to put things into perspective for her. Melissa always had a unique way of looking at the world. Tiffany discovered this was the biggest drawback about being Kurt. She felt lonely.

The thought of calling up one of Kurt's friends to hang out with was more frightening than reassuring. Although she had promised Kurt she'd learn Centipede –

But she knew things could be much worse, and besides, the good things about being a man were numerous.

As she drove, she continued to think about the various manly aspects she could actually grow accustomed to. She enjoyed eating as a man. There was a freedom to be mildly gluttonish without anyone judging her. If she'd fed her female form the way she fed Kurt's, people would definitely have gawked.

The truth was this body was simply larger, and it craved different types of food than she'd normally eat. That was unexpected, wasn't it? You would have thought that personal tastes would be ingrained into your sense of self. Tiffany had never been a big meat eater. But she had deep urges for burgers now, burgers and onion rings and beer. That's what she wanted for dinner. For the first time in her life, she believed she could really appreciate the taste, and she had no idea why. Beer – cold, imported. That and martinis – straight up with an olive.

Her mouth actually watered thinking about one.

Oh, and she was going to try shellfish. She'd never been able to have any of the delicious San Francisco soups and salads: clam chowder, Shrimp Louie, crab ... Before she got her body back, she would definitely need to head down to the wharf. While Kurt was stuck with her shellfish allergy, she could indulge.

But first, she was going to hit the gym. She found herself looking forward to working out Kurt's body. Sure she'd given him a bit of flack for adding this as an item to his list, but she actually didn't mind. Working out was one of her favorite activities, and she looked forward to feeling the sexy ache in her muscles afterwards. Tiffany had been a bit of a gym rat since her first weight-training class back in high school, but once at Kurt's gym, she quickly learned that her man's body could handle much more weight. There was something exciting about moving the weight bar to a number she'd never fathomed before.

Cripes, Kurt's body was strong. Not rip-a-phone-book-in-half strong, but he was powerful. She could feel the ladies' eyes on her as she pumped iron, and she felt some of the men checking her out as well, which gave her a rush of pleasure. Her workout had a competitive edge that she had never felt before.

She returned from the gym and took a quick nap between Kurt's newly laundered sheets, surprised when she woke half an hour later in the midst of having an erotic dream. Her hand went automatically to her cock. Insane, wasn't it, that she already thought of it as hers. She wondered briefly why she had landed so easily on the word 'cock'. She'd never given the name of this important part of the male anatomy much thought. But dick didn't work for her. And penis was just unpleasant sounding. No, this was definitely a cock. As her fingers explored, she found herself rock hard and ready. Was this why Kurt always seemed raring to go any time of day.

She discovered that he had a bottle of lotion next to the bed – she'd never really thought about what it was doing there. *Now*, she understood. A little lotion in her palm, a little pressure, more pressure, actually, than she'd ever used when she was giving him a hand job, and then – man, instant pleasure.

Tiffany discovered that she fantasized differently in this body. Generally, she told herself X-rated stories when she touched herself, intricate tales that she built on time after time. Occasionally, she read erotica for inspiration. As she started to touch herself in this body, however, she learned that words alone didn't satisfy her cock. She wanted something more, the way she'd wanted a cigarette. She had a vague sort of longing.

Walking naked across Kurt's now immaculate floor – who knew he had a rug under all those clothes? – she opened the lowest drawer in his dresser. Here was the collection of porn she'd discovered while cleaning his place. Without a moment to talk herself out of it, she lifted one DVD and slid the silvery disc into the player across from his bed. Her cock throbbed as she grabbed the remote and headed back to the mattress.

Yes it seemed that moving images were what turned this body on. She built on those pictures, fantasizing about starring in the movie: bent over, pressed against a wall, in the shower, outside. Her thoughts took her to both the male and female roles, now that she'd had a chance to play both parts.

This technicolor fantasy life was intense, different from when she inhabited her normal body. She decided to give in to it, to deal with these urges as if they were nothing more than a natural side effect to the situation. There was only one problem – she couldn't help but wonder who Kurt was daydreaming about.

Chapter Seven

Kurt couldn't believe the difference shopping as a woman. As a man, Star Baby Lingerie was like some sort of mystical Mecca. A place with huge plate-glass windows featuring mannequins wearing glittering outfits straight from the sexiest pages of his most secret fantasies.

He went into the store every once in a while, looking for a sultry Christmas or Valentine's Day gift for Tiffany, feeling intensely out of place amidst the racks of push-up bras and teensy thongs, the animal print and Victorian lace, the velvet and marabou-trimmings. Of course, that fish-out-of-water feeling was part of the thrill in buying Tiffany lingerie. Being in a woman's private paradise gave him a bad-boy sensation that often worked for fuel for future erotic times together.

Now, as a man in a woman's body, he felt like a spy in the sexually charged store. Yes, he was supposedly there to help Melissa choose something to turn on Rick – a thought which made him grimace. He didn't want to know *anything* about Melissa and Rick's bedroom life. But the fact that he was there in the form of an assistant wasn't going to stop him from enjoying the event. He had a plan of his own – once Melissa was sorted out, he was going to take armloads of the lingerie into the dressing-room. He would be near other women trying on undergarments, which was as close to heaven as he could imagine. Truthfully, he couldn't believe his fucking luck.

'You know, you really look good in that,' Melissa said from behind, making him spin around toward her voice. 'I almost didn't recognize you. What happened, Tiff? Did you run out of black?'

Kurt grinned, more pleased by the compliment than he would have imagined. 'I wanted a change.'

'It's great –' she nodded, taking him in from top to bottom, '– although I don't know what I think about the shoes.'

That was the one part of the look he'd been confused by as well. He'd chosen a denim skirt of Tiffany's that she rarely wore but that he always liked, and he'd paired it with a bright red V-necked shirt that fit her body perfectly. But then he'd gone over the top with black knee-high leather boots. He hadn't trusted himself to walk in any of her scary heels.

Melissa gave him another once-over. 'No, they look fine. Very Go-Go girl. The whole outfit looks really nice, especially with your hair like that.'

He was glad she liked the look, because he'd had no other choice.

'And the jewelry –' Melissa tilted her head, taking in Kurt's whole outfit. Had he lost his head with the accessories? He'd worn a ring, necklace and bracelet – ones that he'd bought Tiffany himself. Did girls usually wear that much at once? Why hadn't he paid more attention to Tiffany's day-to-day style? He breathed a sigh of relief when Melissa simply admired his adornments.

'Maybe I should get a pair of boots myself,' Melissa continued, 'and wear them on the honeymoon. Rick's always had a thing for girls in go-go boots, you know. Like Renee Russo in that remake of the thief film. What was that called? *The Thomas Crown Affair*? The original one starred Steve McQueen, I think. God, I always thought he was so hot –' Melissa was walking as she talked, and Kurt nodded, dumbfounded, traipsing along after her as Melissa continued. *Did girls always talk so much?*

'I want to be a fantasy come true for Rick. I want to shock him every single night.'

Now, she hesitated, and Kurt realized Melissa was waiting for him to say something. Once again, he wished he'd listened to Tiffany and paid more attention to her list idea. Had she put on conversational starters? Or given notes on how she and Melissa usually spoke to one another? He took a deep breath and said, 'I'm sure you'll rock his world.'

Melissa seemed to be fine with that idea, and together the two continued to browse through the many racks filling the lingerie store. Kurt had no idea how a woman would be able to cull through the clothing. There were just too many choices. He wanted to try on everything. How could he ever have been bored when shopping with Tiffany in the past? This was exciting. Maybe she'd been right about the *Style* section. Maybe he should pay more attention in the future.

Of course, he and Tiffany did have different tastes. She would always choose elegant over slutty. He craved to see her in costumes that featured cut-outs over the nipples, or corsets that hugged her curves in tightly. Tiffany tended to favor loose silken robes, flowing nightdresses, satin pajamas. But now that he was Tiffany, he could dress her body as he desired.

Lost in thought, he got separated from Melissa as she moved quickly from one rack to another. He had to hurry after her to catch up. She had a definite personal style, one which turned out to be racier than he would have thought. She chose almost entirely black and see-through, tiny little nightgowns with slits to the waist, underwire demi-bras to emphasize her cleavage. She giggled as she showed him the ones she was going to try on, and then disappeared into the hallway of dressing-rooms.

'Stay close,' she called out, 'I might want your opinion!'

Kurt wondered how he was going to deal with that. How would Tiffany feel about him looking at Melissa in her knickers? From her reaction to his scoping Melissa at the hotel room, he knew she wouldn't be thrilled. But she'd gotten a definite kick about the fact that he was spending his afternoon in a lingerie store. Well, it couldn't be helped. Both he and Tiffany knew that she was the one who had gotten them into this situation. He wasn't going to beat her over the head with that fact, but he also shouldn't let himself feel bad for things he had no control over.

Like now, when Melissa walked out of the dressing-room wearing a floor-length satin robe. She looked like a forties screen goddess, and Kurt told her so, barely catching his breath when she flashed him what she was wearing under the robe.

'Oh, my –'

'I need a different size,' she explained, traipsing on tiny petal-pink marabou-trimmed slippers toward a rack in the front of the store. 'Why don't you choose a few things to try on, too, Tiff? That's one way you can make it up to Kurt.'

'Make what up?'

'You said the two of you had a little spat, right?'

'Oh, right,' Kurt nodded, realizing that he really needed to keep with the program a bit more. 'Yeah, we did. He was behaving like a total idiot.'

'So what are you waiting for? Pick out something that will make his brain stop working. He won't even remember what he was mad about. Men are so easy,' Melissa shot over her shoulder as she disappeared between the racks.

This was precisely what Kurt had been waiting for, but now he turned around, trying to decide where to start first.

'May I help you?' a petite blonde co-ed type asked him. He hadn't even seen her lurking there, and her proximity made him a little uncomfortable. He wondered if anyone could guess how out of place he felt. But when he looked into the girl's green eyes, he simply saw dollar signs from a possible commission, not outrage that he was impersonating a woman.

'No,' he said, startled from his reverie, then 'well, maybe –' He'd just realized that he didn't know Tiffany's bra size. In the past, he'd usually bought her sexy nightgowns. Those were easy – Small, Medium, or Large. She was definitely a small. But bras came with numbers. Numbers and letters. A secret female code that made no sense to him.

It would seem strange to let Melissa know that he didn't remember his size, and as he fingered one of the black lace underwire bras, he realized he had no idea how to dress his new body. He looked around quickly. Melissa was already back in the dressing-room, so she wouldn't see this little encounter.

'I've gotten into shape recently,' he told the girl, coming up with this lie on the spot. 'And I'm not sure what my bust size is now.'

This didn't seem to faze the girl in the slightest. She had a tape measure in her pocket and proceeded to measure him up right there in the corner of the store. Women touching women! Did this thing happen all the time? Why hadn't Tiffany told him about it? He would have loved to fantasize about her being felt up by a lithe young shopclerk like this girl. Oh, if he'd still had a cock, the thing would have been at full mast in a flash. Instead, his heart just raced and he felt his cheeks redden. Tiffany's body was quick to blush, just as she was quick to be ticklish. He had to force himself to stand still and not laugh.

'Thirty-four,' she told him, 'and I think a C-cup would fit you nicely.'

He nodded his thanks at her, not trusting his ability to speak. His nipples were erect, and what he suddenly wanted more than anything was to go back home for another round with Tiffany.

'Let me know if I can help out further,' the girl told him before returning to the front of the store.

'Thank you,' he murmured as he began to pile up all of the different outfits that he liked the best. He knew that Tiffany always wore matching bras and panties, although he didn't know why. Who, aside from himself, would ever see that she had a matching set on? Personally, he liked the concept of putting two different patterns together. Or two different colors. Black on top, white on the bottom. Polka dot boyshorts and a striped tank bra.

Was he secretly a cross-dresser?

The thought stopped him for a moment, his hand outstretched toward a floral baby doll. He didn't think so. All right, so yes, he was having fun at the thought of dressing Tiffany's body in these outfits. But he would have had just as much fun if he had been himself and Tiffany had let him dress her. Wouldn't he?

As he entered the dressing-room and took off his clothes, he only wished he were slightly more adept at the fastenings. The tiny little hook-eyes running the length of the corset were impossible to get right. He tried three times before discarding that piece of difficult lingerie in favor of one with bows. Much easier ... both to tie and untie.

'You there, Tiff?' Melissa called to him from the room next door.

'Yeah.'

'I have something new to show you. I think you're going to like it.'

'Wait a sec, I don't have anything on.'

The door opened before he could cover up. 'Like being naked's ever stopped me from barging in,' Melissa scoffed. 'There's nothing I haven't seen before.'

But there was stuff Kurt had never seen before – like

Melissa in a similar corset to the one he'd been fumbling with, paired with a set of panties that had tiny red bows at the hips. She was wearing a different pair of slippers, these ones with red marabou trim, and she had pulled her hair back with two combs. Kurt felt guilty looking at her at all, and he tried to keep his eyes focused on her face rather than her breasts.

'You like?'

Kurt nodded emphatically, reaching for his shirt and pulling it over his head. 'Very va-va-va voom.'

'You think Rick will think it's sexy?'

'Oh, yeah,' Kurt told her seriously. 'He'll love that.'

'Good.' Melissa smiled at her own reflection in the mirror. 'One down. Thirteen to go.'

'Excuse me?'

'We'll be in Paris for two weeks. I want a different look for each night.'

'That Rick's a lucky man,' Kurt told her.

'I know,' Melissa said as she shut the door.

Kurt swallowed hard and returned to his own dress-up games. *I'm a girl*, he reminded himself over and over again. *I'm a girl. I'm a girl. I'm a girl.*

Chapter Eight

'What *did* you wear?' Tiffany demanded. She was staring pointedly at the simple Diane von Furstenberg tie-at-the-waist dress she'd left out for him. She had chosen the dress carefully, thinking that this would be one of the easier outfits for Kurt to put on correctly. She didn't want to drive him mad with one of the more intricate outfits she owned.

Kurt, now clad in a comfy pair of bright crimson drawstring pants and a cobalt-blue spaghetti-strap tank top he'd bought himself at the lingerie shop, gave her a don't-mess-with-me look. 'I told you I could dress myself.'

'I just want to know what you wore. Is that such a big deal?' She tried not to sound accusatory, but she couldn't help herself. If Kurt had gone out dressed like he normally was, people would think she'd had a mental breakdown.

'Why?' he asked her fiercely. 'Don't you trust me?'

Tiffany took a deep breath and crossed her arms over her chest. 'Look, Kurt. I trust you to dress yourself, but not *my*self. I know your taste, and I don't mean any judgment here, but it's not the same as mine.'

Kurt didn't say another word. He simply pointed to the corner of the room where he'd left Tiffany's outfit in a small untidy pile. He rolled his eyes as she quickly picked up the different items and refolded and hung each one. 'With those boots?' she quizzed him.

He nodded. 'Melissa thought they looked nice.'

'I would have chosen that pair,' she explained, pointing to a pair of stacked-heel black shoes with a silver buckle on the toe.

'When I put them on, I was very unsteady. How *do* you women manage to walk in those things.' Kurt was indicating the row of shoes in Tiffany's closet. 'They're fucking impossible.'

'Anything's possible.' Wasn't that the truth? Just look at

them. They were living proof that the impossible could come true. In a heartbeat. When you least expected it. Kurt was having none of her attitude.

'Not walking in four-inch pumps. Believe me, I've tried. I haven't fallen on my ass so many times since I learned to ice skate.'

'You know how to ice skate?'

'Of course.' He glared at her. 'I played ice hockey for years. I've told you that.'

'Well, walking in pumps isn't nearly as hard as ice skating. You did fine last Halloween.'

'That was one night. And my feet were killing me afterwards. And if you hadn't shown me the tricks to it, I would have truly embarrassed myself.'

'It gets easier,' Tiffany assured him. 'It just takes practice.' She grabbed a pair of patent-leather heels. 'Slide these on. Melissa lent them to me.'

Kurt obeyed her command, but gave her a look of incredulity. 'Do women all wear the same size shoes?'

'Of course not, you moron. Melissa and I are just lucky. We can borrow each other's whenever we want. That doubles our shoe wardrobe.'

'So instead of two hundred and fifty pairs, you guys have five hundred?'

'Now stand up,' Tiffany insisted, ignoring his comment.

'No.'

'Come on, Kurt. I can't teach you how to walk if you won't try.'

'What will you do for me?'

'Do for you?'

He gave her an evil smirk. 'Yeah, what will you do for me?'

'I'll –' She looked around, thinking. 'I'll fuck you in them –'

'Okay.' He seemed appeased. 'What's the trick?'

'Well, first show me how you do it.'

He took a step and fell over, barely catching himself on the edge of the dresser.

'You're putting your weight on your toes. That's the problem. You want to walk heel-toe, heel-toe, with confidence. Tip-toeing will throw you off balance.'

Kurt tried to do what she said, but wrapped one leg around the other and fell.

'Slowly,' she told him, helping him to his feet. 'Go slowly.'

'Being a woman is too much work,' he insisted. 'I'd go barefoot all day if I were you.'

'You say that now, but you like the way I look in the Christian Louboutins, don't you?'

'The what?'

'The shoes with the scarlet color on the bottom.'

'Who cares what color it is on the bottom?'

'Women do,' she insisted. 'So you'd better pay attention.'

'Tomorrow, I'm going out to buy you some Tevas.'

'I would never wear them.'

'Doesn't matter what you would wear, does it?'

'Kurt, don't granola me up,' Tiffany begged. 'I need to look professional when I meet people.'

'Professional is one thing. In serious pain is something else entirely.'

'Well, how about you?'

'What do you mean?'

'I played basketball this afternoon at the gym, and I got elbowed so hard in the ribs I'm going to have a monster bruise.'

'That's the price to pay when you play with the big boys.'

'I don't want to play with the big boys.'

Kurt stared at her. 'You have to. The team's counting on you, Tiff. I'm their secret weapon. Nobody beats my three-point shot.'

'Yeah, but it's your shot. Not mine. Your body is strong as anything, but the athletic prowess didn't transfer over when we switched. I'm incredibly lame out on the court.'

'It just takes practice,' Kurt assured her.

'You learn to walk in those shoes, and I'll learn to make a three-point shot,' she told him. 'Do you want to shake on it?'

'No,' he shook his head. 'I want to do something else to seal the deal –'

Kurt was bent over in front of Tiffany, his hands splayed out on the floor. In this position, he could see how chipped his toenail polish was. Tiffany had told him that she'd fuck him in the shoes, but that had turned out to be more difficult than sexy. He kept tipping over until he'd gotten smart and kicked them off into the corner.

He wondered what you might call the color of the polish. Bruise? Vampire? The hue was darker than blood, and matte not iridescent. Tiffany definitely would not have allowed her toenails to get to this stage. He wondered if he should try to paint his toenails himself, or if he ought to make an appointment at a salon. Women definitely were higher maintenance than men. His legs could also use a shave – he shook his head, chagrined.

Was he actually having these thoughts while they were fucking? This was ludicrous. The thing of it was that Tiffany wasn't touching him correctly. Not in a way that would raise his heart rate. He'd been in the mood to make love when they started. In fact, he'd been more than ready. After putting on one of his favorite CDs, he'd done a mini fashion show for Tiffany, traipsing out of the bedroom in the different lingerie he'd bought for her earlier in the day. By the time they'd made their way to the bathroom, he'd been positively dripping wet.

But now, he just wasn't feeling that aroused.

Was she messing with him for laming out on her in a similar position? He looked over his shoulder at her.

No, she had her eyes shut. She was off in bliss, not meaning to be rude, but too far gone in pleasure to pay attention to his needs. Without a word, he pulled forward, releasing her, and then stood.

'Wh –' she stammered.

'I don't think I'm ready yet. I mean, *your* body isn't.'

Tiffany was hurt. She felt as if he were blaming her for his inadequacy. She couldn't help the fact that he wasn't turned on. 'How do you know?' she asked. 'It's not the same as with a guy. We don't get hard, you know. There's nothing that obvious. We're much more subtle.' She could have continued, defending women all the way back to Eve, explaining their intricate plumbing to this newest member of their ranks, but Kurt stopped her.

'Look, I know all about getting women in the mood. I'm just not ready,' he said. 'I can tell.'

'What do you want me to do about it?'

'Well – what turns you on, Tiff? What's the best thing for you?'

God, she wouldn't. She couldn't. Not to herself. 'You know,' she started. 'But I don't think I can –'

'Well, what else?'

'Close your eyes,' she instructed him, 'and play out a fantasy.'

'Is that what you do?'

She nodded.

'Every time?'

'Sometimes.'

He considered her words, but he didn't think that idea would work for him. His fantasy life was rich and detailed, yet he never needed to prod himself to climax with a mental masterpiece. Instead, he decided that he wanted to experiment with a new position. 'Let's try it like this,' he countered, hoisting himself up onto the bathroom cabinet and spreading his legs. Tiffany didn't argue. She seemed willing to attempt whatever position he wanted. With his legs wrapped around Tiffany's waist, Kurt settled back on his hands for support.

This was instantly better. The friction between their two bodies created a heat that spread swiftly throughout him. He sighed and brought his hips forward, and Tiffany thrust into him, hard, sealing her body to his. Her cock throbbed within him, filling him up in the most delicious manner. Kurt felt his mood switch as he grew steadily more aroused.

To reward Tiffany, he started to drag his fingernails down her chest. Instantly, she began to moan. He loved that sensation himself, and he could tell that this was something that worked for his body no matter who was within its skin. Physiologically, there were some things that couldn't be denied. Some pleasures that ran deeper, to nerve endings, to the very center of his self.

He watched as Tiffany discovered that pleasure. As she made it her own.

Bucking forward, she lifted Kurt off the counter top, cradling his ass in her hands. She pressed him back up against the wall, supporting his weight, slamming her body into his over and over, biting into his collar bone as she reached her limits.

But once again, he was left hanging.

After crying out with her climax, Tiffany smothered him with kisses, and he accepted each one, feeling lost somehow. Left out of a party. One that he desperately wanted to attend.

Chapter Nine

Over breakfast the next morning at their favorite cafe, Kurt searched his mind for a way to broach the topic. In the past, he'd always been extremely blunt when something was bothering him. He and Tiffany were polar opposites in this manner. She would often worry an issue to death for several days, or even several weeks, and then explode over an insignificant situation when both she and Kurt were least expecting it. Bam! Everything would come spilling out of her. He hated when she went off, like a human time bomb. It sometimes took them hours to figure out what the real problem was, and by the end they'd both be exhausted.

Kurt wasn't like that at all. When something bothered him, he wouldn't hesitate to speak up. He couldn't understand why Tiffany didn't realize that this was a trait that helped him in many aspects of his life. At work, with friends. There was never any of that wondering where you stood with Kurt.

But being in this new body had given his confidence a violent shake. So that now he wasn't quite sure how to explain his dilemma. He'd actually found himself paging through several of Tiffany's magazines, looking for a clever conversational starter, one that would allow him to explain the issue without hurting Tiffany's feelings.

The problem right now was sex. Yes, he was enjoying the various positions and the new-found freedom with which Tiffany seemed to feel comfortable to express her fantasies. Who would have thought that she was such a tigress? She clearly enjoyed taking charge, flexing her muscles, lifting Kurt and holding him up against the wall, gripping his wrists together above his head, biting into his bottom lip hard enough to leave marks. And he'd had a whole afternoon of mental foreplay by dressing up in ladies' lingerie the previous afternoon. But Kurt felt that something was lacking.

At first, he'd told himself that this was simply what it must be like to be a girl. Maybe women didn't get to experience the sort of pleasure that men did. But when he'd been reading Tiffany's magazines, the descriptions inside had forced him to think that was incorrect. So many of the articles were geared around sex, discussing clitoral orgasms, vaginal orgasms, ways to massage the G-spot. Sex seemed to be a major focus for the female mind.

Then he started to feel as if he were starring in the 'Emperor's New Clothes' about their encounters. Tiffany was clearly over the top when she came. Kurt wasn't so sure he was even close to reaching the finish line. It wasn't exactly that he'd been faking so far, but he hadn't really seen what all the excitement was about. Something, he'd decided, was definitely wrong. He wished he could ask someone for advice. He couldn't talk to Rick about it. He felt disloyal to Tiffany at the thought of discussing his sex life with Melissa; he *had* to bring the topic up with Tiffany.

'So what did you want to talk about?' Tiffany asked as the waiter brought them their usual. She lifted the cup of mocha to her lips and was about to take a sip when the waiter interrupted her with a surprised expression.

'No, no,' Joe said to Kurt. 'That's *his* espresso. Here's your non-fat, half-decaf half-caf mocha!'

Kurt looked surprised, and then quickly figured out the problem. 'Don't worry,' he told Joe, 'we're trying something new today. We're each going to have the other's regular breakfast.'

Joe walked away, shaking his head, while Tiffany sipped her mocha appreciatively.

'Look,' he said softly. 'I don't think I'm actually coming.'

'Coming,' she replied, her mind working to catch up with him. 'Coming where?'

'Not where, when. Well, that's not right either. Coming when we have sex.'

She looked stricken. 'You've been faking?' This was awful news. And here she thought she'd been doing such a good job. Hadn't they had fun in the bathroom the night before? She'd loved looking in the mirror while they were doing it, lifting him up when she came, feeling the strength of her muscles . . .

'Look, I can't describe the problem all that well. But it's been great, what we've been doing. You're awesome. It's just that I don't think I'm actually reaching the climax with you. I feel a build-up, and a lot of pleasure, it's just not . . . well, it's not as good as chocolate, I can tell you that for sure.' Tiffany's body did love chocolate. He'd never had much of a taste for it himself, but his spirits definitely rose each time he had a bite from the stash in her cookie jar.

Tiffany hung her head. She wasn't going to be an insensitive male lover. Not if she could help it. And here she'd been congratulating herself on her expertise, on her prowess, on her ability to hold back, to rein in the big dog.

'I think it might have to do with the fact that, you know, mentally I'm not wired to be –' he couldn't stop stammering for some reason, '– the receptor.'

'Well, how does it normally work for you?'

'I don't get it up while fucking a guy.' He hadn't meant to be that blunt, but there it was: Classic Kurt.

'You don't get it up at *all* anymore –' she corrected him, yet again, and she couldn't help grinning this time. Kurt was so adamant. But did he protest too much? He had told her more than once that if men could give themselves blow jobs they'd never have a reason to leave the house.

'The thing is that you're harder to turn on than I would have thought,' he conceded.

She took offense. 'Meaning what, precisely?'

'Masturbating, kiddo. Look, I tried it at the hotel in New Orleans in the shower –'

So he had! He'd been taking liberties with her body, just as she'd guessed!

'And again last night after you fell asleep. I mean, I generally jerk off quite a bit, Tiffany, I'm used to some form of release on a regular basis. I'd consider myself something of an expert.' He didn't mean to sound so pompous about this, but he couldn't restrain the note of pride in his voice. 'But in this new body, I just can't get it to work. It's like you're broken.'

'Broken?'

'Not *totally* broken. Because I am getting sensations that

signal pleasure. But you're sort of out of order.' He kept talking, even as he saw her eyes widening with anger. 'That's not to say I haven't been enjoying myself. I do have quite a good time playing with your tits.'

Now, she was incensed. She hated when he used that word, and he knew that perfectly well. 'You must not be doing it right.'

'I did everything I usually do with you.'

A flush crept slowly across her jawline. She could feel it. Shoot, she had no idea how to hide her embarrassment in his body. She averted her gaze, swallowing great gulps of the too-hot mocha, but Kurt seemed to sense something was wrong. He grabbed her face in both hands and forced eye contact. 'What –?' he demanded.

She said nothing, but her silence was incriminating.

'Don't you get off when we're together?'

'Yeah,' she said, vaguely, heart pounding.

'Always?'

She pulled free from his grip and turned to look out the window.

'Usually?' he tried next.

'Sometimes,' she said, refusing to look at him. 'Most of the time.'

His response surprised her. 'Why didn't you say anything before?' His tone was soft, compassionate even.

'Look, it's not something I really want to talk about.'

'You'd better talk about it. We don't know when this spell is going to wear off. And I'm not going through life without coming. I'll fucking explode.'

She couldn't help but laugh. *He* was sexually frustrated, and he wanted answers. Well, in spite of her embarrassment, this was at least one area where she could help him.

'Did you try The Rabbit?'

He looked mortified. 'You're not into animals, are you? Please, God, tell me that you're not. I don't think I could handle that after everything else.'

'The Rabbit,' she repeated coldly, trying to emphasize the capital letters of the name of this magnificent device. 'The Rabbit Vibrator.' In any other situation, confessing that she occasionally used a battery-powered appliance to get off would have mortified her. What she did at home late at night by herself was none of his damn business. But what sorts of secrets did they need to keep from each other now? She'd been through all of his drawers. She manhandled his unit when she went to the men's room. He'd told her the trick of shaking after urinating. There was no space left for secrets.

'A sex toy?' His eyes suddenly gleamed very bright.

'Yeah. The mother of all vibrators. You'll like it. I promise.'

For a second, she wished they could try it together. But she had promised him that she would go to practice at the Y. It was something he did with several of his buddies every Saturday, and she couldn't let him down. Not when all of this was officially her fault.

'How's it work?' Kurt's mind was still focused on the toy that waited for him. He was eating his breakfast very fast now, literally stuffing forkfuls of scrambled eggs into his mouth.

'Turn on the button and let the magic start.'

He stood up so fast, she thought he was going to tip the table. 'Thank God,' he said, wiping his lips on one of the cafe's paper napkins. 'I need some relief.'

She watched him walk out of the restaurant, and it took her a moment to realize that he hadn't even offered to split the check.

'Fuckin' broads,' Joe murmured, in sympathy.

'You know it,' Tiffany said, slipping an extra few dollars in with the tip.

Chapter Ten

Kurt had tried rubbing. He'd tried lotions. He could feel this new body growing excited whenever he and Tiffany were making love, but he couldn't get past that teetering, breathless edge to orgasm. Up until now, he'd assured himself that if they continued to remain in one another's bodies, he would ultimately get the hang of it. The truth was that he hadn't wanted to tell Tiffany that there was a problem at all. He understood this was a very male thing. Like not wanting to ask for directions when he was absolutely certain that he was lost. Or not admitting that he didn't know how to fix the broken motor on his Mr Coffeemaker, which was the real reason the machine remained unused on an upper shelf in his hall closet, and the truth behind why he never kept any fresh coffee beans in the house.

In that same stubbornly masculine way, he'd been unwilling to confess that he couldn't get the hang of making Tiffany's body climax. But now he had a solution, and he could hardly wait to try it out.

With shaking hands, he rummaged through her bedside table to discover the sex toy hidden there. Thank Christ she'd told him. He'd gotten to the point where he had been sure there was something wrong with her – not with the methods he was employing. Now, he knew that wasn't the case.

But what else was in that magic drawer of hers? He rummaged further and discovered several dog-eared paperbacks, books that were so thoroughly mangled they looked as if they might have fallen into the bathtub on more than one occasion. The cover of one was completely gone, but when he looked at the second, he saw the type of steamy romance cover that he and his friends always scoffed at as *girl porn*. He actually glanced over his shoulder to make sure that Tiffany hadn't quietly followed him back to the apartment before he picked up one of the books and got comfortable on her bed.

The start was a little slow, too much plot for him, so he scanned the pages until he found a particularly lusty passage, one that Tiffany had clearly enjoyed in the past, as the corner of this page was creased over . . .

But this afternoon, the lens of the camera recorded two women making love for the first time, and Cameron Sweeney couldn't believe his fucking luck. There was nothing like the cheesiness of porn movies about the situation. Yet here were two totally gorgeous girls, getting to know each other in a very personal way, only moments after having met. Perhaps that part was like an X-rated movie, he thought. The plot. Or what wasn't actually a real plot, just a 'cute meet'. You know, cut to the chase. Whatever you called it, the scene turned him on. He stared at the screen, hand wrapped tightly around his cock, and he pulled hard as he watched his favorite girlfriend lick another woman's cunt. How sweet that was, the way Isabelle's hands caressed the girl's thighs, then moved back, obviously cradling her ass.

From the women's positioning, he couldn't see Isabelle's face clearly. That was because his blonde nymphet had pressed her mouth against the new girl's pussy. He thought about Isabelle's knowledgeable tongue as he watched the brunette sigh in true pleasure.

As he continued to read the words, he felt himself grow more and more aroused. Oh, this was nice. He was dripping wet; he knew it even before he slid one greedy hand inside of his panties. So wet. He kept on reading, thrusting himself into the scene, flipping pages to find the sexiest part, until finally he felt that he was ready for the toy.

But first he took a good long look at the thing. The vibrator was an incredibly bright pink. It was a tube shape with a tiny bunny attached to the base, fitted with softly rounded ears.

How ridiculous that the tool was in the shape of a bunny! He would have designed the thing to look like a mammoth cock. But maybe that was too gauche for someone with

Tiffany's sensibilities. Maybe bunnies were more innocent, or sweet, or something. Yet Tiffany wasn't all that innocent at all, was she? Not with books like this lying around! He was pleased to have discovered that she owned smut. The paperbacks made such an agreeable change from the books in the living-room, the ones that never appeared to have been opened.

He flipped a few more pages until he found another passage he liked, and as he read, he touched himself with the sex toy:

Bailey was a number-one sex fiend. It was one reason they'd been so good together. The way she moved her lithe body underneath his had made him come like no one else ever had. The way she slid up and down when they did it with girl-on-top drove him crazy. Sometimes she'd push up on her thighs until he was almost completely exposed, and she'd grip onto the rod of his cock, grip firmly and squeeze, her blue eyes focused on him, reading the need she saw there. Other times she'd simply fuck him until she came, riding him like a cowgirl. The girl was game for anything, for going out to his favorite erotic night club and engaging in a sex act on stage in front of strangers, letting him tie her down and blindfold her. 'No' wasn't in her vocabulary. She refused to give a safe word, took anything he had to give. That's what he'd liked best about Bailey – she knew how to take what she wanted. Which is why she'd taken off from him and gone to his partner.

The vibrator was heavenly. Almost as soon as he rubbed the tip of the ears of the rabbit against his clit, he felt the pulses of pleasure begin to swell deliciously inside of him.

Oh, yes, he thought. *God, yes.*

When he rotated the toy, he could stimulate both his clit and his inner pussy lips. The power of the vibrations could be controlled as well, growing stronger or weaker with a little twist of the knob at the base. Kurt lost himself in the erotic experiments, tickling his clit with a low pulse from the rabbit, then upping the power until he felt as if his breath had been knocked out of him.

In the throws of pleasure, he heard the phone ring. There

wasn't a second in his mind when he considered answering it, and when he heard Melissa leaving a message, he felt extremely relieved. The woman called way too fucking much. He hadn't noticed how often she and Tiffany talked to each other when he was himself. But it seemed as if Tiff's best friend called at least six times a day. On and on she went, about some minute aspect about the wedding. No, not the wedding this time. The bachelorette party.

He took a deep breath, trying to get back into the mood. The rabbit helped considerably. He was able to pick up immediately where he'd left off.

If he had known about this toy from the start, he would never have left the house. He would have spent every waking minute with his legs spread. The rhythmic pulsing was divine, the most perfect sensation. And he was so excited by the fact that he could control the pressure, upping the vibrations, then sliding them back down again. He could peak and crest, peak and crest. He could drive this sex however he wanted to. It was totally unique to the experience of coming like a man, where the build-up continued until the expected release and then it was over.

He shut his eyes, then opened them immediately as a new wave of pleasure broke over him. Why hadn't she told him about this sooner? She hadn't even trusted him to dress himself. Clearly, she could have figured out that he needed help in bed.

Slowly, he let the toy slip between his nether lips and enter him. His hips arched automatically, and he began to buck ever so slowly with the rhythm of the vibrating machine. It took him a moment to realize that the sound beneath the buzzing, the soft humming sound, was his own little tuneless song of bliss. *He* was humming with satisfaction, growing increasingly aroused, wetter than he had been since the change had taken place. Wetter than wet.

But a thought suddenly occurred to him that made him drop the device.

She didn't always come with him.

This was both a major disappointment and a big kick to his ego. He turned off the vibrator and sat up in the bed, thinking about what she'd told him. For years he'd considered himself a talented lover. He'd been with more than twenty women, although he'd halved the number when confessing to Tiffany back when they were still in the getting-to-know-you phase: 'How many girls have you slept with? Really? Ten!' The look on her face letting him know he was correct in not coming totally clean with her. And all of those women in his past had seemed pleased enough with their encounters.

There was Jinny, first, way back in high school. She'd been a senior, he a sophomore, and she'd shown him a thing or two about maneuvering around a woman's body, helping him to find his way. And then he'd been with two sorority sisters – at once, mind you – as a junior in college. That had wowed the guys in his fraternity. They'd practically erected a statue in his honor. What was college for if not engaging in the occasional threesome?

He wasn't a total slut, but he'd had a few one-night stands scattered before and after two long-term relationships. There'd been no one since Tiffany. He hoped she knew that. He assumed she did. He'd had a minor office flirtation the first year they'd been going out, but he hadn't acted on it, although turning his back on the woman had taken serious willpower. She was a tall redhead who had wanted to do him in the boss's private bathroom, and he'd declined.

He'd wanted to tell Tiffany that he'd remained faithful in spite of powerful urges, but he'd assumed that she wouldn't see it as a positive. Not like he did. After his last breakup, when he started to fall for a girl, he'd made sure to distance himself from her right away. He wasn't into getting hurt, emotionally crippled, what have you. But this time, he'd rejected the easy way out, and had stayed true.

And look where it had gotten him.

He was a girl.

He closed his eyes and reached for The Rabbit again, starting the thing up with a flick of the dial on the base.

Thank God for small favors.

Tiffany couldn't fully figure out the controls on this body. It was as if she were in a brand-new car and had never read the manual. And that wouldn't have been like her at all. She kept all the manuals for every device in her apartment, sometimes long after the device was no longer working.

Kurt teased her about that, making fun of her for holding onto paperwork for a vacuum cleaner that had died at least two years previously. She couldn't explain why she kept it.

Oh, if only she had a manual for Kurt.

She had been sort of testing the body in random ways, from the very beginning trying almost casually to see if she had access to Kurt's memories, his feelings, his secrets. But she had decided that wasn't the case. If her whole self were here, trapped in the vessel of Kurt's body, then it made sense that his self – his core, his soul, whatever you wanted to call the part that made him Kurt – had traveled along the same journey to her body. This both frustrated and relieved her. She had no desire for Kurt to go rummaging through her most private thoughts, even if she'd hoped to do the exact thing to him, paging through his mental secrets like a snoop going through a lover's diary.

But back to the controls – she'd always known how strong Kurt was. Whenever she had trouble opening a jar, she simply handed it to him and he twisted the lid off with no apparent effort. He could carry huge pieces of furniture by himself. He was innately athletic, graceful even, out on the basketball court, managing to shoot three-point shots in almost every game. Unfortunately, the abilities hadn't come with the body.

For the hell of it, she moved the dining-room table, seeing immediately that the power behind the body was there. Then she tried to do the complicated Tai Chi moves she sometimes watched Kurt engage in. No such luck. She looked like a moron – and felt like one, too.

So there were rules to the switch.

Well, that was good to know. Inauspicious, in some ways. It meant she had no more of a grasp on what Kurt did at work than she ever had. And it meant that all of her skills had left her body as well. She'd had a miserable time playing basketball at the Y, but that didn't mean she had to live with that misery. After changing into a fresh pair of sweats, she headed out to her own gym. She would sign him up as a member, and go and do a yoga class. That would ease her mind. Yoga always did.

She wondered how Kurt was getting along with The Rabbit.

Chapter Eleven

'What's this?' Kurt asked Tiffany, running his fingertips softly over his pussy lips. Was it wrong for him to feel as if he owned them?

She looked over at him from her side of the bed. He was touching himself again. The man was too much! Every free moment, he seemed to have a hand in his panties.

'I didn't shave the last few days. And you didn't either.' She said this matter-of-factly, because he could have figured out the concept for himself.

'Shave?'

'You don't think I'm hairless, do you? You shave your beard. I shave mine.' This was generally true, although she hadn't shaved her face since she and Kurt had been transplanted. Tiffany looked at the razor each morning, but found herself terrified of nicking Kurt's jaw. She'd watched *Queer Eye for the Straight Guy* often enough to garner tips on shaving. Take a shower first. Get the skin nice and warm. Lather abundantly. Work slowly. Yet the thought of cutting him made her hands shake.

Still, she couldn't understand why Kurt was looking so shocked, until he continued. The start of the soft, downy fur wasn't what he was questioning. It was the color. 'But you're blonde. Your hair is so fair. *This* is dark –'

So that was the problem. Inwardly, Tiffany groaned. Men were so – so *obtuse* sometimes. Tiffany had never told him that she dyed her hair because ... well, because she just hadn't. Her choice of hair color wasn't any of his business, was it? She wasn't ashamed of herself. Her true color was a light and, in her opinion, rather mousy brown. She'd been blonde as a child, and now a little peroxide helped her remain one. No harm in that. No reason to share the fact, either. Her hair appeared natural with her fair skin and bright blue eyes. Kurt had never questioned her about this before.

'I dye my hair,' she said, when he continued to look confused. 'And usually, I shave down there. Or get a bikini wax. I didn't when I was on vacation, because there was no point. Melissa had no reason to be looking. You weren't there to care.'

'What other secrets have you kept from me?'

Would you listen to him? Tiffany thought. As if she'd betrayed him.

'I don't know what you mean.'

'Are you really thirty years old? Do you really weigh a hundred and fifteen –' As he spoke, he hopped out of bed and ran toward the bathroom. Tiffany could just guess that he was getting on the scale. So what? Her driver's license said a hundred and fifteen. And she was generally within a few pounds of that. In many ways, Kurt had behaved in a far more deceptive manner.

'A hundred and nineteen!' he called from the other room as if he'd caught her in a major lie.

'So hit the gym tomorrow,' Tiffany yelled back. 'Don't each so much pizza. I'm not going to stress on a few pounds.'

Kurt looked flustered when he walked back in. 'The gym. As a girl? What would I do? Lift the pretty colored weights instead of the real man weights?'

'Fuck you,' Tiffany said, and Kurt immediately gave her a thumbs-up for swearing. 'I do the metal ones. I can curl twenty pounds and I use the twenty-five pounders to do the over-the-head set.'

'Oooh ... Twenty-fives.' Kurt was clearly messing with her. She knew now that he curled a lot more than that, but she didn't care. He could bench press her whole body – probably twice of her – but she was proud of the workouts she could manage.

'How about you? You told me you'd quit smoking. That's a bigger lie than all of this put together.'

'Trying,' he amended. 'Trying to quit.'

'And what about all the porn you have?'

'I never lied to you about that.'

'You never told me about it, either, which is about the same thing. I couldn't believe your stash. When I was putting new shelf paper in your dresser, I found an entire drawer full of porno: magazines, DVDs, videos.'

'Shelf paper?'

Tiffany gave him a look.

'Did you watch any?'

She turned away from him so that he couldn't see her face.

'You did,' Kurt demanded. 'You watched one, didn't you?'

Tiffany nodded, refusing to make eye contact.

'What'd you think?'

What did she think? She'd been slightly uncomfortable to come across the collection in the drawer, but when she'd popped in one of the DVDs the other day, the pictures had opened up a whole new sexual world for her. She and Kurt had never watched any porn together, but from her new body's response to the images on the screen, she thought that they might try it at some point. She'd especially liked a video that showed men and women in Victorian era clothing. Women in white petticoats. Men in breaches. A girl wearing a pirate's patch over one eye.

Right now, however, she wasn't ready to acknowledge she'd enjoyed several of the scenes. Instead, she said, 'Why do you have so many?'

He shrugged. 'There's only four or five. That's not so bad. I've had most of those tapes since college.'

'Oh, so you're saying that they're sentimental?'

'Something like that. You're not always with me, Tiffany. A man has needs, you know.'

'So does a woman...' She eyed the drawer where she kept her rabbit vibrator. Kurt took the hint. He sat down on the edge of the bed and looked at her, a serious expression on his face.

'You've never come when we do it?' He sounded wounded. Tiffany felt bad. 'I thought sex was good for you.'

God, men were so lame about stuff like this. Why did it hurt *his* ego if she were the one who had an occasional lapse in orgasm.

'It's not never – I always come when you, when you –' She swallowed hard. Was it crazy that she found it difficult for her to explain things like this? The magazines she read always had articles about discussing your sex life with your man. But the advice in the articles never made speaking out any easier for Tiffany. Now, she looked directly into Kurt's eyes. 'I always come when you go down on me.' There, that hadn't been so bad. 'And sometimes in the reverse cowgirl position, and spooning, especially when you touch me while you're thrusting. But it's just that I don't always get off on just regular . . . you know.'

'Fucking.'

'Yeah.'

'Well, you should have said.'

She shrugged. 'Sometimes, the more I try, the harder it is. If I told you that I wasn't quite reaching it, I'd feel more pressure and that would make things even more difficult.'

'Pressure?' he asked. 'From me?' The wounded look had increased. Tiffany didn't know how to explain.

'Just pressure,' she said. 'I always like having sex with you,' she assured him. 'I come more often than not. I don't have any problem with the way things are.' She hesitated. 'I mean, were.'

'Well, that's not good enough for me,' Kurt said, mildly huffy. 'If you're going to get off, then I am. And vice versa.'

Wow, he sounded emphatic. Tiffany couldn't help but feel a bit pleased. Maybe in the future – if she ever did get back to being herself – he would continue to feel the same way. She planned on reminding him if he forgot.

Unfortunately, he was less emphatic when she changed the conversation to their plans for the evening.

'Why do we have to go?' He sounded like a whiny child.

Kurt was not yet dressed in the clothes Tiffany had laid out for him. The full effect of the pieces compiled one of Tiffany's favorite outfits. The blue polka-dotted skirt was short and pleated and would swing out around her when she moved. Or when Kurt did. She hoped Kurt would get into the scene, yet at the moment, he had thrown himself down on the mattress, pulling a tantrum like a three-year-old.

'Because I promised,' she told him plainly.

'Break your promise.'

'I can't.'

'See?' Kurt said. 'That's one of your biggest problems.'

'What is? That I keep my word?'

'No, that you won't ever change your prescribed course. If

you have a plan, you stick to it. You're absolutely ruthless when it comes to a schedule. What if you change your mind? What if you don't feel like keeping to a regular routine? What if you don't want to go out dancing? Because I don't want to go!'

'I thought that having a routine was one of my better qualities. It's why I make such a damn good party planner.'

'Sometimes inflexibility is an excellent quality,' he agreed, 'but not tonight.'

'I'm helping the teacher. I promised. Izzy's going to be short-staffed tonight as it is, and she's expecting a big turnout. I don't want to let her down.'

'But I don't know how to dance.'

'Sure you do.' What was he talking about? 'You've partnered with me hundreds of times.'

'Not as a girl.'

So that was it. 'You'll figure out the moves. No problem. Half the time when I'm helping out, I end up playing the guy part. It's not that difficult to switch. In fact, I read that it's good for the brain.'

'To do what? Dress as a girl?'

'To do the opposite of what you're accustomed to.'

'If that's the case, then I'm going to be smarter than Einstein when this is all over.'

Ignoring him, Tiffany adjusted her outfit in the mirror. She adored the way she looked, in a navy-blue zoot suit, with dark violet suspenders, a crisp white shirt, and two-toned shoes. She'd bought the outfit for Kurt several years before when she'd taken him to one of her swing dancing celebrations in hopes that he would fall in love with the style of dancing as she had. No such luck. Kurt had flat-out refused to wear the outfit, claiming that he felt foolish all dolled up in the old-fashioned clothing. She'd tried to convince him that he'd get used to the look, to no avail.

Now, she felt vindicated. His body looked nothing less than magnificent. All she had to do was convince him to attend.

'I can't go to the dance.' He sounded like Cinderella. So where was his fairy godmother? Or in his case would he need a fairy godfather?

'Fine,' she told him. 'Stay home and mope then. Play with

your fucking rabbit. I promised Izzy I'd be there. And I'm going.'

Kurt didn't care. He would not be made to feel guilty. He'd been a good sport about this all, hadn't he? Nobody could have expected more from him – from *anyone* in the same situation. He'd gone lingerie shopping. He would have gone to the fucking cake-tasting if the appointment hadn't been canceled. He was driving around town in that pepto-bismol-pink car. Pepto-*dismal* in his opinion. And he was destined to get all dolled up in a freaking purple maid of honor dress if something drastic didn't happen shortly – he'd do it, too. He wouldn't let Melissa down.

But this was too much.

He glared at the outfit that Tiffany had set out for him, then touched the fabric casually, and was irked to discover that a small part of himself wanted to see what he would look like in the skirt.

There was something to be said for women's clothing. Being a girl tickled him a bit. He was actually undressing and sliding into the clothing before he knew it. She'd put out a pair of stockings for him, and he slid these over his legs with an unexpected delight. Stockings felt divine, especially now that he'd shaved his legs. And what a trial that had been. He'd almost slipped in the shower, had been forced to contort himself into the strangest positions in order to maneuver the razor around his calves.

He didn't have to go to the dance, but he could preen in the mirror and see what he looked like.

The skirt spun when he twirled. Ooh, you could see his panties. He'd have to watch out for that. And what was going on in the rear? The stockings had seams that ran up the back. He had to bend over and straighten them all the way up the backs of his legs. Had Tiffany chosen these ones on purpose, to punish him for something? No, she always wore clothes like this when she went to her dances.

Should he go? He might have fun.

Maybe. But he had no desire to embarrass himself at one of Tiffany's fancy swing dancing parties. He lay back down on the mattress and glared out the window.

* * *

Tiffany attended the dance solo, anger flaring through her even as the music worked its very best to soothe her mood. Yes, she understood that Kurt had a genuine reason to be furious with her. But if they were stuck like this indefinitely – and they appeared to be, at least until one of them came up with another clever idea – then he ought to be a bit more flexible. Swing dancing was important to Tiffany. She'd been part of the dance scene for more than a decade, into the trend before it was trendy, sticking with it long after those memorable Gap ads had faded.

When she walked down the row of dancers, she started to feel the anger leave her and trepidation begin. Technically speaking, she understood how the male partners were supposed to dance. But she was a master at following, not leading. Would she be able to pull off the charade without being discovered? What would Izzy think if she fumbled?

Her teacher was on stage already, talking with the band. Tiffany walked up the steps to meet her, and she saw Izzy's rain-gray eyes widen in surprise. 'Hey there, Kurt, what are you doing here? Where's Tiffany? What are you wearing?' The questions were all spoken together in a rush, as was Izzy's general way of talking.

'Tiff isn't feeling well,' Tiffany heard herself say, inwardly wincing at the lie that felt so wrong. She was feeling just fine, thank you very much. It was Kurt who was being the problem. But that would make Izzy's already deeply fried brain positively crackle. 'So she sent me to help. Said you'd be able to tell me what to do.'

'You don't dance much, though, do you?'

'Privately, Tiffany's showed me a lot of moves.' That was true. Not that Kurt had ever attempted to master any of them.

'Wonderful,' Izzy cooed. 'Then you can go work with the beginning ladies. Off in that corner. I'm sure you'll have a line of willing chickies to choose from in no time.'

Izzy was right, if a bit understated. Tiffany had more than enough partners to choose from. And she knew why. Eligible male partners were difficult to come by. Many of the best dancers were already partnered up. Some of the others weren't really interested in dancing, just in what it might mean to be partnered with a pretty girl in a short skirt. But after a few twirls around the floor, Tiffany – as Kurt – was easily identifiable as a damn fine dancer, and not a letch.

Tiffany had no desire to hold another girl too close, to caress her anywhere inappropriate, to grope her in a way that might promise something she wasn't offering. She had too much on her mind as it was, trying to lead. She'd played the male role occasionally in dance class, and she had a good idea of what it meant. But dancing in Kurt's body wasn't simple. It took so much concentration that she didn't immediately notice when Kurt entered the dance hall.

He looked nervous, eyes roving over the multitude of dancers. When he spotted her watching him, his shoulders seemed to sag with relief. He hadn't gotten all dressed up for nothing. Tiffany ended the dance with the partner she was with, and hurried to his side. It was clear that he didn't want to dance with her, but he still allowed her to steer him out onto the floor.

'You're right,' he said as she spun him around.

'I am?' She was charmed to see that he was doing his very best not to lead. It appeared to be a concentrated effort on his part.

'If we're going to be stuck like this, we ought to try to make it work.'

'That's what I said.'

'I know.' He frowned at her. 'I'm apologizing.'

'That's how you apologize?'

'Tiffany –' As he spoke, he seemed to forget who he was, and he made a wrong move, switching positions so that he was leading. She pulled him back to the proper form, shaking her head.

'*Tiffany* –' she repeated, hissing the word at him. 'You're going to have to do better than that. People are going to start to think it's odd if we call each other by the wrong names.'

He nodded, and then let her spin him. Amazingly, he didn't stumble. Tiffany watched as the skirt flared out around him. He'd dressed exactly as she'd hoped, minus the shoes. He was wearing one of the few pairs of flats she owned, and he still seemed to be having a bit of trouble

with them. She registered just how much he was trying –
for her – and she felt herself start to melt.

'Tiffany,' she said, pulling him close. 'We'll make it work.
We have to.'

Kurt tilted his head up for a kiss, and even though she
generally didn't go in for public displays of affection, Tiffany
gave in. Oh, it was good to kiss him. Always, always good.
Tiffany felt her heart start to race and her body respond as
it did nowadays, quickly and fiercely, the lust generating a
need of its own.

When they broke apart, Kurt went up on tiptoes to
whisper in her ear, 'Now take me to the bathroom and fuck
me like a man.'

She led here, too. Undoing the fly on the navy slacks, she
released her hard-on and began to stroke it, shaft to tip,
while Kurt gazed at her, hunger wet in his eyes. They were
in a unisex bathroom with a lock on the door. There wasn't
a chance that they'd be interrupted. With a nod of her head,
she motioned for him to bend over the ivory-tiled sink, to
grip onto the edge of the counter.

He did so immediately, pausing only to slide his panties
down his thighs. The music continued to swell in the other
room, building in sound almost as if the band leader knew
what the two were doing back here. The crescendo of horns
accompanied Tiffany as she held Kurt around the waist and
thrust once inside. He was slippery already, and she could
tell how excited he was.

Kurt lowered his head, and Tiffany bucked against him.
Up until now, she had found that it was easiest for her to
make love when she pretended she was back in her own
body. The thought of fucking herself didn't work nearly as
well as imagining Kurt was taking her. It also helped her to
last a little longer if she visualized just what she liked Kurt
to do to her. Now that she knew he'd had trouble climaxing,
she was trying with all of her might to make sure he came.
Tonight she upped the ante, stroking her hands along the
blouse she'd chosen for Kurt to wear, pinching his nipples
through the fabric, then moving the palms of her hands
lower and lower.

She recalled the video of his that she'd seen. Almost all of the scenarios featured multiple partners. This must be what he was into. She bent to whisper in his ear. 'I wish we had another man in the room.'

'Yeah?' Kurt murmured, breathing hard.

'So I could take you from the front, and he could take you from behind. You'd be filled in both holes. Would you like that?' Tiffany couldn't believe how gruff her voice was.

'Oh, yeah –' Kurt sighed, tossing his hair forward. All Tiffany could see in the mirror were his lips, done in a glossy almost indecent red. Kurt was getting better with make-up, and Tiffany noticed for the first time that he was using different colors than she favored. Had he gone out cosmetics shopping?

'He'd fuck you hard, baby. So hard you'd scream.'

'Oh, yeah –'

Tiffany could envision the scenario, plucked from Kurt's video. It suddenly didn't matter who was who. She would have found it just as sexy to be in the male role as the female, and for the first time since the switch, she mentally remained a boy as she fucked him. She used her hands to slightly spread apart Kurt's rear cheeks, and then trailed one fingertip down the crevice between. Kurt shuddered all over and moaned even louder.

In her mind, Tiffany could imagine one of the other male dancers taking up this place, spitting in his palm and then lubing Kurt's rear hole, while Tiffany entered Kurt from the front, creating a sexual sandwich –

'Keep talking,' Kurt begged.

'Dirty girl,' Tiffany hissed. 'You want to be filled, don't you? You want to be demolished –'

Each time she thrust forward, she rewarded Kurt with a tap of her fingertips against his pussy. And with each tap, he sighed and squeezed onto her, creating spasms of pleasure within her.

God, it was hard to be a guy. She worked her best not to let Kurt down.

Fucking in public was one of Kurt's big fantasies. Having sex while still partially clothed, as if they didn't have time to strip, was one of Tiffany's all-time favorite desires. Why they'd never done this at a dance before seemed suddenly odd to Tiffany. Did it take a shake-up like they'd had to become honest with one another?

'Harder,' Kurt demanded, and Tiffany felt her body go weak. 'Fuck me harder, baby –'

She did, her fingers gripped tightly into his waist, the feel of the soft fabric of the skirt caressing her skin, the way Kurt's hair felt against her face when she buried it in the back of his neck making her groan with pleasure.

Everything came together, dazzling her, taking her to a higher level, taking her over the top.

Afterward, Kurt had an evil look in his eyes.

'What?' Tiffany asked, knowing that something was up. Even within her body, Kurt had certain ways of behaving that were easy for her to recognize.

'Nothing –'

'Don't be like that. Tell me.'

Kurt tilted his head coyly, but remained silent, doing a fairly decent impression of Tiffany herself when she had a secret.

'God, you're picking up all my tics, aren't you?'

He grinned. 'Well, I just wanted to make it clear that you owe me.'

'We're keeping score?'

'We will be. Soon.'

'What do you mean?'

'Basketball at the Y. Friday night.' Kurt looked positively gleeful now.

Tiffany shuddered. 'I'm not good enough. Kurt, really,' she pleaded. 'I tried. I failed. There's no way I can play without letting down your teammates.'

'Then I guess you'd better keep practicing.' Kurt smiled. 'The boys are all going to be counting on you.'

'Kurt, team sports are just not my thing.'

'Swing dancing's not really mine.'

Point taken, Tiffany thought. Oh God. 'All right. You go with me. Tell me what to do.'

Chapter Twelve

On Monday morning, Tiffany stood in front of Kurt. 'What am I missing?'

'It's what *I'm* missing,' Kurt said, looking forlornly and somewhat comically down at his groin.

'No, I'm serious. I mean, look me over.'

Kurt did so begrudgingly. 'You look too good.'

Tiffany beamed at him.

'I've told you before, Tiff. I don't ever get this dressed up. You look like you're running for office.'

'It never hurts to put your best foot forward.'

'Yeah, but I'd never wear those fucking shoes.'

She shrugged. The Kenneth Cole loafers had been on special. She'd bought them as a Christmas present for Kurt, and now she got to wear them herself. What fun! 'I've got your keys, your Nicorette gum, your cell phone, your wallet –'

'About the whole wallet thing –' Kurt did not look pleased about what he was about to confess. 'You shouldn't try to use the VISA.'

Tiffany waited.

'Just for a couple of days. I paid it, but I was a little late. So until they get the check, you ought to stick to American Express or MasterCard.'

Tiffany sighed. 'Kurt, why don't you pay via computer? It's easy to sign up for bill pay, and the bank gives you the service for free. I checked it out for you months ago, don't you remember? I even printed out all the information and left it on a file on your desk.' She hated to sound self-righteous, but she couldn't help herself.

He remembered that file. Tiffany was constantly printing out articles to help him to improve himself. 'I stare at a computer screen far too much as it is.'

'You're so good at computer games. You never complain about that.'

'Paying bills isn't a game.' Wow, that sounded lame, even to Kurt.

'You're right. It's not. So why are you always late? Then you have to deal with extra fees, and all the hassles –'

He shrugged. 'Slips my mind, that's all.'

She was going to sign him up for automatic bill pay. First thing. Once she had all his bills entered on line, he would be able to see that she was right. As she was thinking this, her cell phone rang. Automatically, she reached for the little silver camera phone, but Kurt got to the cell first, swatting her hand away. In an extremely professional voice, Kurt answered, 'Tiffany Mitchell, Precision Party Planners.'

Tiffany watched him work the phone. She had to give him credit; he was getting better. He sounded just like her, patient and calm, even smiling as he talked, in the way she'd coached him. People could hear the smile in your voice.

'You go,' he mouthed to Tiffany. 'You don't want to be late for work. I can handle this.'

She took one last look at him, watching for a moment as he made his way to her desk and began writing notes, then realized she simply had to hope for the best and made her way out of the apartment.

Melissa called almost as soon as Kurt hung up the phone with the florist. He sighed and closed his eyes, listening to her fast-paced, one-sided conversation. Kurt couldn't believe how often this girl wanted to talk. Didn't she ever have to do any work? 'Hey there,' he said begrudgingly, when she paused to take a breath. 'What's up?'

'You busy today?'

Kurt glanced at Tiffany's schedule. She had cleared off as much as she could for him, not wanting to overwhelm him with too many appointments. Much of her work could be done via email and phone calls. Still, he was able to honestly say, 'Pretty busy.'

'Want to do lunch? I'm in the mood for sushi.'

No, he did not want to do lunch. And he hated sushi. He knew Tiffany never ate the fish, but he despised even the basic seaweed-wrapped veggie rolls.

'I'm meeting Ti– Kurt,' he said lamely. Man, he was going

to have to get better at that, and quickly. *She's Kurt*, he reminded himself again. *I'm Tiffany.*

'Maybe coffee tomorrow? I don't have to be in until ten. We could go over the tables again. I have a new idea of how I want to do the centerpieces. You know, I was thinking of putting disposable cameras at each table, so that the guests can take candids. But what if we decorated the cameras with ribbons to match the decor –'

'Sure,' he said, only half listening, already planning to cancel later on. 'Coffee sounds great.'

He looked back at Tiffany's computer after getting off the phone. There was a file on the desktop called 'Kurt'. He hesitated for almost a millisecond before opening it.

Tiffany's heart was racing. Over and over, she repeated what Kurt had told her, until the story became like a mantra. A famous local deejay had been fired for making a derogatory remark about the manager of Tommy's beloved ball team. Tommy worked the security desk downstairs at Kurt's office. Tiffany was supposed to say something to him about this recent turn of events. As Tiffany purposefully flashed her ID badge, Tommy said, 'You hear about that son of a bitch, Weston.'

'Man,' Tiffany replied. 'What a fucking racist.'

Tommy nodded. 'Had it coming to him, didn't he?'

'You bet,' Tiffany said, and then froze as Tommy looked at her badge and then back up at her. Had she failed? Did he sense something was up? Tommy tilted his head to the side – 'You growing a beard?'

Tiffany felt relief wash over her. 'Maybe. I'm going to see how it looks.'

'Your lady like it?'

'She's not complaining,' Tiffany replied, smiling as best as she could.

Tommy nodded at her, and Tiffany headed toward the bank of elevators, feeling as if she'd just finished the first mile of a marathon. She'd passed. But she still had a long way to go.

Kurt continued to click open the different files in the folder with his name. If he'd been looking for something damning, he was way off base. Here were the files about on-line bill pay, and ones about contests where he could enter his photographs. At the bottom, was a file titled 'Health'. Here, Tiffany had gathered pages of information about how to quit smoking. She'd downloaded reports from a wide variety of websites, some homeopathic, others filled with cold, medical facts.

Kurt settled himself in her plush desk chair and read each one.

Tiffany headed down the hallway to Kurt's office. She'd been here often enough to visit her beau, and she knew her way around the place. Yet this was different. She wasn't visiting Kurt today – she was *being* Kurt, from his new Armani sweater – also an early Christmas gift – down to his blue-and-white striped boxers. She had to remain on her guard all day long. Someone might easily trip her up if she wasn't paying attention. Look at how scared she'd been when Tommy had hesitated for a second glance at her new appearance.

Kurt had given her a detailed description of the different people he worked with and the potential problems that might arise. The good news, he'd said, was that most people worked on their own projects. This meant that she wouldn't have to interact with too many coworkers at once. Not until there was a big staff meeting, and those rarely occurred more than once a month. If she was lucky, she would never have to attend one.

She tried not to gaze around too much as she headed toward Kurt's corner office. It would be strange if she appeared like a visitor, drinking in the surroundings, rather than a worker, someone who saw the images every day. Kurt claimed that he didn't even notice the art on the walls – he'd seen the pictures so often that they disappeared from consciousness. Yet to an outsider like Tiffany, his work environment was mesmerizing. The hallways were decorated with huge blow-ups of photographs. Some black-and-white pictures of buildings, stark and unadorned. Other four-color photos of landscapes. Pictures of couples kissing. A close-up of a woman's bright red lips.

Kurt worked in a photo service bureau, run by a variety

of artists such as himself, and the place was hip and youthful. The carpet along the hall was a deep fuchsia, no brown-and-gray industrial Burber here.

Tiffany entered Kurt's office and sat down at his desk. She looked at the phone messages waiting for her. She looked at the computer. And she realized, in a frightened flash, that she had no idea what Kurt actually did.

Kurt finished reading the files and crossed his arms over his chest, contemplating the information he'd just absorbed. Then he recrossed his arms. Here was a standard pose that no longer worked for him.

Breasts, though fun to look at and amazing to touch, got in the way. For instance, Kurt had always slept on his stomach. Now, he couldn't get used to the sensation. He was worried about crushing these twin peaks of pleasure. Breasts were a pain when running as well. He'd worn a bra ever since Tiffany had patiently explained how to work the clasp, but still ... whenever he had a need to sprint, he felt as if he were re-creating a slow-motion movie scene, with his breasts bouncing up and down to a heavy drum beat.

But the breasts weren't the worst things to deal with. He'd simply never imagined being a woman was so extremely time-consuming. Yes, he'd complained about 'high-maintenance women' with his friends in the past, but he hadn't understood, hadn't realized, precisely what that meant.

Tiffany had never seemed to be over the top with her various routines. After some of the divas he'd dated, she was positively easy. Yet keeping her looking the way she liked to look was wearing him down. And her lists kept growing.

Grooming was insane. Mascara was impossible and the little eyelash curler – heated, no less – looked like a torture device. How did women do all of these things and still have time, and energy, for work, for the gym, for sex?

He couldn't say all this to Tiffany, though. He didn't want to let her know how hard it was for him. He wanted to do a good job at being a woman, as ridiculous as that sounded to himself.

He wanted to show her he had it in him.

At that thought, he remembered her gym appointment. She worked out with a man named Rolf twice a week. Kurt quickly pulled his hair back into a ponytail and reached for the workout clothes in Tiffany's middle drawer. He still couldn't believe how organized her stuff was. All of the pants were folded in one stack, the T-shirts to the right, the workout bras in the middle. He had seen her dress for the gym often enough to know that she liked to wear all one color: black from head to toe, or pale blue, or an iced green. Feeling rebellious, he chose a pair of navy gym pants, a pink racer-back bra, and a white T-shirt. He knew the bra would show through, and he didn't care.

He checked the clock on the bedside table. Why was he always running late in Tiffany's body?

That was easy – because he was always running late in his own.

Tiffany left the office and headed back to the elevators. Kurt had said to eat a cake donut in the morning. Dunk it in coffee while reading his email. She hadn't paid that much attention to this concept, but now she had an idea.

At the nearest bakery, she bought two dozen donuts in all different varieties: pink iced, sprinkled, jelly, glazed, chocolate and cake. Then she headed back to the office. She knew from years of party planning never to attend an event without a hostess gift. People always responded well to food. She was sure that by bringing in a treat, she'd be able to win over Kurt's coworkers in no time. And they might even be able to help her figure out exactly what it was she was supposed to be doing.

Did Rolf actually touch Tiffany like this all the time? Why hadn't she told him? Because the man definitely had his hands on Kurt, on the backs of his thighs, on the small of his back, twisting and turning Kurt's body into the proper positions. He was impressed by the amounts of repetitions Rolf expected from Tiffany. She did a mean workout, he had to give her that. He wished he was on his own, though.

In one of Tiffany's magazines, he'd read that men were more lone wolves in their preferred style of workouts. They liked to go for solitary runs, long-distance bike rides. If they were at a gym, they didn't chitchat. The women in Tiffany's gym perfectly fit the descriptions given in the magazine. They were working hard, but talking while on the elliptical trainers, chatting about inane subjects that Kurt had no interest in. Why did women care about the sex lives of movie stars? How on earth could that conversation trump the latest offering on the History channel?

'Stay focused, Tiffany,' Rolf said suddenly, bringing Kurt back around with an innocent little squeeze. Was it all that innocent? *Humph*, Kurt thought. The man was a man. In his point of view, there was no innocent touching between a guy and girl. Why didn't Tiffany use a female trainer?

In spite of himself, he felt mildly aroused by all of the unexpected touching, and he also felt a bit put out. Did Rolf turn on Tiffany as well?

This was something he'd definitely have to bring up with her. When he had a second to catch his breath.

Mari-Beth walked into the office looking like a model from *Vogue*. No, that wasn't right. *Cosmo*. One of the cheezy pin-up-style girls, in a crocheted sweater over a tight spaghetti-strap tank top and a form-fitting mini skirt. Who dressed like that to go to work? The answer was given to Tiffany almost immediately: *she* did. In walked Kurt, dressed almost identically to his assistant. Was this really what he thought girls should dress like? Tiffany looked back and forth between the two 'women'. She actually thought like that – 'women' in quotes when she saw Kurt. Because she knew he wasn't one, but that was such a strange feeling.

Clearly, he'd taken his fashion cues from his nubile assistant, and just as clearly, Mari-Beth was charmed with the transformation.

'Oh, my God,' she gushed. 'Tiffany! I just adore your outfit.'

Of course she did. It was almost identical to the one she had on. Kurt had tramped himself out in a tight red skirt, pairing that with a black tank top and a semi-sheer jacket. Where had he gotten those clothes? Not in her closet. She shook her head. They *were* from her closet! From a Halloween costume she'd put together several years before when she'd gone as a naughty devil.

'What are you doing here?' she asked when Mari-Beth had left.

'I want to show you something.'

'Your god-awful taste?'

Kurt looked hurt. 'You always say nice things to Mari-Beth about her clothes. I thought –'

'You're crazy. I think she looks like a whore.'

Kurt's eyes went big. 'But –'

'Women are phony, Kurt. Get used to it.'

Kurt seemed to shrug this off as information he wasn't interested in processing. Instead, he flipped the lock on the office door and began to undress.

'Really –' Tiffany began. 'I've got work. Mari-Beth just told me that I have a meeting ... You said I wouldn't have to deal with one. I've been going through all of your files, trying to figure out what I'm supposed to be doing.'

'Don't worry. Carly will run the show. You just nod and smile and kiss her ass.'

She wrinkled her nose. The image wasn't pleasing. Carly was built like a linebacker. 'Regardless, I have to be there.'

'They never start on time,' Kurt assured her.

'Maybe you just never get there on time.'

He shook his head. 'Everyone's always late around here. All of the staff have artistic temperaments. We've got at least twenty minutes.'

'Twenty minutes for what?' What was he doing at the office, anyway? Did he actually think she was going to have sex with him here? She was still mired in the most basic details of keeping his work life on track. Sex was the last thing on her mind. At least, it was until Kurt began to slide up the hem of his skirt. Her cock, apparently sensing the mere possibility of impending pleasure, hardened fervently against her inner thigh.

'Here?' She was mortified. What if Mari-Beth came in? Or Kurt's boss? How would she recover?

'I've always wanted to, Tiffany. You're the one who has a problem with the idea.'

'Yeah, but –'

'No buts about it. I want to do it on my desk.'

Tiffany hesitated. Then shrugged. Why not? What were her fears about the situation? Being caught. That was the only one. Being found out. But things like that seemed so trivial now in comparison to what she and Kurt were going through. Without a word, she pushed the few papers on her desk aside. They fluttered gently down onto the floor. Then, with a grin, she lifted Kurt onto the desk.

God, she loved how strong she was in this body. Lifting him previously would have been impossible. The only time she'd mastered the task was when they'd messed around in a hotel pool while on vacation, the clear turquoise water making him almost weightless in her arms. Quickly, he'd reversed the position, slipping her tangerine bikini bottoms aside and taking advantage of the fact that they were the only couple craving a dip after midnight.

Now she sat him on the edge of the desk and spread his legs, her body slipping easily between his open thighs. Maybe this outfit wasn't totally awful. She ran her fingers along the jacket, and slowly massaged Kurt's arms through the thin fabric. As she began to kiss him, Kurt sighed and gripped onto her hair, pulling her even tighter against him.

Tiffany was at full-mast now. All thoughts of making it to the meeting on time had evaporated. She began to move down Kurt's body, kissing into the hollow of his neck, breathing in an unfamiliar fragrance. Tiffany always wore Coco Chanel, had since college. But what was this? She breathed in deeper. Poison. The new one. She recognized the scent from one of her magazine inserts. Was that where Kurt had gotten it? Had he been culling through her ladies' magazines, lifting out the different pretty fragrances he wanted to try?

The concept delighted her, but before she could ask, Kurt spoke up.

'Tell me about your trainer,' he said, and she pulled back.

'What do you mean?' Was that his idea of sweet talk?

'Does he turn you on, Tiffany?'

She gazed at him, and she saw what jealousy looked like echoed back from her own face. 'You've got to be kidding. I don't go for muscle men.' No, that didn't come out right. Kurt looked even more upset. 'Not that you aren't strong,' she amended quickly. 'But Rolf is a rock. All he wants to talk about is obliques and traps and curls and reps. I work out with him because he's good.'

'That's what the women in your locker room said.'

Tiffany's eyes widened. It hadn't occurred to her that Kurt would need to venture into the girls' dressing-room. She didn't know why, but when these sorts of things came up, she found herself surprised every time. But she only said, 'Good in what way?'

'Apparently, in bed –'

'Not with me, though.'

He stared at her.

'Come on, Kurt.' She looked down at her grandfather's watch. In Kurt's body, the watch suited her more. She knew that Kurt really should have been the one to wear it, but she felt naked without the timepiece on her wrist. 'We only have a few minutes. I thought you wanted to play.'

'I only need a little reassurance. That's all,' Kurt said, and as soon as the words were out of his mouth, he blanched. He sounded just like Tiffany.

'Don't worry.' She grinned at him, feeling her hard-on throb once more against her leg. 'You're the only girl I want to fuck.'

Chapter Thirteen

Kurt was going to surprise her. That was his plan for Tuesday. Tiffany had insulted his manhood by claiming that he'd never be able to handle a bikini wax, to say nothing of a Brazilian. Well, when she got home that night, he'd be waiting for her, with one of the sexy new thongs he'd bought while shopping with Melissa. He'd show her what he was made of. Maybe he'd even do that retro thing he'd read about in one of her ladies' magazines: wrap himself up in sheer cellophane and wait for her by the front door, martini in hand, nothing else on his body at all. Just like that famous Marilyn Monroe quote: 'It's not true I had nothing on. I had the radio on.'

The concept turned him on immensely. He wondered why Tiffany rarely did the things he'd been reading about. *Cosmopolitan* featured actual perforated cards you could tear out of the magazine, with pictures illustrating different sexual positions to try. The cards were somehow linked to your horoscope, but he hadn't fully understood that part of it. Still, he enjoyed shuffling through the deck, and he lost himself in visions of trying out several of the new positions.

Was he usually this horny? Maybe. Now that he'd gotten the hang of using her vibrator, there wasn't much else he could think about. Fucking himself with the toy. Surprising Tiffany with new and exciting ways to do it. Dolling up this new body that he was in so that his female form fit his different fantasies.

With a wax job on his mind, Kurt looked through her address book until he found the name of her skin-care salon. It took him several minutes to locate the right one. Apparently, she went to different locations for different procedures: one for manicure/pedicure. One to have her hair cut and styled. And this one, for skin. He'd ventured there once before, to buy a gift certificate for Tiffany one Valentine's Day. He'd been surprised at the cost, but felt like the perfect boyfriend at Tiffany's surprised reaction when she'd opened the envelope. She'd told him how hard it was to get an appointment, and that thought echoed in his mind as the receptionist penciled him for later that very day.

Lucky for him, the receptionist told him, there'd been a cancellation. Otherwise, he would have had to wait until Tiffany's actual appointment – two weeks down the road. The word cancellation reminded him of Melissa. He was supposed to have coffee with her. But waxing was far more important.

Tiffany's trick of bringing in donuts seemed to work. One by one, her coworkers stopped by her office, thanking her. She got the feeling that they might come to expect the treats, as she'd brought them in for two days running.

Dunking donuts into her coffee didn't make Kurt's job any easier, but the friendly atmosphere definitely helped. She went through his emails, organized his filing cabinet, displayed his new desk set. Her concept now was to nod and agree with anything anyone said to her, and then quickly call Kurt on her cell phone to ask him questions. So far, she'd gotten by just fine.

The salon was so froo-froo Kurt thought he was going to retch. He'd forgotten how girly the place was. There might as well have been a big sign that read NO MEN – or at least NO STRAIGHT MEN – on the front door, along with the note already posted about no dogs or children under twelve. The décor baffled him: little golden pots of potpourri stood on every table, pedestal and shelf. He hated the batches of dried flower on sight, and on smell, and the scent of the potpourri seemed to clash with the great huge vases of overly fragrant flowers standing on the reception desk.

Did women really like stuff like this?

What was wrong with a room smelling like a room? When did the scent of 'room' go out and 'pine cone' come in? He thought longingly of the old-fashioned barber shop he'd been patronizing in the Mission District for years. That place smelled comfortingly like Brylcream and Barbasol. A manly place for manly men. They even had *Playboy* magazines out in plain sight. This salon was its opposite. No, that wasn't true. Corabella was – Jesus, not womanly – Barbie-esque, he decided. Tiffany wasn't *totally* a Barbie girl. That was one of the things he liked about her the most. Yes, she was pretty and perky and up until recently he'd thought she was blonde. But even though she had an unshakable fondness for pink, she didn't mind getting dirty. She was willing every once in a while for a game of frisbee, for a hike, for a bike ride in the Marin Headlands. But he acknowledged, as he looked around the salon, that she had a girly side to her, too.

While he waited, he flipped through the salon's brochure, and suddenly he noticed the prices. He was going to be billed $85 for this? He ought to just go home and shave the thing himself, but no. This was a challenge. A Herculean show of his inner strength.

Still, when the receptionist asked him if he'd like a glass of water, he nodded, thinking he ought to get his money's worth. She brought him a tall iced glass with slivers of cucumber floating in it, and he looked up at her, horrified. Who drank shit like that? Cucumber-flavored water? Ugh. Did they give cucumber water to every woman who came into the place, or had the receptionist somehow guessed he was an imposter and was setting a test for him. If he drank it, she would know he was a man ... like in that fairy tale 'The Princess and the Pea'.

'Hi there, Tiffany –'

He looked up from the brochure to receive another shock. The waxing technician was a babe. Hands down, one of the sexiest girls he'd ever seen. She had a thick Russian accent that went with her thick blonde hair, wide-set blue eyes, nubile figure – or what he could see of it draped in a white lab-like coat. For the first time in his life, he realized he found women in lab coats appealing. Perhaps that was something else he ought to buy for Tiffany to add to the collection of lingerie he had already splurged on.

The blonde led him to a tiny room down a narrow hallway. He wondered how many other technicians there were, and his mind took a brief fantasy trip involving fucking each one. He'd walk into a room, have a tryst with the technician therein, and then make his way to the next open door. He was only half listening as the woman told him to take everything off from the waist down, then cover up with the white paper sheet folded neatly on the burgundy leather-padded table.

Everything off from the waist down. Thank God he'd worn a skirt today. That made for easier access. Kurt quickly did what she said, first slipping off his thong and then his skirt. In spite of his complaints, he'd decided that he actually liked thongs. They didn't leave panty lines, and were really pretty damn sexy. But where did women put their clothes during a procedure? He set the skirt down on top of the thong, hoping that was right, then settled himself on the leather table.

When the waxer returned, he thought for the first time that he was glad he was a woman. Having this girl adjust him, lift his legs into the proper angles, move him around on the table the exact way she wanted him, had him very excited. Did Tiffany get turned on when she came here? Was it a faux pas to become wet during a waxing? That was something he hadn't yet read about in Tiffany's magazines. Maybe he should write in the query himself to one of the advisor-type columns.

'All right,' the woman said, breaking through his thoughts, 'this is going to be a bit warm.'

She was right. Warm and sticky. Super sticky. Like honey, or molasses.

'Now, a deep breath in –'

He sucked in his breath, and then bit back on a monster of a yell as the girl ripped the wax off with a strip of fabric, and ripped off most of his skin down there as well, from the feel of it.

Oh, my fucking god, Kurt thought. *What the hell was that?*

Why hadn't Tiffany ever told him about the experience of being waxed? Maybe she had and he hadn't been listening, which was a definite possibility – or maybe women didn't feel pain the way that men did. But that didn't make sense. He *was* a woman, wasn't he? And he was feeling some serious fucking pain –

'A deep breath in –'

Shit, the bitch was going to do it again. He did not believe it. Was this something Tiffany actually underwent on a regular basis? This was pain the likes of which he'd never truly experienced before. All he could think of was that his girlfriend could tolerate this, yet she whined whenever she got a papercut. Crazy women.

'And another –'

Oh, fuck. Fuck, fuck, fuck! thought Kurt, eyes squeezed shut. This was torture. Plain and simple –

'And we're all done.'

Whew. The pretty Russian girl had lifted up a small mirror and was showing off her handiwork. Kurt looked through wet eyes at the reflection, and he had to concede, she'd done a good job. But there was no way in hell he'd tip her. Not for pain like that.

Carly stood in Tiffany's office, rambling on about the important meeting with clients coming up the following week. Tiffany did what she always did in situations like this: she took copious notes. On her new note pad. One that matched the new desk blotter and pen holder.

She didn't fully understand everything she was writing down, but that didn't matter. Later, she could go over all of the information with Kurt, and he could explain the concepts she'd missed.

PowerPoint. That was something Carly seemed especially focused on. It was Kurt's job to create a PowerPoint presentation. Tiffany nodded and wrote down word for word what Carly said.

'Like the beard, by the way,' Carly said before she left.

'Thanks,' Tiffany told her, gazing down at her notes.

What the fuck was PowerPoint, anyway?

After all of that pain, Kurt decided to reward himself with a massage. He expected to be given a rubdown by one of the pretty nymphets he'd seen chatting up front with the receptionist, waiting impatiently for one to enter the room, bottle of hot almond oil in hand. When the door slid open, however, a tall, lean man stood in the doorway. 'Hi there, Tiffany.'

'Hi,' Kurt squeaked out. *Who the fuck was this Ken doll?*

'Is your back still bothering you?'

Shit, it was someone she'd been to before. How was Kurt going to deal with that? By his new policy of being vague and mildly ditzy. That seemed to work best.

'No, it's good,' Kurt said swiftly. 'In fact, maybe I don't need a massage after all –'

'Such a kidder.' The man smiled. 'Close your eyes now, and just relax.'

Easier said than done, Kurt thought to himself, imagining this handsome man rubbing Tiffany all over. Actually, that didn't take much imagination at all, as that's what the masseur *was* doing. Why hadn't Tiffany ever told him that her masseuse was a masseur? Or once again maybe she had and Kurt simply hadn't been paying attention. That was probably the truth. You know, he was going to have to start listening to her.

'And exhale,' the man said soothingly. 'Come on, Tiffany. Waxing's over. This is the fun part. This is the reward.'

Kurt realized suddenly that he had been holding his breath. With great effort, he slowly forced himself to exhale, then inhale, then exhale, as the masseur's strong hands worked their magic over his shoulders, then down his arms. A warm tingling sensation began to build up inside of him.

Kurt had received massages previously. A few regular massages and one 'special' massage way back in college, where the rubdown itself had been less than mediocre, but the hand job at the end had more than made up for the lack in technique. He'd felt a bit dirty afterward, but that had been part of what made the trip exciting.

This particular massage was legitimate. He could tell. Yet this body of Tiffany's was responding a bit as if it was receiving a 'special' massage. Kurt did his best not to groan as the masseur's hands slid under his back and began to work out the knots.

Oh Lord, did that ever feel good. No wonder Tiffany liked this place. He'd been wrong about the salon. So what if they had froo-froo potpourri? So what if they put cucumbers in their water? This was worth it.

Those strong hands continued their way to the small of his back. Kurt sighed with pleasure. If he could have, he would have started to purr. Oh, yes, he thought, knowing that he sounded just like Tiffany. That's lovely.

He closed his eyes and felt his thoughts float away.

* * *

You can do anything you set your mind to. That was another of Tiffany's slogans. It had gotten her far in the past. Whenever she was faced with an unexpected hurdle, she buckled down and pushed through.

But learning PowerPoint wasn't like learning to write calligraphy. Or ordering sugar cubes with tiny flowers. Or tracking wedding gifts that had gone astray. Besides, she really didn't understand what the presentation was supposed to be about. Carly had mentioned wooing these new clients. But wooing them how? She thought about going to Mari-Beth and asking for help, yet that would seem weird. Instead, she barricaded herself in Kurt's office and made sure that his computer was flashing image after image, as if she were culling different pictures for use in the presentation. Then she dialed up Melissa, knowing that she couldn't have the conversation she wanted, but needing to hear her friend's voice nonetheless.

'You see?' he asked, defiantly. 'I *can* stand it –'

'Stand what?' Tiffany asked. She hadn't even looked over at him, her face hidden behind the computer screen, her whole body completely focused on the work in front of her. She'd put in a regular day at Kurt's office, and now she was following up on the day-to-day chores for her party planning business.

'Look at me when I talk to you –'

Tiffany jumped. Wow, did that sound familiar. It was something she said to Kurt nearly every day. Sometimes, she said it when he was playing a hand-held video game. Other times, when he was clearly *pretending* to listen to her, but his eyes were on some faraway spot on the horizon. To hear her own voice echoing these familiar words had a profound impact. She looked up at Kurt immediately.

Kurt had changed his mind about meeting her at the front door encased in an entire boxworth of SaranWrap. He'd actually gone out and bought a tube of the stuff, but had wound up feeling extremely claustrophobic after only wrapping up his midsection. Plus, the stuff made him too hot. Whoever had come up with that idea had definitely not been a woman. Instead, he was holding a pose in the doorway between Tiffany's home office and hall. Tiffany shook her head when she saw him. His hair was up in an early Britney-Spears style of braided pigtails, and he was wearing a trenchcoat –

Did she own a trenchcoat? She didn't think so. Had he gone out and bought more clothes for her? Was she going to have to keep the clothes once they were able to switch back to themselves? It would be rude not to –

He let his trenchcoat fall open to reveal that he was wearing a marabou-trimmed cardigan and a plaid school-girl skirt.

Shaking her head she said, 'This is how you like me?'

As she spoke, Kurt showed her his secret, lifting up the skirt to display his freshly waxed bikini area. For a moment, Tiffany was speechless. Then she walked forward, intrigued.

'How'd it feel?'

'Hurt like fucking hell. But I have to say –' he looked down at himself, '– I'm somewhat enamored with the sensation. Panties feel so sexy now. The silkiness. I've been walking around for the past hour almost coming simply from the way the material feels on my skin. And I wanted to –' As he spoke, he started to reach for Tiffany's slacks. 'You know. Fuck –'

Kurt was right. The wax job was sexy. He'd even gone in for a design, Swarovski crystals glued to his skin in a spiral pattern. Tiffany was charmed. Who would ever have thought Kurt would be the type to pay such attention to minor details? Perhaps he didn't think the details were so minor when they had to do with his own body.

She bent down to look closer, and couldn't help but kiss up and around the designs. His skin was so smooth, so soft. She used the tip of her tongue to trace the crystals. They gleamed wet in the light when she moved back to admire him once more.

This was something she hadn't done yet. She'd occasion-ally fantasized about a ménage à trois with another woman, but of course she hadn't put herself in the male role. Now, Kurt leaned back against the door frame, his hands still holding up his skirt, his eyes shut tight. Tiffany couldn't resist. She tricked her tongue between his pussy lips, search-ing out for his clit. In an instant, she'd found it, ready, bursting. He had told her the truth. Simply walking around after the wax job had clearly been a turn-on. Kurt was as wet as he'd been so far.

Without any thoughts of what she was doing, Tiffany gripped his hips and pulled him hard against her face. She clicked the tip of her tongue against that ripe little pearl, making Kurt groan and twitch in her arms. He was trying to press himself as hard as possible against her mouth. He wanted more. She could tell. Tiffany overlapped two of her fingers and slowly slid them inside of Kurt. He clamped down on her immediately, and she felt him squeezing and releasing, over and over. Had he practiced on the vibrator? Was he doing his Kegels?

Her cock throbbed against her, letting her know that it wasn't at all happy not to be partaking of the action. But Tiffany was busy. She flipped Kurt around so that his hands were on the wall, and she lifted the pleated skirt up in the back. Now, she began to lick him from behind, and Kurt arched his back, groaning even louder. This is what she would sound like if she ever granted his wish and let herself go. The moans and sighs he let loose flowed over her, making her cock as hard as she'd ever felt it. She couldn't hold off much longer.

Standing upright, she undid her slacks and pressed her body against Kurt's naked backside, letting him feel the satin of her boxers against his skin. He shuddered all over and started to beg. 'Fuck me, Tiff. Fuck me –'

She plunged inside of him immediately, desperate to feel that warmth around her, ravenous to be inside Kurt once more. She might not have any idea how to do his job at work, but she felt she was getting damn good at fucking like a man.

Chapter Fourteen

Burn a candle, get a wish –
   Different candles. Different wishes.
   What do you want? Money? Fame? Love?
Why had she thought that being Kurt would be easy. She realized how pathetic her wish had been. One month in his body, and she'd shake everything back into place. That was so conceited of her.

She'd never tell Kurt this, but she realized during the first week in his office that she was floundering. Up until now, all she'd known was that he was an office manager; it's how she had always introduced him to friends and acquaintances. But he really was more like a kindergarten teacher, trying to keep everyone in line. There were so many personalities to be wary of, and different people's soap-opera love lives to complicate matters. Mari-Beth could occasionally be seen in tears when she'd had a spat with her girlfriend. Jarred got on everyone's nerves by disappearing for long stretches of time. Carly was a power-crazed bitch, only happy when she was making demands. And through it all, Tiffany took notes and tried her best not to appear like a moron.

She hadn't worked in an actual office setting since temping in college, and she'd forgotten how difficult it was to be in one place for nine hours at a time. With her own company, she felt as if she worked constantly. But she wasn't chained to a desk. She could get a manicure in the middle of a Wednesday if she desired. She could have coffee with Melissa, or go shoe shopping, or watch *Entourage*. Now, her back ached by mid-afternoon, and sometimes she just wanted to leave the building for some fresh air.

'That's why I smoke,' Kurt explained when she confessed on Friday to being mildly overwhelmed.

'Makes zero sense.'

'It's an excuse to leave, though,' he said. 'You can't smoke in the building, so you sneak out for ten minutes. Maybe twenty.'

'So why are nonsmokers penalized? You're actually polluting the air. I should be rewarded. I should be able to get ten free minutes to do yoga, or something.'

'You actually can slip out every once in a while,' Kurt informed her. 'You just have to pay attention to what Carly's doing, and tell Mari-Beth you're running a quick errand. She'll always cover for you. How are things really going, anyway?'

She didn't want to tell him about her failure with PowerPoint. Instead, she said simply, 'I'm trying to be the best man I can.'

'The best man!' The words jarred something deep within Kurt, and he spilled the coffee he'd been pouring. 'You're Rick's best man, aren't you? Melissa was blathering on about that today. I forgot to remind you.'

'She doesn't blather.'

'Oh, yes she does. I still don't get why she calls so fucking much.'

'Do you ever call her?'

'I call her back.'

'Well, you need to call her first sometimes.'

He shrugged that off. 'Jesus, Tiffany. You have to go to the bachelor party.'

'I know. I've been worried sick over it. They're going to be able to tell something's wrong. Some of those guys have known you since college.'

'But they're all idiots.' Kurt grinned, regaining his sense of composure quickly. 'They shouldn't notice anything, as long as they get drunk enough.'

'And you know what that means?' Tiffany asked, treading carefully. She'd wanted him to figure this out on his own.

'That you're going to be with strippers all night?'

'No, that you have to go to the bachelorette party.'

Chapter Fifteen

On the way to Melissa's, Kurt was pulled over by one of San Francisco's finest – a motorcycle officer in a dark navy uniform. Kurt swore when he saw the flashing lights in his rear-view mirror. This wouldn't be his first ticket. What an understatement. He couldn't even do traffic school this time. There was a limit to how many times that little loophole device would save your insurance rates.

Shit, he fumbled for his wallet, and when he came up without the battered black leather filled with ID cards, driver's license, insurance verification, he swore harder. How was he going to talk his way out of that? And where the fuck had he left his wallet, anyway? Only when he saw the small beaded purse on the seat at his side did he remember who he was.

The realization temporarily stunned him. He *would* be able to go to traffic school after all, because he knew that Tiffany had never had a single ticket in her entire life. She'd probably never even run out of time on a parking meter. He was still wide eyed when the officer reached his side of the vehicle.

'Evening, officer.' Kurt smiled as best as he could.

'You were going pretty fast there, miss,' the dark-eyed cop told Kurt. Well, that was different. Kurt had never been spoken to by a police officer with anything other than direct sternness. He wondered if the cop's respectful tone of voice had to do with the outfit he'd chosen tonight. He thought he was getting a bit more adventurous with his style.

'Emergency somewhere?' the officer continued, yet his tone remained even, not flippant. Not even all that annoyed, actually. He was talking to Kurt in an almost conversational manner, as if they had run into each other at a neighborhood bar.

Kurt shook his head. He could feel himself blushing,

which mortified him. Blushing was a sign that he was in the wrong, yet this body sometimes seemed to betray him in spite of his best intentions. He took a deep breath, trying desperately to picture how Tiffany would act in this situation. The thought of Tiffany speeding in the first place was impossible to imagine. But if she had – perhaps done so unintentionally – what would her response be? That was simple: she'd apologize, definitely, and be extremely contrite. And the truth was that she wouldn't be faking it.

'I'm so sorry,' Kurt gushed, his eyes still wide, but open like that on purpose. 'I was going to my friend's bachelorette party, and I guess I got sort of excited.' He indicated the frilly wrapped present on the seat at his side.

The man's stony expression actually softened. Kurt couldn't believe it. Gaining confidence, Kurt continued, in a rush, hoping to keep the cop in a friendly frame of mind. 'Yeah, she's been my best friend since elementary school, and I spent so much time choosing my outfit, that I'm going to be late.'

Was the officer buying any of this? He seemed to be, because he actually appraised what he could see of Kurt and said, 'Nice dress you landed on.'

Kurt shrugged. 'I didn't know exactly what to wear. We're staying in, but there'll be about ten of us.'

'My sister had fifteen at hers. Stayed up all night having some sort of slumber party thing.'

They were bonding! This was unbelievable!

The cop was now staring at Kurt's hands on the wheels, and suddenly Kurt realized the officer must be looking for a wedding ring. The nerve! Still in flirt mode, however, and dying to get out of the ticket, Kurt asked in a light-hearted voice, 'How'd they dress? Do you think I look appropriate?'

Again, the cop appraised the outfit. Kurt had tarted himself up a bit tonight, enjoying the freedom of dressing Tiffany's body however he wanted. There was a thrill in choosing stockings and bra and panties that were all totally mismatched, in sliding on a form-fitting dress, in shaking out the blonde foil of Tiffany's mane of hair. This was another instance where Tiffany's unending supply of fashion magazines had come in handy. He'd been able to do his research, page through the volumes until he'd found something suitable, something he might be able to piece together from Tiffany's overflowing – and intimidating – wardrobe, or from Melissa's, who always seemed to want to come over and borrow or trade with him.

As a kid, he'd never played with dolls. He was a boy's boy all the way to his unkempt toenails, even if he had been raised by a feminist mother who often played *Free to be You and Me* to her children. Kurt had not gone for that 'William Has a Doll' mentality. But as he'd dressed himself this evening, he'd suddenly understood the fun of design, of working with beautiful materials, of making the most of a bad situation. At least, that's what he'd told himself while primping in front of the mirror.

'You look lovely,' the cop told him, a little too seriously, and now Kurt started to wish he had gotten a ticket and was already driving away. 'If you all go out later, where might I meet up with you?'

Kurt shrugged. 'I have to confess, officer, I have a boy-friend,' he said, even though he knew this was his moment to escape without a ticket. Something he'd never done. Something he'd have remembered forever.

Rick picked Tiffany up at Kurt's apartment early. He called her up from his cell phone and told her to meet him downstairs. She gave herself a final once-over in the mirror on the back of Kurt's bathroom door, nodding in approval to the clothes she'd chosen. She was modeling herself this evening on Tom Ford, her all-time favorite designer, going for a classic look of gentlemanly excellence, something Mr Ford might wear himself. No doubt about it, she looked striking – Brad Pitt, step back! she whispered to herself, then headed out of the apartment.

When she went outside, she almost started laughing. Parked in front of Kurt's building was a long, blindingly white Hummer limo. The thing was a cock on wheels. Tiffany winced with embarrassment as she watched Rick get out of the car. God, did you even call things this big 'cars'? 'Monster' was more like it.

'Dude,' Rick said, slapping Tiffany hard on the back. (Why did men do things like this? What was wrong with a simple handshake or a brief hug? Why did they have to slap each other, to punch each other, to act like big dogs?) 'Can you believe this, man? We're going to stay out all night.'

'Dude,' Tiffany said, trying hard not to laugh. 'You had to get the Hummer?'

'If it's good enough for the Governor.'

'Right. Because you and Arnold Schwarzenegger have so much in common.'

Rick flexed. Tiffany would have giggled, but she stopped herself knowing that wouldn't be too manly, would it? As Kurt she just said, 'In your dreams, man.'

'Well, Arnold and I both like the ladies,' Rick settled on. 'So which club are we going to hit first?'

Tiffany mumbled something unintelligible as she climbed into the car, hoping he wouldn't ask her again. She didn't know the names of any strip clubs. That was aside from the O'Farrell Theater. But they wouldn't go there, would they? It seemed too clichéd. In any other party planning situation, she would have done research beforehand, but she hadn't been looking forward to this night, and had done her best to put the thought of it out of her head.

Kurt had assured her that she'd do just fine, but she felt extremely nervous. He had tried to get her to one when they first started dating, claiming that she'd find it sexy to watch pretty women dance. She hadn't gone for it then. How odd she was going to go now, without him, but *as* him. Why had she made such a big deal of not wanting to go when he'd asked. It had only been as a turn-on, she understood now. A fantasy for him. She shouldn't have been so uptight.

Three of Rick's friends were waiting inside the gargantuan vehicle. They all had beers in hand – here was the true beauty of being chauffeured around for an evening. They had a paid designated driver, which meant that there would be no holding back as far as the drinking was concerned. Tiffany took a deep breath. This was going to be difficult. Kurt always said she was a lightweight, and it was true. How was she going to match them with alcohol consumption? Rick immediately handed her a Heineken. She grinned and toasted the rest of the guys, then took one quick swallow.

'Ladies,' she grinned as she set the beer between her legs. That was something she'd heard Kurt do in the past, call his friends 'ladies' when he entered a room. As the car pulled into traffic, Rick handed her a second beer. Her heart sank. Did he think she could actually drink a beer in less than a minute? Would Kurt have done so? Yeah, she knew she had more body mass as Kurt, but she also knew that she didn't have any idea what it felt like to be drunk as a man. And she wasn't all that sure that she wanted to find out.

Kurt could not believe how fucking loud these women were. There were only about ten girls together in one room, but from the giggling they sounded as if there was a stadium filled with young co-eds. Now, *that* was a sexy thought, while this was rather more on the ear-splitting side.

'We did it,' Marlena whispered to him.

'Did what?' he whispered back, thinking, Mmm, she smells good. Spicy. What was that scent? Was it something he ought to buy for Tiffany, or himself? So far, he'd tried out Dune, Obsession, and the new Poison.

'Got the guy –'

Kurt played along, nodding enthusiastically with his eyes wide open in the same spirited expression he'd used with the police officer, but feeling totally lost nonetheless. The guy. *What* guy? How did they get one? Get one for *what*? His thoughts would have spiraled out of control if one of the girls hadn't explained.

'The *stripper*,' Eleanor said in a hushed tone. Kurt was thankful for only the second time since this switcheroo had taken place that he no longer had a cock. The proximity of the pretty bridesmaids on his right and left would have turned him on visibly in a heartbeat. As it was, he squirmed on the sofa, hoping he wouldn't leave a wet spot when he stood. How did women deal with this sort of thing? Should he have worn jeans instead of the thin leopard-print dress he'd ultimately plucked from the very rear of Tiffany's closet? He hadn't realized that almost all of the clothes he'd found enticing were Tiffany's former Halloween costumes.

'The stripper.' Kurt grinned now. 'Cool.' It took a moment for him to realize that they meant a male stripper, and then he bit down on the reaction that threatened to slip out – *Shit, I have to watch a guy take off his clothes.*

'Melissa has no idea,' Eleanor explained. 'She thinks this is going to be a tasteful little celebration.'

'Crazy, huh?' Marlena asked. 'She's known us since college. Since when have we ever been tasteful?'

Kurt's expression froze. Marlena was a research librarian at one of the local private girls' schools. What hadn't Tiffany been telling him? Or was this just one more instance of him not paying attention? He vowed not to zone out so much in the future, if he ever returned to his own skin.

'Hey, Kurt, you faggot,' Mike said.

Tiffany turned to look at him, shocked. Was this how guys talked to each other? Should she respond by calling him a fruit? A queer? A drag queen?

'You wearing perfume, Kurt? What's next? Eye shadow?'

She felt her cheeks redden. 'Not perfume, dude. Cologne. There's a big difference, you know.' She hoped they wouldn't look at her hands. She'd gotten a mani/pedi earlier in the day, enjoying every second of having Kurt's rough callouses smoothed, his ragged cuticles tamed. This was something she'd wanted him to do forever. At least, every time his feet brushed against her naked legs in the bed and she squealed in distaste. As it was, she'd used a certificate she'd bought Kurt for his last birthday, one that she realized now he'd never had any intention of redeeming. It was just another thing she'd uncovered when organizing his apartment. That, along with a few joints, a pile of girly magazines and the drawer of porn.

Now, looking down at her hands, she was happy that she'd gone with a simple buff job on his nails rather than the clear polish the manicurist had been pushing. What would they have said about that?

'Oooh,' Axel crooned. 'Cologne. He's a homo. No doubt about it.'

'Not a homo.' Rick laughed gruffly. 'Don't you guys read the papers? He's a metrosexual. Wait, an *übersexual*. That's what Melissa was going off about the other day. Ubersexuals. They're the new "it" men. Strong, yet sensitive. Bono's one –'

'The cologne was a gift.' Tiffany glared at them. She'd read the same article, but she wasn't going to confess to it and get more grief. 'From Tiffany.' Good Lord, men were rude. At the very least, they should have appreciated the effort. She'd been dying to get Kurt to wear cologne for years. She'd given him Aramis, Paco Rabanne, even Polo, which all the boys favored back when she was in high school, hoping that she'd ultimately land on something he would like. She hadn't messed with him too much – hadn't suggested that he wear something silly like Hummer (although that would have fit in with the theme of this particular evening). No, she'd gone classy all the way. Tonight, she had on Black Code by Armani. And it wasn't as if she'd showered in the stuff! She knew about putting on a tasteful amount of a scent – back of the knees, nape of the neck –

'She's got you wearing perfume already? Better watch out. Next comes a leash.' Axel panted like a dog. He looked ugly when he did that. Tiffany narrowed her eyes. She'd never liked Axel much. Right now, she liked him even less. It was easy to see why he was single.

'Leave off,' Rick insisted, and Tiffany looked at him in relief. At least Rick was coming to her defense. 'He's wearing it for the strippers.'

'How quaint.' Axel grinned as they pulled up to the first club. 'You'll have to make sure you get close enough for them to appreciate it.'

They'd ordered a cop.

What a fucking cliché. They couldn't have gotten a chef? Or a football player? Or even a fireman? No, they'd gone with cop. In a navy-blue uniform. With a nightstick. And handcuffs.

Right when Melissa was in the middle of opening up her gifts, the doorbell rang. Melissa asked Kurt to answer it for her, and when he did, he shook his head. Maybe men were easy, but women were so predictable. A fucking cop.

'Where's the party, beautiful?' the stripper asked him. Kurt immediately straightened his back, but that only made Tiffany's tits stand out more prominently. He didn't like the way this guy was looking at Tiffany's body, even if the man most likely was gay. There wasn't a straight male stripper on the planet, was there?

'This way,' Kurt said, motioning for the dancer to go ahead of him down the hallway. He didn't want the cretin to stare at his ass. But the sight of this guy in full-on costume reminded him of his encounter earlier in the evening. When he sat back down next to Eleanor, he told her the story.

'You got off *again*?'

'What do you mean "again"?' Kurt asked before he could stop himself. He was going to have to get better at this. The girls might be a little tipsy, but that was a pretty obvious slip. Yet how could he have known better? Tiffany had never told him she'd ever been pulled over.

'How much have you had to drink, Tiff?' Eleanor asked him. Kurt shrugged and then played a bit drunker than he really was. 'Just a few of these.' They were drinking some horrific pink concoction tonight, and he was pretending for all he was worth to like the stuff. What was wrong with old-fashioned Martinis? Why did girls have to put paper umbrellas in their drinks in order to consider them festive?

'Can't hold your liquor, crazy girl. You got out of a ticket last month, too.'

Kurt nodded, spellbound. 'That's right. Can't believe I forgot!' He giggled moronically, and then worried he'd gone too far when Melissa shot him a strange look. Luckily, Eleanor appeared to be as drunk as he was acting.

'I know. Especially when you were so proud of yourself. Bought rounds for everyone at Harvey's that night. You must have spent more than you saved. Not like the last time. What'd it cost you? Two hundred dollars, plus traffic school.'

Eleanor was interrupted as the cop took off his pants.

'Thank God you didn't have to blow him,' she giggled, and Kurt, full on in agreement with her, nodded.

Oh, cripes.

What if she got a hard-on?

Or what if she didn't?

The women were gorgeous, animal-like dancers, tigresses, spinning around the poles in the center of the stage. Tiffany couldn't stare at any one too long. Making eye-contact was the worst. Each time she found herself captivated by the rotations of one of the dancers, the girl would inevitably come over to her, offer a lap dance, and the guys would hoot and howl their encouragement.

'Which one do you like?' Axel wanted to know.

'They're all lovely,' Tiffany said. No, that sounded lame. Nothing like Kurt would say. Ever. 'I mean, sexy,' she amended quickly. 'Totally fucking sexy.'

'Yeah, but which one's your favorite?'

She squinted up at the stage. Which girl would Kurt like best? The one with the obviously fake breasts? The brunette with the full hips? The girl with tattoos all over her body, an angel's wings over her shoulder blades, a devil's tail snaking around one thigh. She didn't know. But these guys probably did. She almost eeny-meeny-minied it. But finally she said, 'The one in mauve.'

'Oh, shit. You *are* gay, dude.'

'Mauve. What the fuck color is that?'

Tiffany snorted into her beer, trying to recover as quickly as possible. What should she say to cover up her faux pas? She'd never have thought that 'hanging with the guys' would take so much brain power. 'Sorry, boys,' she finally managed. 'Tiff's got me watching all those fucking make-over shows every night. I guess I picked it up there.' She hesitated for one more moment. 'I like the girl in the nurse's outfit best. She'd could take my temperature any time she wanted.'

The other men seemed drunk enough to accept this, and Tiffany let loose a sigh of relief. One that died on her lips as Rick waved the girl over and motioned to Tiffany's lap. No, no, no. She couldn't. That would be too strange.

Rick waved a twenty in the girl's face, and she made the bill disappear into her g-string like magic. Tiffany watched, in awe, as the girl in the crisp white uniform straddled her lap.

She'd never been this close to a girl before.

Never.

And she didn't know what to do about it.

But Kurt's cock seemed to know.

The cop was down to his shimmering metallic panties. There was no other word for them. *Panties.* Kurt couldn't believe the guy was actually as big as he looked. Must have a sock stuffed in his drawers, he thought, precisely as Eleanor whispered the same observation to him.

'A cucumber's more like it,' Melissa countered.

'No, a salami!'

Who knew girls could be this crude? And were they pleased that the guy was stuffing his knickers, or did that turn them off? He just couldn't tell.

'You do know your meat,' Eleanor teased.

Oh, he wished the girls wouldn't get so close to him. He'd never be unfaithful to Tiffany, and he clearly *couldn't* be in this new situation, but their proximity made him feel like a letch. Every time they pressed against him, he felt giddy, then guilty. He wondered how Tiffany was holding up on her night out with the boys, and then he relaxed against the sofa, knowing that no matter how difficult this was for him, her night must be equally trying.

She was harder than hard. How bizarre. This must be an innate physical response, because her mind wasn't in on the game. Or maybe that wasn't entirely true. She'd always enjoyed looking at other women, and every so often one frisky female would make her way into Tiffany's fantasies.

She hadn't confessed this to Kurt. He'd have taken it the wrong way, wanted to act it out, wanted to make Melissa a third. And she'd never been willing to cross that barrier between fantasy and reality.

As the nurse slid her hips against Tiffany, she tried her best to put on an excited expression. The girl grinned at her and licked her lower lip. Tiffany found herself drinking in every motion. Maybe she would do a striptease for Kurt someday, if they ever got back to their own bodies. Or maybe the two of them would come together to a club like this. Watching the girls was a turn-on. She had to admit that now. And even if she wouldn't say so verbally, her cock was beating out a morse code of pleasure against her thigh.

'How's it going?' Tiffany asked softly. She'd crept back to the hall in the rear of the building and dialed Kurt on her cell phone. His cell phone. *Whatever*, she thought, tipsy enough not to care.

'You didn't tell me about the stripper,' he said accusingly.

'Neither did you.'

There was a silence while both registered what the other was talking about.

'Rick buy you a lap dance?' Kurt asked her, seeming to guess what she was talking about.

'Two.'

'And did you like it?'

From the sound of Kurt's voice – well, her own voice, but the cadence of it – she could tell that Kurt was aroused at the idea. That made sense. Here was one of his all-time favorite fantasies come true. Every so often when they were in bed, he'd talk about taking her out to North Beach to do exactly what she'd spent this night doing. Going to see girls undress together. Buying a lap dance for her. He'd never pressured her into actually going through with an evening of girl-watching, but she could tell that the thought thrilled him.

'You go first.'

'The cop did nothing for me, but Melissa seemed to enjoy herself. He cuffed her and then made her watch him strip down to nothing but a little golden g-string.'

'I think on guys those are called "mankinis".'

'Yeah. That. Don't ever buy me one of those.'

'I'm wearing one now.'

There was a silence again, and then Kurt laughed. 'You've got a wicked sense of humor, Tiff.'

'I have to.'

'Hey,' Kurt said, 'what did you get Melissa for the gift? You never told me, and she's unwrapping the presents next.'

Right then, the men's room door opened and Rick came out. He looked as drunk as Tiffany felt and in a heartbeat he'd confiscated her phone. 'Hey,' he said to Kurt. 'No calls to sweethearts, spawn or spouses. Those are the rules for tonight. He's doing fine, Tiff. So don't you worry. I'll have him home in time for church.' Laughing, he cut the connection and slipped the phone back into his own pocket.

'Come on, dude. We're off to club number two –'

Melissa opened Tiffany's gift last. Kurt wished he knew what was in the box, but Tiffany had been disconnected before she could tell him. He tried to put a knowledgeable expression on his face, as if he had done hours of shopping in order to find this – the perfect gift for his best friend in the whole world. All the girls were gathered around Melissa in a heap of wrapping paper and ribbons.

'Ooooh,' Eleanor squealed as Melissa pulled out the first layer of silvery tissue.

Kurt couldn't see what was inside of it, not with the cluster of girls so close to Melissa, so he said simply, 'I thought you'd like it.'

'She'll love it,' Marlena murmured appreciatively.

'Especially when Rick's away on business,' another agreed.

'Or when he's asleep.'

Melissa lifted the gift out and held it up high in the air. The girls, giggling, bowed down before it as if the gift were an idol.

Tiffany had bought her best friend The Rabbit, and Kurt couldn't hide the bright crimson blush that colored his cheeks.

At the next club, Tiffany was surprised when she saw Rick heading to the back room with an Amazonian redhead and a petite Asian in shiny black vinyl. 'Hey,' she called out. 'What's going on?'

'Be back in twenty,' Rick replied, 'or maybe thirty,' and the other men at the table chuckled. But Tiffany thought she saw something in Mike's eyes. He wasn't having as much fun as Axel was. Clearly, he enjoyed the spectacle of the pretty women, but Rick's behavior seemed to perturb him. Mike was the one with the spawn that Rick had been referring to, wasn't he? Tiffany glanced down and saw a gold wedding ring shining on Mike's second finger.

'He's getting a private dance?'

'If you want to call fucking a dance,' Axel grinned, 'which I guess it can be if you're doing a girl who has a sense of rhythm.'

'They're not actually going to have sex, are they?' She said this in a hushed voice, not actually wanting to know the answer.

'If he pays them each the two hundred, they are.'

'Has he done that before?' She couldn't stop herself. 'I mean, since he started dating Melissa?'

'Well, you know Rick,' Axel said, lifting his beer. 'He doesn't consider it cheating if he doesn't know the girl's name.'

Chapter Sixteen

'He *didn't* cheat,' Kurt insisted. 'Tiffany, I know the guy. He's all hot wind and big talk. But he loves Melissa. Truly. Sometimes he just puts on an extra macho manner when he's with the guys. You know what an alpha-male Axel can be? He brings out the worst in Rick.'

Tiffany didn't believe it. 'Look, you weren't there,' she said fiercely. 'You didn't see what he was like. He wasn't pretending.'

'But I've been with him before at places like that. He likes to act like the man –'

'Yeah, the man who fucks strippers in the back room for four hundred dollars. Axel didn't seemed surprised by this, Kurt. I don't know why you're defending him.' She took a deep breath. 'And when were you at a strip club with him?'

Were they really going to go there? Kurt glared at her. 'Occasionally guys venture to strip clubs after work, Tiffany. I've never hidden that fact from you.'

'You mean you've never told me about it, but you've never denied it, just like your cache of pornography.'

'Well, how about your overly friendly trainer at the gym?'

Tiffany felt her cheeks turning a dark shade of purple. 'There's nothing going on with me and Rolf.'

'Oh, Rolf,' Kurt cooed. 'Come on, Tiff. You never told me anything about him either.'

'Because there wasn't anything to tell!'

'He seems to know an awful lot about you.'

'I work out with him twice a week. Are we really going to talk about this right now? I wanted to discuss Rick and Melissa.'

Kurt was silent. He'd known that Rick considered himself a player, but he hadn't ever seen actual evidence that the boy was cheating. 'Tell me from the start,' he insisted. 'How do you know that he fucked her? Did you see him? Were you in the room?' An instant image of that scenario came unbidden to Kurt's mind, and he was mildly embarrassed to realize that he found the concept arousing, the thought of Tiffany – in his own body – doing something sexy with an alluring stranger. He wouldn't even have been upset with her; he would only have wanted to know all the dirty little details.

'I didn't go back there,' she admitted with distaste. 'But he was different when he rejoined the party. He had one of the girl's panties in one hand, and he was all greasy looking. Blurry around the edges.'

'He wanted you all to think he'd nailed her. That's what it was.'

'Talking about her choking on his sausage –' Tiffany shuddered. 'Are men generally like that? All night long. If they weren't talking about laying pipe, then they were making meat references or fart jokes.'

'Axel, you mean.'

'Yeah, mostly him, but Rick seemed to be in that sort of mood as well. Is this what you all are like?'

Kurt said, 'Well, are all you women as stupid as Eleanor?'

'Hey –'

'I'm serious. That girl doesn't have two brain cells to rub together.'

'She's sweet –'

'In a kill-me-now sort of way. I've never had to talk to her before for any length of time, thank God, but I can see why she's single.'

'I was thinking the same thing about Axel.'

'Maybe we should get the two of them together –'

'Come on, Kurt. I fucking *hate* him.'

'And I'm feeling the same way about her. You should have heard her go off about the stripper. And she couldn't shut up about the fact that I bought Melissa The Rabbit, which I wish you would have told me about ahead of time. I was so embarrassed when she pulled that sex toy out of the box. My cheeks were scarlet –'

'You know, this isn't about Axel and Eleanor. Or a bunny-shaped vibrator. It's about Melissa and Rick. What are we going to do?'

'You must mean what are *you* going to do,' Kurt said,

hands on his hips. 'Because *I'm* not going to stick my nose in other people's affairs.'

'Kurt –'

'I'm not,' he insisted. 'I mean, Tiffany, haven't you gotten into enough trouble lately when you've tried to fix things?'

When he put it that way, Tiffany realized that he was right. She'd just have to keep an eye on Rick and hope for the best. In their present situation, there wasn't much more that she could do. Still, she felt like punching the man's lights out.

She looked over at Kurt, who had now settled himself on the sofa, and she watched, bemused, as he bypassed the History channel in favor of a repeat of *Sex and the City*. They were changing. That was certain. But were they changing for the better?

Chapter Seventeen

'Melissa talks too fucking much.'

'What do you mean?'

'Some days she calls me up five times.'

'Only five?' Tiffany felt herself grinning. She and Melissa spent hours on the phone. They spoke on their cells while doing laundry, or driving, or shopping at the grocery store. They talked on land lines from home or work. They instant-messaged each other while checking email.

'What can you two possibly have to talk about? She's always ringing me up. And if I try and screen the call on the machine, she just talks until I have to leave the apartment.'

'She's giving you a chance to pick up if you're there.'

'And every single second she wants to discuss the wedding.'

'Well, there's your answer. *That's* why she's calling.'

'But sometimes she calls and doesn't seem to have anything to say. Anything at all. It's destroying me. I can't get anything done.'

Tiffany sighed. Did he *really* not understand? Girls liked to talk to each other. Had he not been around her for the past four years? Did he really not notice? As if on cue, Kurt asked, 'Do you two talk that much normally?'

'Yeah we do. We could be stuck together on a desert island and never run out of things to say.' This was something she dearly missed since becoming Kurt. She loved to talk to Melissa. Every once in a while, she had rung up her friend since the transformation, but she knew Melissa would think it strange if she called too much as Kurt.

'But why are the conversations so damn boring? I don't want to talk about which celebrity is banging her costar. I don't want to know what Melissa is thinking of eating for lunch. And I definitely don't want to discuss who's going to be on the next fucking *Oprah*.'

'You're making that up. She doesn't watch *Oprah*. She rarely gets home before eight.'

'Well, whatever.'

Tiffany eyed him. '*You're* watching *Oprah*, aren't you?'

He turned away from her, and she could hardly stifle her laughter.

'You are!'

'Look, sometimes she's got interesting guests on,' he said defensively.

'And I'll bet you're reading my magazines.'

He scowled. 'All you have in the place are ladies' magazines. If you really loved me, you would keep some men's rags around.'

'What, like *Maxim* and *Hustler*? You could buy new ones if you wanted to.'

'I did buy a *Penthouse Variations* the other day at a newsstand, but the cashier gave me such a lecherous look as I was paying that I didn't want to go through that again. Anyway, your magazines have some interesting articles,' he confessed. 'Although they don't have the one I could really use –'

'Which is?'

'"How to keep your relationship from going sour after your girlfriend switches her body with yours".'

Tiffany gave him a mean look. 'We aren't going sour.'

'Okay, well, how about, "How to deal with a best friend who won't shut up"?'

Tiffany's glare intensified. 'How about your tastes?' she said, turning the conversation around to him. 'I hate almost all of your CDs.' Although their musical tastes overlapped – they both liked Talking Heads, Tom Waits, Peter Gabriel – each had their own favorites as well. In a strange twist, Tiffany was the one who had a penchant for old rock and metal bands: Led Zeppelin, The Stones, Cream, while Kurt favored female vocalists: Natalie Merchant, Annie Lennox, Sam Phillips. That chick from the Cowboy Junkies. 'Thank God I have my iPod.'

'You could experiment a little more,' Kurt told her. 'Listen to new things for a change. Now that you're surrounded by other musical styles, you might broaden your horizons.' He sounded surprisingly like Tiffany when he said this, but she wouldn't acknowledge that fact.

'I'd have to find all your CDs first, wouldn't I? You keep them scattered everywhere. How do you possibly live like that?'

'What do you mean?' He sounded concerned now. 'What have you done to my pad?'

'Your pad,' she said huffily, 'was a disaster. I cleaned it. I set one of your monster clocks to the real time.'

'Which one?'

'Honolulu. Until you're rich and famous, you need to be able to get places on time.'

Kurt sulked. 'I told you not to mess around too much with my stuff. I know where everything is.'

'Great. So where is your detergent?'

'What detergent?'

'For washing dishes?'

'I don't have any.'

Tiffany didn't understand this answer. 'Do you mean you ran out?'

'No, I never have any.'

'Why don't you have any detergent, Kurt?'

'I don't do dishes.' He sounded like a crazy person, and he knew it. 'I mean, I try not to. I do them rarely, how about that?'

'How do you wash your plates?'

'I don't use plates.' Kurt seemed to understand how utterly insane that sounded, because he continued quickly, 'Come on, Tiffany. I hardly ever eat at home. You know that. And when I do, I just put the sandwich or pizza slice on a paper towel, then crumple it up at the end, and voilà – no plate. No mess. No detergent.'

'Classy,' Tiffany said.

'Sarcasm's not your best feature, speed demon.'

'What's *that* supposed to mean?'

'Eleanor told me all about how you talked your way out of a speeding ticket –'

'You should talk!' She flushed even as she spoke.

'I do talk. I tell you each and every time I'm pulled over. Why the great secrecy act?'

Tiffany was silent. She hadn't told him because she'd been so superior when he'd gotten his latest ticket, going on and on about the increase in his insurance payments, and blah, blah, blah. Underhanded of her, yes, but she hadn't wanted to – what? Seem less than perfect. That was it. She blinked hard to make the thought go away.

'Anyway, I got out of a ticket on the way to Melissa's.'

'You were pulled over in my car?'

'Yeah, and it wasn't even my fault. That thing of yours just wants to fly. You wouldn't guess it looking at the little bug, but when you get inside –'

'I know. It cruises.'

'Any other secrets you want to share with me?' Kurt asked. Tiffany looked at him. Were there? Before she could think, the phone rang.

'Oh, fuck me,' Kurt said as he glanced at the caller ID. 'Would you believe it's Melissa? Again. I can't do this, Tiffany. I can't keep talking to her about hair designs and pearl necklaces and stockings. Old, new, borrowed, blue. Who the fuck fucking cares?'

The machine picked up and the couple listened together to the message.

This time, Melissa was calling with good news.

Her luggage had finally arrived.

Chapter Eighteen

Kurt and Tiffany looked at each other over the unlit wick. The candle was fat and cobalt blue – almost the exact same shade as Tiffany's eyes.

'Who's going to make the wish?' Tiffany wanted to know. She tried to make her voice sound light-hearted, but inside she was quivering with excitement.

'It should be you, right?' Kurt asked. He looked as nervous as she felt. 'After all, you made the wish that got us into this. I don't mean it like that,' he said quickly, but she shook him off, understanding exactly what he was talking about.

'But do you think it would be better if you wish for the reverse?' she asked.

'How'd it work in *Big*?'

'I don't know. That was a long time ago. Plus, that was a movie, not real life –'

'Well, this *feels* like a movie,' Kurt insisted.

They stared at each other in silence, then looked back at the candle.

'Why don't we light the fucking thing and say the wish together?' Tiffany suggested.

'Wow, you're really starting to sound like me!'

Tiffany grinned at the compliment.

'Did you say it out loud in the shop?' Kurt wondered.

She shook her head. 'We'll *think* it together, then. We'll both wish as hard as we can to be back in our own bodies. All right?'

Kurt nodded.

Tiffany's fingers were shaking as she tried to light the match. Kurt didn't rush her or make fun of her. He was staring intently at the candle, waiting for the moment. Tiffany finally got the match to light and brought the tip to the candle wick, her whole hand trembling now. When the wick lit, she shook out the match. Then she and Kurt both closed their eyes. The scent of the candle seemed to swirl all over her. She tried to place herself back in the shop, willed herself to have that same moment one more time.

I wish I were me again!

Tiffany focused on this statement, concentrating as hard as she could until she felt as if she could see the words outlined in neon red in her mind.

I wish I were me again!

She hoped that Kurt was taking this seriously. She was really ready to be back in her own body. She missed herself, missed being a woman, dressing in girl clothes, putting on make-up, dancing as a follower rather than a leader. She missed it all. And she was tired of being Kurt, tired of going to his office, tired of dealing with his coworkers, tired of trying to play basketball.

After a moment, she tentatively opened her eyes, only to see herself staring back at her. The change hadn't taken place. She was still trapped inside of Kurt's masculine body.

'But it took the whole night last time,' Kurt reminded her, obviously thinking exactly the same thing. 'Right? We woke up in each other's bodies. Maybe that's what will happen again.'

'That's right,' Tiffany said, relieved.

They looked at each other in the darkened room.

'So?' Kurt asked. 'What do we do while we wait?'

'Well, I think we have to go to sleep for the magic to take effect.'

'But it's only seven. There's no way I'm going to fall asleep before eleven.'

They stared at each other again.

'Do you want to play a game?'

'What kind of game?'

Tiffany shrugged. 'Poker?'

'Strip poker?' Kurt immediately countered.

'Sure.' She grinned. 'Why not?'

Kurt had never been all that great at poker. When he got together with the guys, they generally combatted each other over video games, or played basketball, or got stoned.

Tiffany enjoyed cards. Sometimes, she played poker on line when she couldn't fall sleep.

This evening, she trounced Kurt without trying too hard, and Kurt had to take off the blouse he was wearing. Next came the pencil skirt, the garters, stockings, until he was down to bra and panties and Tiffany had only lost her tie. She coiled it carefully and set it next to her on the table.

'Why don't you wear ones that match?' Tiffany wanted to know, appraising Kurt with an observant eye.

He shrugged. 'I just think it's more interesting like this. Why do you dress so formal?'

'Because men's clothes are fun to play with,' she said without even thinking. 'The cool belts. The crisp shirts. There's something so sexy about putting on a tie.'

'Or taking one off.'

They stared at each other for a moment, thoughts of the card game disappearing. When Tiffany looked into Kurt's eyes, she had an idea of what he wanted, but she couldn't quite believe it.

'Are you game?' she asked, his standard query when they were going to try out something new.

He held her gaze for another beat, and then nodded. In a flash, she had the tie off the table and was bending on her knees on the floor. Thinking of how he'd bound her in the past, she fastened his wrists behind his back to the chair with the silken tie, and then turned the chair forward. With a deep breath for courage, she began to kiss him. Kiss his lips, then his breasts, working her way down his concave belly to his parted thighs.

Kurt groaned and arched his hips. He wasn't so firmly bound as to be uncomfortable, but this was the first time he'd ever given up his power like this. In all the times they'd been together, in all the ways they'd ever played, Tiffany had never had the upper hand during a bondage game. Now, he wondered why not. There was nothing wrong with giving into a submissive side.

Tiffany could tell from the expression on his face that he liked everything she was doing. Still, she checked in with him verbally. 'You okay?'

'More than okay,' he told her, before biting into his

bottom lip. She watched as he took a deep breath through his nose, his entire body shuddering. He was waiting for her to give him pleasure – even though he was the loser in their card game, he was going to be the winner tonight.

Tiffany thought about the videos of his that she'd watched, and she remembered the different scenarios that had given her the most enjoyment. Working slowly, she kissed her way back up the insides of his legs, moving ever closer to the place between his thighs, still covered by his red satin panties. She could breathe in the aroma of his arousal, and could see that he was wet. Very wet. She wondered if he'd been thinking of this moment during their card game.

Then she thought about the books she'd bought by sex guru Violet Blue – *How to Go Down On a Woman and Give Her Exquisite Pleasure*, and the matching title for Kurt. She'd been astonished about the techniques that she'd never even thought of before. As a woman, she'd assumed she knew all there was to being pleased orally. She'd been surprised to discover ways she'd never considered in the past. Perhaps, if they did get their bodies back, Kurt would begin to employ some of the new tricks on her. Until then, she would show him her fancy new tonguework.

Because she always liked this when Kurt did it to her, she started by kissing him through his panties – working through a fabric barrier somehow extended the pleasure for her. Kurt groaned and shuddered in the chair. Tiffany, inspired, continued to tease him, her mouth sealed to the split between his legs, her tongue tripping up and down the seam of the panties.

Maybe Kurt was right. Maybe there was something sexy about not matching. She admired the way the crimson panties went with the black lace bra. Kurt was definitely having fun with ladies' lingerie. Who would ever have guessed he'd be so interested in what went on underneath his own clothes? As a man, he never gave any thought to his underwear. He only had cool boxers because Tiffany bought them for him.

Now, she focused harder on the job at hand, continuing to make rotations with her tongue along his panties, until Kurt groaned and urged her to continue to the next level.

Tiffany untied his wrists and carried him to the sofa. She slid down his panties and pulled Kurt on top of her, accustomed now to the way it felt when she first thrust inside of him.

They made love for hours, ultimately falling asleep in the living room, not even making it to the bed.

Nearly six hours later, the candle finally spluttered and went out. The smoke tendrils woke Tiffany, and she looked over to see the orange glow at the tip of the wick fading gently to black. She realized that she'd forgotten all about the candle. Forgotten about the magic.

In the hazy light of dawn, Tiffany reached out one arm to touch Kurt's back, running her short fingernails along his naked skin. She looked at her outstretched hand.

She was still Kurt.

Rubbing one hand over her eyes, she got up and headed to the bathroom to take a shower. It was time to face another day – and she'd have to do it as a man.

Chapter Nineteen

'Hold on!' Kurt yelled through the door. *'I'm in a fucking towel!'* The last part he added under his breath. It wasn't totally true. The towel had fallen down and now he was totally nude. He still didn't have the hang of doing that classic wrap-tie thing that Tiffany did whenever she got out of the shower. The breasts got in the way. And he liked to look at them anyway. Why Tiffany didn't walk around naked all the time was beyond him. If he were her – and, of course, he was – he'd be naked twenty-four seven – which he had been whenever possible.

Regardless, he wasn't decent enough to open the door.

'Hey, Tiff. It's Rick –'

Rick. What the fuck was Rick doing here? He wondered for an instant if Tiffany had been right about the guy, but then he pushed the thought from his mind. He was sure that Rick was here in total innocence, and he was also sure that it wouldn't be prudent for him to open the door without a stitch of clothing on.

'Just a minute!' Kurt ran down the hall and got into a pair of panties and a bra. And jeans and a T-shirt. Then he shook back his hair and glanced at his reflection. No make-up. He hadn't put any on yet, because he hadn't been expecting guests. Since the candle trick had failed, he and Tiffany had simply continued on their chosen course, acting like one another while hoping something would happen to break the spell. Now, they were banking on the magic lasting the full month Tiffany had wished for. This meant that Kurt would be going as Tiffany to Melissa's wedding. It also meant that Tiffany would be making a big presentation at Kurt's office.

He added mascara and lip gloss, since Tiffany had told him in no uncertain terms never to face people without them, and he wasn't going to spoil her reputation as a natural beauty. At least these two items weren't all that hard to get the hang of. Because he thought he could use additional references, he'd gone out to Borders and bought two make-up books, one by Cindy Crawford, on whom he'd always nurtured the fondest of crushes. The other was by some chick named Bobbi Brown. Both authors tended to favor a lighter side to cosmetics, which is what Tiffany, herself, liked. Kurt had to say he thought the look was a bit boring, which is why he'd tried to be ever so slightly adventurous.

Although he'd confess this fact to nobody, he actually enjoyed lipstick shopping when he'd been out with Melissa the afternoon following the candle failure. The color names were so much fun. His favorite hues were Crushed Rubies and Cherries Jubilee, deep almost burgundy lipsticks, but his favorite color names were Spank and Bitten. Who would have thought women's cosmetics had such slutty names? There were also two nice blushes called Orgasm and Sin that he mixed together with a fluffy brush.

All right, so the liquid eyeliner had been a disaster. He'd ended up looking as if he were trying to emulate Cleopatra or Siouxsie from Siouxsie and the Banshees. But he did feel that he was a bit of a fast learner with a mascara wand. Lip gloss was unnerving. He didn't understand how to wear it without having his hair plastered to his lips. He'd bought a clear gloss called Triple X by Nars that had been so sticky, his mouth felt superglued shut, although the effect had been seriously sexy. Since then, he'd decided only to wear gloss if he put his hair in a ponytail, and he'd stuck to a trio by Philosophy called 'A Few Good Men'. He'd read in one of Tiffany's magazines that wearing flavored lip glosses was an inexpensive way to lift your spirits. Bubble baths were also recommended. Kurt had been a shower kind of guy since – well, since forever. But he'd enjoyed pampering himself with fruit-scented bath gels.

Christ, Rick was still knocking.

After slipping on a pair of flip-flops with spangled straps, he raced back to the door. Shit, even these shoes hurt. They dug into the delicate skin between his toes. Who would ever have thought being a girl was so fucking painful?

As he sprinted to the door, he realized that the History

channel was playing on the TV. This wasn't something Tiffany would ever watch. He knew this from her complaints whenever he landed on the station while channel surfing. He clicked over to the DVD player and hoped for the best. As he opened the front door, he inwardly sighed with relief. The familiar theme song to *Sex and the City* had begun.

'Hi there, Rick,' he said, as he swung the door shut behind Melissa's fiancé. He forced himself to keep from adding, 'Hey, my man. What about them Giants?' Instead, he said, 'What's going on? Where's Melissa?' God, he sounded just like Tiffany. It was almost frightening.

'That's what I wanted to talk to you about, Tiff.' Rick walked into the room and perched himself on one of Tiffany's red vinyl barstools. If he thought the messiness of the place was odd – the towels draped over the arm of the sofa, the newspapers spread out all over the coffee table – he kept that to himself. 'I think something's going on with Kurt and Melissa.'

Kurt started laughing. He couldn't believe it. This was too fucking much. 'No,' he said, quickly shaking his wet hair. 'No, there's nothing between them.' At Rick's serious expression, he stopped laughing and added, 'I know Kurt. I'd know if he were cheating on me.'

'They've been spending a lot of time together lately. I'm sure you've realized that.'

Kurt couldn't believe this. Not on top of everything else. He walked into the kitchen and started looking through the fridge for something to offer Rick. 'Really,' he said, 'I'm sure there's a simple explanation. Maybe they're planning a special gift for you . . .'

'I think Melissa senses something went on at the bachelor party.'

This was news to Kurt. He looked up from the refrigerator. Tiffany had a bottle of pink wine in there, but he hated pink wine. What was it called? Rosé? It was such a fucking chick drink. No self-respecting man would ever order a glass of pretty wine. Ah, at the back of the fridge stood two lonely beers. Should he offer one to Rick? Should he pour it in a glass?

'Well, *did* anything happen?'

'I'm sure that Kurt told you.'

Kurt – as Tiffany – shook his head. At the moment, he wanted to know exactly what had happened at the bachelor party from Rick's point of view.

'Really? He didn't?'

Kurt held up the Grolsch beer and when Rick nodded, reached for a glass. 'No, she didn't – I mean, he didn't say anything.' Oh, shit. Would Rick notice the slip? He didn't seem to.

'We were plowed, man. I mean, plowed . . .'

'So you looked at the strippers –'

'Well . . .'

'And got a lap dance –'

Rick downed almost his whole beer. He slammed the bottle on the counter and Kurt winced in an extremely Tiffany-esque way.

'*More* than a lap dance?'

'I didn't mean to, Tiff. You've got to understand that. But Kurt was there, forcing the girls on me. One after the other. I sort of went out of my head.'

Kurt didn't like the way this was going. No wonder Tiffany had seemed so incredibly down after the party. She'd learned that her best friend's fiancé was a fuckhead. And now, apparently, he was blaming Tiffany for his indiscretion. The slime.

As Rick continued to blather on, Kurt tried to think like a girl, but felt a miserable failure. What he wanted to do was punch Rick in the mouth. Lost in these thoughts, he was surprised when Rick came around the hatch into the kitchen and put his arms around Kurt's waist. 'Oh, Tiffany – I just don't know what to do.'

Kurt's entire body stiffened. He was going to have to kill this guy. And it was going to feel good. But first he needed to find something out. Was this something that had ever happened before? Had Rick and Tiffany gotten together? Nausea swam through him at the warmth of Rick's chest and arms around him, and he knew he had to think fast –

'You're Melissa's fiancé!' he shrieked in his most soap-opera-star manner. Thank God he'd been watching a few of these shows.

'But I've always liked you. You're so much sweeter than Melissa is.'

'She's my best friend!' Kurt pulled out of Rick's embrace and stalked over to the refrigerator. Rick pursued him, drawing Kurt effortlessly back into his arms.

'Don't you feel it, Tiffany? You can't deny it.'

'Yes, I can.' Kurt struggled, but Rick held fast. So this was what it was like to be a girl in trouble. Did Tiffany have an ice pick anywhere nearby?

'I knew you'd say that. You're so good and kind. It's why I like you so much –'

'You're getting married, Rick.'

'That's one more reason why we should give into this feeling now –'

'Get away from me,' Kurt demanded. He squirmed, but suddenly they were back in the initial position, with Rick behind him, pushing up against him. Kurt was forced against the refrigerator, and he felt Rick's hands on his breasts, and – oh, fucking Christ – Rick was hard, pressing his cock against Kurt from behind. What was wrong with this guy? Had Kurt thought of him as a slime? He was worse than slime. He was pond scum. Slug trail. Kurt spun around in Rick's arms, trying to get away. Rick was much, much stronger, and held on tight.

Quickly, Kurt executed his next move, neatly kneeing Rick in the groin with every ounce of Tiffany's strength.

Rick doubled over, coughing. Kurt's eyes narrowed. He knew all about that specific kind of pain, and he knew that Rick would be incapacitated for several moments. Feeling a strange kind of glee, Kurt leaned against the counter and picked up the beer, drinking directly from the bottle. Rick looked at him, eyes wet with pain.

'Don't be like that, Tiff –'

'You need to go,' Kurt said. He had the bottle in his hand like a weapon, and he planned to use it if Rick didn't clear out. He had a feeling Rick understood this plan.

'You won't tell Melissa, will you?'

'No.' Kurt shook his head. '*You* will.'

He watched Rick leave the apartment, then settled down with the rest of his beer in front of *Sex and the City*. It really was a pretty decent show. At least, the characters took his mind off what he was going to have to say when Tiffany got home.

Chapter Twenty

'I'm sorry,' Kurt said. He had his arms around Tiffany. 'You told me, and I didn't believe you. He's a fucking scum bag.'

Tiffany didn't say 'I told you so'. She didn't have to. All she could think about was what would have happened if Rick had come onto her when she was in her own body. Would she have been able to fend him off as well as Kurt had done? She shook her head, aghast at the image. 'So what are we going to do?'

'I told him that he had to tell Melissa tonight. That if he didn't, I would. That was the deal.'

'And he agreed?'

'I took his whimpering in pain for an agreement. Maybe it wouldn't stand up in court, but we'll just have to see, won't we?'

As if on cue, the phone rang. Kurt looked at the caller ID. 'Ah, Jesus, it's Melissa.' He looked afraid of what would happen if he answered the phone.

'Do you think he's gone over there already? Do you think he's told her?' Tiffany asked.

Kurt shrugged. 'Get it.'

'You get it.'

The machine picked up. Melissa was in tears. 'Tiffany, are you there? I need to talk to you.'

'Pick up the phone –' Tiffany insisted, her eyes wide.

'I can't do this,' Kurt said. 'I'm fine for quick meetings, short phone calls. The occasional visit to Sephora. But this situation is over my head. You know it, too, don't you, Tiff?'

Immediately after the beep on Tiffany's answering machine, her cell phone started to ring. She dug it out of the purse Kurt had been using and glanced at the LED display. 'It's Melissa,' she said in a hushed voice. 'Kurt, really, you have to talk to her. She needs someone.'

He shook his head. 'She doesn't need me anymore. She needs you.'

Tiffany looked as if she were going to cry, just listening to Melissa's pleading message. 'All right,' she sighed, reaching for Kurt's new leather motorcycle jacket. She zipped up the sleeves and fixed the collar. 'I'll go over there, and –' She hesitated.

'And do what?'

'And comfort her.'

'As me?'

'Look, if it gets to that point, I'll explain the whole thing to her.'

'She's never going to believe you, Tiffany.'

'I've got to make her believe. She's my best friend.'

Melissa was in a state. 'What the hell are you doing here?' she demanded at the sight of Kurt on her doorstep. Her eyes were rimmed with red and she had a balled-up pink tissue in one hand. She looked equally distressed and livid, and Tiffany had to call upon her extra charge of courage in order to press the issue.

'We need to talk.'

'I don't want to talk to you. I want to talk to Tiffany. Rick was just here and he said that she –' Melissa started crying again. 'That she –'

'That she what, Melissa?' Tiffany asked, but somehow she already knew. It would be just like Rick to put the blame on someone else. Still, she didn't think he'd actually stoop so low.

'He said that she came on to him. That she was trying to kiss him, and –'

Oh, the fucking asshole. Tiffany would have beat the man to a pulp if he'd shown his face. There was a small sense of satisfaction in the fact that she knew she actually could crush him if it came to that. Kurt was much stronger than Rick and in much better shape as well.

'Melissa, it's simply not true,' she told her friend as calmly as she could.

'How do you know?' This was a howl as Melissa spun away from the door and headed back into her living room. 'Clearly, things aren't going well between the two of you.

Maybe she's jealous of how happy Rick and I have been. Maybe she wanted him for herself.'

'You don't really believe that, do you?'

'I don't know what I believe.'

'What do you mean?'

'The two of you have been acting so strange. Ever since we got back from New Orleans.'

Tiffany took a deep breath. Now was the time to confess. But first she wanted to know where Rick was.

'He left. He said he didn't want to talk about it anymore. I wanted all the details and he claimed I was being too lawyerly for him. He went out on a walk to calm down. When he does that, he's sometimes gone for hours –'

All right. So Tiffany had some time. But first she went and mixed them each a drink.

Kurt wondered how things were going with the two women. Tiffany was brave if she thought she'd be able to convince Melissa that she was herself, only trapped in a man's body.

He wondered if he should have gone over to Melissa's apartment with her. That might have helped the situation.

No, it was better to stay put and watch the next episode of *Sex and the City*. You know, he was really starting to like this show. Except for when that Carrie girl was wondering. She was always wondering about something. She couldn't help but wonder – that seemed to be her main state of mind. Bewilderment. But the sex scenes were fun – especially the ones with Miranda. Did he have a thing for redheads that he'd never known about?

He glanced into the mirror over the mantle. How would Tiffany look with red hair?

'No, I *don't* understand.'

Tiffany tilted the vodka bottle again, refilling Melissa's glass. The clear liquid gleamed in the crystal. Tiffany considered it, and then took a sip from her own goblet before she started to explain again. They'd gone past Cosmos now, to drinking the vodka straight.

'I'm Tiffany.'

'Kurt, you're even drunker than I am.'

'Melissa, listen to me. *I'm Tiffany.*' She took a deep breath and then tried again from the beginning, describing the Witches' Shoppe in great detail. Explaining everything that had happened up until now.

'Prove it,' Melissa slurred, egging her on. 'What's my favorite ice cream?'

'Rum raisin.'

'That's an easy one,' Melissa said as if Tiffany had been the one to suggest the query. 'Tiff could have told you that at some point, or you might have remembered.' Melissa shut her eyes, deep in thought. 'Okay,' she said, when she opened them again. 'What's my favorite current lipstick color?' She emphasized the word 'current'.

'Perplex by Chanel.'

'Favorite *discontinued* lipstick color.' Melissa had a 'You'll never get this!' expression on her face.

'Sealilly by Cutex. You used to buy it in junior high, but they don't make it anymore.'

Melissa looked a little disconcerted, and Tiffany felt as if they might be making progress. 'Favorite perfume,' Melissa said in a soft voice.

'You don't have just one. You like to layer several. Right now, you're into FCUK for Her, Lolita Lempicka and Amour, Amour. I don't know how you get the mix just right, either.'

Melissa's forehead wrinkled. 'All-time favorite fantasy.'

'You and Jon Bon Jovi in a woven net hammock in Hawaii. At sunset. With the golden rays of light caressing your naked bodies. But trust me, that would never work out. You'd flip over and someone would break an arm, and what's so sexy about that? Besides, isn't it about time that you updated your dream man? Ashton Kutcher's hot. Or that Heath Ledger.'

'You always say that,' Melissa pouted, and then she realized what she'd said and turned her huge dark eyes on Tiffany. 'Oh, my God, it's really you. That's why you've been acting so strange. And why Kurt has.' She put a hand to her head. 'Jesus, I should have known. Our phone calls had become so weird all of a sudden. You were always trying to get off the phone. I mean, *he* was –'

She was speaking so fast now that Tiffany held up a hand. 'Slow down. I know it's hard to take in.'

'But I'm just so relieved,' Melissa explained. 'I thought I'd done something to offend you. And that time at Star Baby Lingerie when you – I mean he – was trying on clothes that just didn't seem like you at all. And he seemed absolutely unable to look at me in my underwear. He wouldn't look anywhere except straight in my eyes.'

'Really?' This was gratifying for Tiffany to hear. She hadn't wanted to believe that Kurt had intentionally gazed at her best friend in knickers alone.

'Oh, Tiff. I can't believe you didn't tell me.' Now, she looked a little put out. '*Why* didn't you tell me?'

Tiffany gave her a sheepish grin. 'I was trying to fix this –'

'Yeah? That's what seems to have gotten you into this in the first place.'

'That's what Kurt said.' Tiffany was the one to pout now.

'But what is it like?' Melissa gazed at her friend in total awe. 'I mean, being a man.'

'Hard to describe,' Tiffany said, pacing around the room. 'Sometimes I actually forget what's happened, and then I catch a glimpse of myself in a window, or I look down and see these huge feet in a pair of leather loafers, and everything comes slamming back to me. It can be jarring.'

Melissa eyed her curiously. 'Boxers or briefs?'

'Boxers,' Tiffany said, going red. 'But I could have told you that before.'

'I should have guessed something was wrong,' Melissa said in a faint voice. 'The way you started swearing and Kurt stopped entirely. And Kurt becoming so interested in talking to me on the phone. At one point, I actually thought he wanted an affair.' She was quiet for a minute. 'Oh, and Kurt was wearing your watch – I mean you wearing your own watch, of course. Oh, my God, it's making my head hurt.'

'I know you thought it was strange that I was calling you,' Tiffany explained, feeling relieved herself at how well this conversation was going. 'It's just that I wanted to hear your voice. I felt desperate. Sometimes things have been difficult at work, and I didn't want to worry Kurt, and I just have needed to vent –'

'So what are you going to do?' Melissa asked her, seriously.

'Don't know. Live as Kurt. Be all I can be.'

'That's the army's slogan, Tiffany. And I'll kill you before I let you join the reserves.'

'All right, then I'll just be the best man I can be.'

'Wait, that's from *Tootsie*, isn't it? "I was a better man with you as a woman than I've ever been with a woman as a man." No, that's not right, is it? Something like that. He's saying it to Jessica Lange.' She squinted her eyes as she tried to remember the exact wording.

'Doesn't matter what the quote was, does it? I'm just trying my best –'

'And Kurt?'

'Well, he was doing fine for a while. But we had a problem –' Tiffany explained the situation with the candles not working. Melissa looked concerned.

'I wonder why it didn't work?'

'We thought of everything.'

'Well, maybe you can't cancel out one wish with another. Maybe the first one needs to run its one-month course.'

'That means we still have two weeks left, and I don't know whether we can pull this off. Kurt has this big presentation coming up, and I can tell that he's really nervous at the thought of me doing it instead of him.'

'You'll be fine.' Melissa shrugged. 'Look what you were able to hide from me.' She eyed Tiffany again. 'Is it good, though? Being a guy.' Tiffany was pleased to see how much better Melissa was acting. It was as if knowing that Tiffany had a problem larger than hers had helped Melissa put her world into perspective.

'You can pee standing up,' Tiffany said with a grin. 'That's the best.'

Melissa lay back on the bed. Tiffany could tell that she was deep in thought. 'So Rick really was lying to me?'

'Look, I didn't want this to come out in this manner. I really didn't,' Tiffany explained. 'But he was acting very suspiciously at the bachelor party. And when I told Kurt about it, he said that Rick just is like that. That it was an act. I was trying to find out for sure whether or not he'd done something with the strippers –' she saw the hurt look on Melissa's face, but kept going '– and then he came on to

Kurt. As me. Kurt gave him one day to tell you everything, and I guess he took the easy way out.'

Melissa nodded. She seemed to have too many thoughts whirling through her head at once. Tiffany understood this sensation. She'd been feeling it often enough since the switch took place.

'What did Kurt do when he found out what happened? When he was trapped in your body.'

'You saw. You were with him.'

Melissa furrowed her brow. 'That's right. He got plastered. And you?'

Tiffany shrugged, remembering. 'I started wearing the nicotine patch, threw away all of his junk food, and discovered his ginormous collection of pornography.' Tiffany thought for a moment. 'And I cleaned his apartment and got his truck detailed.'

'Typical Tiffany.' Melissa shook her head. 'You know, all of this makes so much sense.'

'Are you out of your mind?'

'Not the actual magic. That's crazy as anything I've ever heard. I just mean the way you've been acting. And *he's* been acting. I suddenly understand it all. I thought you were going through some sort of mid-life crisis. I mean, an early one. And I thought Kurt might be a latent homosexual –'

'Just 'cause of one pink shirt?'

'No, everything. The new haircut. The new shoes. The beard. The almost OCD-like tendencies. Do you know that every time you walk in here, you straighten things up? It's positively pathological.'

'Just because I like things clean doesn't mean I have obsessive compulsive . . .'

'Of course not, Tiffany. But it was an odd change to see that behavior in Kurt.'

Tiffany felt herself nodding.

'Anyway, what did he do? Once he finally calmed down.'

'At first, he seemed to be shell-shocked. And then I think he started to enjoy some of it. But I can tell that he's scared. He had clearly told himself that this was like a wild ride he was on, but that the ride would eventually stop and he'd be able to get off. Now, well –' Tiffany raised her eyebrows. 'We don't know how it's going to end. What if this is it? What if I'm always a guy. I mean, forever?' She lowered her voice. Here was something she hadn't wanted to say to Kurt yet, but that she'd been thinking about. 'I always thought I would have kids.'

'You will, Tiffany.'

'But how can I?' She gestured to her transformed figure. Melissa looked at her; Tiffany appeared so totally crestfallen.

'You will,' she insisted. 'Don't worry, Tiffany. It's all going to work out.'

'How can it?'

'Trust me,' Melissa said. 'It will. You can adopt. Or Kurt can have kids. Or you could dump Kurt and marry me.' Melissa sounded as if she were only half kidding.

'What are you talking about?'

'We've always joked about it,' Melissa reminded her. 'Whenever we're both single. That all one of us needs is a cock and we'd be the perfect match. And now you have a cock.'

'But I have Kurt,' Tiffany said.

'You don't have him,' Melissa reminded her. 'You *are* him.'

Kurt glanced at the clock. Tiffany had been gone just over an hour. He understood why it was nice to have a working clock now. He'd never appreciated being on time before, or cared about how much time had passed. But he wondered how Tiffany was getting on.

Should he call her cell?

He pressed the button on the remote, relaxing against the sofa as the next episode started up.

'I really thought he was the one,' Melissa said. They were back to talking about Rick. Her initial anger had broken through to this.

'Yeah, so did we all,' Tiffany assured her, feeling wrecked inside. She knew exactly how she would feel if she'd learned that Kurt had cheated on her. Hell, she'd gone through this exact sort of misery with her ex-boyfriend Ryan, whom she had discovered in bed with a woman one night. Discovered in *her* own bed. For some reason that part had been more hurtful than the rest of it. As if she wouldn't have been as devastated if they'd done the deed in Ryan's office. Or in his car. Anywhere other than on her bed, in her sheets. She'd actually burned the sheets afterwards, in the basement incinerator, feeling a sick sort of glee as she'd watched the flames lick over the fabric, ruining the silk, destroying it.

The person he'd chosen for his transgression had floored her. Tiffany could understand, if not forgive, a situation like Jude Law and his naughty nanny. There was an instance where the girl must have been available all the time, who probably was walking around the mansion doe-eyed. She understood Clinton and Monica. She could fathom Brad Pitt and Angelina Jolie.

But Ryan chose a woman from work he had constantly complained about. It was always 'Diane is such a bitch. Diane made me late. Diane flaked on this important assignment and I had to cover for her –' But Diane apparently was good at one thing – blowing him – because that's what she'd been doing when Tiffany had caught them at it.

What had finally made that pain go away? She tried to remember, having blocked it out as best she could. Time. Lots of time. And support from Melissa. She couldn't imagine what she'd have done without her. Melissa had been there for her every night at the start, had been the one to baby her when she needed that and bully her when she felt that it was time for her to get her sorry ass out of bed and back into the real world.

Now, she held Melissa in her arms, patted her on the back, and told her boy self to stop when she felt her cock start to twitch. Men. Here was an occasion when all she wanted to be was sympathetic, yet Kurt's body was growing aroused from the proximity of an attractive female form, and there was nothing she could do about it. That seemed to go against the rest of the rules she was learning. Perhaps being turned on as a guy was physiological more than mental. Regardless, Melissa seemed completely unaware.

'We were good together.'

'Sure you were,' Tiffany agreed in spite of her desire to trash-talk Rick. 'But some men go a little crazy when they're getting married. They think they'll never have fun anymore, never sleep with another girl. All that shit.' She shifted uncomfortably. *Down, boy*, she mentally hissed. Go *down*.

'What am I going to do?' Melissa was fully crushed. Tiffany had never seen her like this before. Melissa always knew what she was going to do.

'What do you mean?'

'All the invitations. All the people to call.' Is that what was really bothering Melissa? Tiffany guessed that it wasn't, but that Melissa had to focus on one aspect of the situation in order not to think about the fact that the plans she had for her entire life had gone hopelessly astray.

Suddenly, Tiffany had an inspiration. 'Have the wedding anyway.'

'Get married to that shmuck? He almost raped Kurt.'

Tiffany had to laugh at how that sounded and, after a moment, Melissa did as well. 'All right, not raped, but you know. What would have happened if he'd overpowered Kurt? If he'd pressed his size advantage.'

'Kurt wouldn't have let that happen.'

'Still, Tiff. What if it had been you?'

'Don't think about that now. I would have handled him the same way Kurt would have. Fought tooth and nail to the end. So put that out of your mind and think about you. You're the person we need to pamper right now. Have the wedding without the wedding. Have the party. I read in one of my magazines about a girl who did that. She and her fiancé broke up, but she went ahead and had the party, anyway. I think it's sort of in style now. People don't always make it to the altar, but everyone loves a party. Not an "I Do" but an "I Don't". There are even divorce parties, now. I've been asked to plan a few, but I haven't wanted to.'

'But the flowers. The dress –'

'We'll punk out the dress, tear the hem, tie-dye it like Gwen Stefani's.'

'She had Gavin Rossdale.'

They both paused for a moment in silent appreciation of Gavin Rossdale. Sweet, soulful Gavin Rossdale. Then Tiffany spoke up again. 'And you'll have us. It'll be a gas, Melissa. All of your friends will come and cheer you on. His friends won't have the balls to show, and if they do –' Tiffany balled up one of Kurt's huge fists. 'I'll knock 'em out.'

'Tiffany, you're the best –' Melissa was in her arms again, and Kurt's cock was going crazy. Tiffany closed her eyes tight. *Down, boy. Down!* For the first time, Melissa seemed to notice.

'Are *you* okay?' she asked, pulling back. 'You look a little pale.'

'I'm – fine,' Tiffany hesitated. 'It's like buying a new car. I'm still getting used to all the fancy controls.'

'Like –'

Tiffany didn't want to say. She was embarrassed.

'Come on –' Melissa urged, and at least Tiffany saw that she seemed a bit more lively. Tears still sparkled in the corners of her eyes, and Tiffany wanted to do anything she could to keep them from falling.

'Like the plumbing.'

'You mean peeing?'

'No, that's cool. That's awesome, actually. You can do it anywhere. Standing up is totally freeing. Just shake, shake, shake and you're done.'

'So –'

'So the thing gets turned on whenever ... I mean, wherever...'

'You mean like now?'

Tiffany nodded.

'You're hard?'

She nodded again.

'Can I feel?'

Tiffany giggled. 'No, you *can't* feel.'

'Why not?'

'Because that would be like cheating.'

'But why? It's you. I mean, I've known you forever. If it were me, I'd let you.'

'It's not right,' Tiffany said, pulling away. 'Because Kurt's not here.'

'If he was?'

'What are you suggesting?'

'Call him up.'

Suddenly, Tiffany thought she could see where this was going. 'You serious?'

'Well, it would kill Rick, wouldn't it? To know that I had a threesome. That's one thing he talked about forever. You and me and him in bed together. A sort of best-friend sandwich.'

'So you knew? You knew he liked me?' She felt confused that Melissa had never confessed this before. If she'd known, then – Then nothing. She would never have told Kurt, because he would have wanted to tear the guy's arms off.

'I always thought it was just a fantasy . . . I never had any idea that he meant anything by the thought. Or that he might act on it. Everyone's entitled to their fantasies, aren't they? If I had –' Her eyes filled up again. 'God, Tiffany. I was going to make such a pretty bride.'

'You still will,' her best friend assured her. 'Just not yet.'

She patted Melissa gently. Then a little more firmly. And then suddenly, without knowing exactly how it had happened, they were kissing. Tiffany felt herself pull back, but that was only the interior part of herself. Her body was still holding onto Melissa's, stroking her hair, kissing her lips.

'We can't do this,' she said, after pulling back.

'Why not?' Melissa's voice was pleading. 'I need someone.'

'Yeah.' Tiffany understood that perfectly, yet she wouldn't do that to Kurt. 'But it's not right. I can't take advantage of Kurt like that.'

'Call him up.'

'But isn't this exactly what Rick wanted to do . . .'

'Come on, it's different and you know it.'

Kurt was more than happy to come over for two reasons. He had no idea how to deal with the vast list of people to inform that the wedding was off – he was pretty sure this task would fall to him. And he was also deeply curious about what Tiffany and Melissa could possibly have in mind. Tiffany had been more than vague on the phone, simply saying, 'You're in for a treat. But get here quick.'

He knocked on the apartment door feeling as nervous as he had on his very first date with Tiffany. He wondered if she'd like the outfit he'd chosen. And then he found himself worried that he had gone too dressy. Women were so difficult. Their clothes were, at least. Nothing felt as comfortable on this body as his old jeans and T-shirts. Even when he dressed Tiffany's figure in old jeans and T-shirts, the feeling didn't compare.

Today, he had on a pair of capris, mules, a spaghetti strap tank and a cardigan. The outfit was the exact one he'd seen on the mannequin at Ann Taylor. He'd asked the salesclerk to help him assemble it piece by piece, gratified by the transformation in the mirror when he spun around. Tiffany's world of blackness was gone and pastels were in.

Every once in a while he felt a wee bit worried at how much he enjoyed playing dress-up with Tiffany's body. But he tried to assuage those fears by simply saying that he'd have enjoyed dressing her even when she was the one inhabiting her sweet figure. She'd simply never been that concerned about what he thought looked nice.

Still, although he hoped she appreciated his efforts, he had no idea how well he'd be rewarded.

Chapter Twenty-one

'I know,' Melissa told Kurt.

'You know what?' he asked, as casually as he could. He didn't like the way she was looking at him.

'I know who you are.'

'Well, you'd better have. We've been friends for –' He tried to camouflage his hesitation with a phony-sounding cough. 'For fifteen fucking years.'

'Eighteen. Tiffany wouldn't have gotten that wrong. And she wouldn't have said fucking.'

He felt a wave of cold air wash over him, but he did his best to recover quickly. 'What are you saying – "Tiffany wouldn't". Like I'm not Tiffany.' He snorted in a very Tiffany-like way. Anyone else would have thought the girl standing there was Tiffany. But clearly he wasn't fooling Melissa. He could tell from the piercing look in her dark brown eyes. Oh, Christ. What should he do now? He and Tiffany had never discussed what to do if someone flat out accused one of them of being a fraud. The thought of being actually found out had not seemed possible. He didn't believe Tiffany had come clean to Melissa, although she'd said she might.

'You're not Tiffany. You're Kurt. She told me everything. I should have guessed much earlier, I know it. But I had stuff on my mind.'

'Shit,' Kurt said, sitting down on the edge of the bed. 'And you let me go on acting like a fucking idiot.'

'Well . . . it was sort of amusing.'

'Fuck you.'

'But you're doing a good job. At least, you were before this.' She gestured to his new outfit.

'I think I look good.' He stood and preened in front of the mirror. When he stood like that, he didn't resemble Tiffany at all. Kurt's personal confidence shone through, electrifying the way he appeared in the new clothes. Why couldn't Tiffany do that? Melissa had never considered the concept in the past, but Tiffany occasionally had a bit of a self-confidence problem. She always looked put together, but she didn't always seem to know that. Was this why she always wore black? Was this why she never varied her hairstyle or chose an avant-garde necklace or wore a vibrant green eye shadow.

'Yeah, you look excellent. But you don't look like Tiffany.'

'That was sort of the point.'

'Anyway, I know, and I think I can help you guys out.'

'In what way?'

'Well, the candle didn't work, but that doesn't mean that nothing will. I can't believe you two didn't try other sorts of magic.'

'I'm not into voodoo.'

'You should be. Just look at you!'

Kurt nodded, understanding her reasoning, and then swallowed hard as Tiffany entered the room. He'd wondered where she'd been during the conversation. Now, he saw that she'd been undressing. The sight of him, naked save for purple boxers, made his heart race.

'What's going on?'

'Did Melissa tell you about her ideas? She wants us to try –'

'Why are you naked?'

Tiffany hesitated. 'Well, we were thinking –'

Melissa interrupted. 'Tiffany was consoling me, and she asked me what would make me feel better. And I think a threesome would. I've always wanted to try it. I'm probably the last person in San Francisco not to have been in a ménage à trois. Plus, it would kill Rick if he found out.'

'But how would he find out?'

'I'm planning on telling him.' She said this last bit as if Kurt was dense, and then pulled Kurt down for a kiss. When their lips parted, Tiffany was at full-mast, so hard from watching Kurt kiss her best friend. 'You know this is a one-time deal, only,' Melissa explained.

Kurt nodded quickly, visibly shaken. He looked as if he would agree to anything Melissa said, especially after a kiss like that.

'Is this part of the magic?' he asked.

'I've still got the rest of the candles from the store. We could light them all over the room, and then wish for a return to your bodies.'

Now, Kurt shook his head. What if something else went wrong? What if he switched places with Melissa? Or Tiffany turned into Melissa and Melissa turned into him? Could things get even worse?

'I don't know about all that,' Kurt said. Tiffany looked shocked. Was he turning down sex with two women? Or, really, a woman and a man.

'All right,' Melissa said agreeably. 'Skip the candles. What if Tiffany and I simply make another one of your wishes come true?'

Kurt swallowed with difficulty, and then nodded immediately. He was doing a lot of communicating without words right now, having a hard time believing this was real. Yet, why shouldn't this be real? Having a threesome with Tiffany and her best friend wasn't any more shocking than actually becoming Tiffany, was it?

Tiffany came close to him and kissed his cheek.

'Is this okay?' she murmured softly. He squeezed her hand and nodded, having decided not to say a thing. He would do whatever the girls wanted, behave however they required. He was going to do nothing to ruin this.

'You sure?' she asked.

He nodded again.

While he watched, Melissa stripped down to her bra and panties. He recognized the set as one she'd bought at Star Baby Lingerie. Tiffany was already in her boxers. Kurt was the only one overdressed. He quickly pulled off the outfit he'd so carefully chosen, and then he waited looking from one girl to the other. Melissa seemed to be the one in charge. While Kurt watched, she kissed Tiffany, and he squirmed on the edge of the bed as he drank in the vision. He'd always wanted to see his girlfriend kiss another girl. It didn't seem to matter that his girlfriend was doing so as a boy. He knew that it was Tiffany trapped inside that male body.

His girlfriend sighed and ran her hands along Melissa's shoulders. Kurt moved forward from his position, now feeling desperate to take a part in the action. He ran his fingertips along Tiffany's back, still not comfortable touching Melissa directly, but wanting to be close, wanting to be included. That seemed fine with Tiffany. She moaned softly as Kurt started to kiss the back of her neck, then trail his fingertips along her spine.

Melissa pushed herself up on the mattress and spread her legs. Now, Kurt felt as if he could stare at Melissa without fear of disappointing his girlfriend. He noted the tattoo he'd seen briefly in New Orleans. He noted the differences between Melissa's body and Tiffany's. Melissa was more compactly muscled, with smaller breasts and sturdy thighs. When she took off her lingerie, her body radiated power. Tiffany's body always seemed more vulnerable when naked, her long lean limbs like a wild cat's, built for speed.

Now, Tiffany, in his own body, took over. She bent down and began to kiss in a line along Melissa's body, and Kurt knew that if he'd had a cock, he would have exploded right then. There would have been no stopping him. As it was, he pressed one hand against his mouth, wiping his lips over and over, unable to believe that this scene was for real – and that he was right there, in the midst of it.

Together, the threesome fit themselves into the most pleasurable positions. Tiffany slid her body along Melissa's, her cock now sheathed in a Trojan, her eyes wide open to drink in every second of her best friend's pleasure. Once he'd gained enough confidence to participate, Kurt brought his hands to Melissa's breasts, rubbing in small circles around her hardened nipples, then bending to suck first on one, then the other.

Tiffany realized that the trio was unintentionally re-creating one of the scenes she had witnessed on her favorite of Kurt's porno videos. Two girls and a guy. That's what they were, regardless of how their sexes were currently shuffled. Why had she fought against doing this for so long? She couldn't imagine anything sexier.

When Kurt began to kiss Melissa, Tiffany thought she wouldn't be able to hold back. She thrust again and again, harder and harder, her gaze unwavering from the sensual image. Two girls kissing – it was beautiful, those full lips together, Kurt's long blonde hair so perfectly contrasting Melissa's inky black bob.

'Oh, God,' Tiffany groaned, reaching her limits and shuddering all over. She moved aside, her body limp from release, and watched, mesmerized, as Kurt took his place between Melissa's spread thighs and began to dine.

Afterwards, Melissa struggled to maneuver herself next to Tiffany. She pushed up on one arm and stared hard into her friend's face.

'What are you doing?'

'Trying to see if I can see you in there. The real you.'

'What do you mean?'

'Well, eyes are the windows to the soul, and all that.'

They were so close that Tiffany finally pulled back.

'I'm in here,' she told her friend. 'You're going to have to take my word. This wasn't some fairy tale Kurt and I told you in order to get you to fuck us.'

'But do you think Rick would be able to tell?'

'If you couldn't, why would he?'

'You're sure . . .?'

'What else do you have in mind, Melissa?'

Chapter Twenty-two

Rick turned away, hurrying back in the direction he'd just come from. Kurt was moving toward him with a ferocious intensity, and now Rick had only one thought in his mind: *He knows.* Or, maybe two thoughts. *He knows* and *Run!* Kurt's eyes were on fire, but it was the expression on Kurt's face that made Rick the most scared. Kurt looked as if he wanted to kill him.

Crap, why had he done that? Why had he come onto Tiffany in the first place? Because he was afraid of getting married? No. That wasn't it. Yeah, he was afraid of getting married. Fucking hell yeah. But that hadn't changed ever. It was the fact he'd always liked Tiffany. That was the honest truth. Cute and blonde and hadn't Kurt said she was a tiger in bed? When he'd heard from Melissa that she and Kurt were having some difficulties, it had seemed like a natural thing to do.

Make a little bedside visit from Dr Rick.

Oh, fuck me, he thought, hitting the rear of the restaurant and realizing there was no place to go but to the men's room. Would Kurt follow him back here? Rick pushed through the swinging door and disappeared within.

There was more to being a guy than choosing a cologne and discovering what a jock strap was for. Tiffany couldn't exactly describe it, but there was an essence of being a man – something within her that hadn't been there before. Something that swelled inside of her when she looked at Kurt. A desire to protect him. A need to keep him safe. To provide for him. It was why she went after Rick.

In the dingy men's room, Tiffany banged her fist on each individual stall, causing the swinging cream-colored doors to fly open. Why did all men's rooms look and smell like this one? Ladies' rooms generally were bearable. Some were even pretty –

Rick was in the last stall. Miserable fucking coward.

'Look,' Rick started as soon as Tiffany was in front of him. 'Look, man, nothing happened.' There was no sense pretending that this scene wasn't about Tiffany. Kurt looked more enraged than Rick had ever seen him, as if he really wanted to tear Rick apart.

'You miserable –'

'Really, Kurt, I swear.'

'What did you think you were doing? I thought you were a friend.'

'She called *me* –' Rick insisted. 'She said she wanted to talk to me about the wedding. About minor details. We had a few drinks while we were talking, and it came out that the two of you were having a little bit of trouble...'

Jesus. Tiffany couldn't believe her ears. He was going to blame her for this. Or him for this. Or whatever. She'd always thought Rick was somewhat shallow. He sold expensive cars for a living, and that seemed like a soulless thing to do. But she'd done her best to withhold judgment. At least, she had until now. 'Get the fuck out of there.'

Rick wouldn't move. He seemed to understand that if he came out of the stall, he was going to be pulverized. He'd never been good in fights, although he had a mouth on him that tended to get him into trouble. But he'd always paid attention to his surroundings, rarely mouthing off unless he had plenty of back-up around. Back-up that occasionally included Kurt. Now, he had no one. Rick prayed that someone else would enter the restroom. Someone who might intervene.

'I said get out.'

'Really, dude. Really. She was all over me.'

Tiffany almost laughed. She tried to see it in her head. Kurt kissing Rick without vomiting. No way. Rick seemed to take her silence for a desire to hear more. He kept talking, swiftly, practically tripping over himself to denigrate Tiffany.

'She opened the door fresh from the shower. Only in a towel. I don't know what she told you, man. But she was the one. She started it all. She said she'd had a thing for me since I first took out Melissa. Said she was the one who wanted to be married. I guess that's what you all fought about, right? When you were going to get married.'

Tiffany leaned against one of the cold, porcelain sinks. What did Rick honestly think was going to happen now? That after lying about Tiffany, Kurt would nod his head and say, 'Oh, well, thanks for pointing out that she was a tramp.' Then would they go get a beer? Was this how guys operated for real?

'Get out of there.'

Rick moved slowly, as if attempting to take up the tiniest space possible. He slid his back against the stall and then out into a corner of the small bathroom. Tiffany eyed him, making a plan as she did. 'So Tiff was all over you?'

Rick nodded emphatically. He looked relieved to see Kurt buying his story.

'Like this?' Tiffany took a step closer and Rick's eyes widened. When Tiffany reached out and stroked Rick's face, the man whimpered.

'What are you doing?'

'Was she on you like this?' Tiffany pulled Rick into an embrace and kissed him forcefully. Rick struggled to get free, but Tiffany held on tight. She started to undo Rick's belt and the man kicked out, desperate to get free, but Tiffany held him in place. Thank God for Kurt's muscles. 'Did she purr all over you, kiss your face, rub her body on yours?'

'What are you doing?' Rick asked again, his voice high-pitched and girlish. He seemed more terrified now than he had been at first sight of Kurt's imposing form in the bar.

'I'm just trying to understand what it was that Tiffany did to you.' Now, Tiffany had Rick's belt undone and his zipper opened. She reached in one hand and grasped onto his limp dick. 'Did she blow you, Rick? Or just jack you off?'

'Hey, man. Stop it. Don't do that.' Rick was shaking. He didn't seem to want to believe this was happening. And yet from the terror in his eyes, Tiffany could tell that he knew Kurt meant what he said.

'Did you choke her on your salami like you did with that stripper?'

'Really, Kurt –'

'Turn around.'

'Kurt, come on. You know I don't swing like that.' He was trying desperately to make a joke of the situation.

'*Turn around.*' Tiffany could feel the power in her voice. Could feel the fear rising off of Rick. Christ, she could smell his fear, a putrid scent. 'Tell me what she said to get you to fuck her.'

'I didn't fuck her. Really, God, Kurt. I wouldn't do that to her. To you. I didn't fuck her at all. We just kissed a little.'

'Oh, kissing. That's it, huh?' Tiffany switched positions so that she could kiss Rick again, powerfully, then bit his bottom lip hard. Rick looked as if he might pass out. What a fucking weenie. 'Did you touch her breasts? Did you cop a feel?'

'I don't know. I might have. When she was pressed against me.' He still wouldn't let up on this. Why didn't he realize that the more he blamed Tiffany, the more outraged she got?

'In her towel. Right? You said she only had on a towel.' As Tiffany spoke, she pulled Rick's pants down to his ankles. What had Melissa ever seen in this pig? Fine, he was handsome. But handsome only took you so far in life.

'Turn around,' she said again. 'And take down your boxers.'

'Oh, my God,' Rick moaned, 'come on, man. Don't be like this. We're friends.'

'Close friends,' Kurt reminded him. 'I was going to be your best man. You don't get much closer than that, do you? But you can. You really can. You and I are going to be much, much closer than you've ever wished before.'

'And then what happened?' Melissa wanted to know.

'I fucked him,' Tiffany said simply, doing her best to keep a straight face.

'You didn't!'

'No,' Tiffany laughed. 'Course I didn't. The guy's an a-hole. I don't do a-holes.'

'But he thought you were going to?'

'He confessed. That's all I really wanted. He told me that he was the one who came on to Tiffany –' She looked at Melissa. 'He apologized until he was nearly hoarse, telling me that he was the one who pushed himself on her. That he even got a little forceful, but that he was sorry.'

'It really is so weird to hear you talk about "Tiffany", as if you're not really her.'

'I know. But you know what I mean. It wasn't me at the time, was it? Rick pushed himself on Kurt. He's lucky Kurt let him off as easy as he did, you know it?'

Melissa nodded.

Tiffany continued, 'As soon as those boxers were down, he started talking faster than I've ever heard anyone. *He* was the one who did all the flirting, all the pressuring. And he apologized tearfully to me for it. Next, he's going to apologize to Kurt, and if he doesn't –' Tiffany slammed her fist into her palm, '– well, we'll see how it goes.'

Chapter Twenty-three

The Chili Peppers was one of those bands that Tiffany went on and on about and Kurt never listened to. At least, not if he could help it. If he was at Tiffany's and he had no choice, then he merely tolerated them, zoning out the sound by simply not paying attention. This was something that he was good at. He didn't hear a whole variety of bands: The Peppers, Jane's Addiction, Jesus and the Mary Chain, The Smiths, NIN, all bands Tiffany had liked in high school, when Kurt was almost out of college and listening to other, more mature music, he liked to think.

But the Peppers were in the CD player, and it wouldn't hurt to play Tiffany's music while he was here. What if the neighbors noticed a change in her tastes? What if a friend stopped by and he was playing someone Tiffany couldn't stand?

He had heard a few cuts off the album: 'Californication' and 'The Other Side'. When 'Purple Stain' came on, he played it again, a dull fear spreading through his body. Why hadn't he considered this before? Because his mind was on other issues, he supposed. Because something like this had never come up previously in his life. He had her on the cell phone before the song reached the ending a second time.

'When are you due?'

'Due?' She was confused, he could tell.

'Due,' he insisted. 'When are you going to get –' Oh, fuck him, he didn't even want to say it. 'When's your period due, Tiff?'

She laughed out loud. The thought of him dealing with that particularly personal issue had definitely tweaked him. Tiffany knew that he had a difficult time simply buying 'ladies' products' for her at the grocery store when she asked.

'Don't laugh. Just tell me.'

'You don't have anything to worry about.'

'Yes, I do. I don't want to go through that, Tiffany!'

'You won't. I'm on a new birth control. I only get my period four times a year. Hopefully, we'll have this all sorted out long before then.'

'Why didn't you tell me –'

'I did,' she said, and now her voice had grown cooler. 'I guess you weren't paying attention.'

He tried to feel bad about that, because she was right. Sometimes he went away in his head when she was talking, missing out on important soundbites. Often, he was imagining photographs that he wanted to take, or visualizing pictures that he already had. But right now he was too relieved to feel bad. Thank God. That was one aspect of being a woman that he had no desire to experience. He sunk into the sofa, wiped out by the sudden panic and resolution.

'Where are you anyway?' he asked.

'Where do you think?'

He looked at the clock. 'Not at the office?'

'Yeah, I'm brushing up on a few things. There's that presentation –'

A new worry began to build within Kurt. 'But we worked that all out, right? You know what we're doing?'

'Sure, I know. But I always get nervous before a big presentation –'

Kurt knew this was true. Often Tiffany had to present her company to prospective clients. But this was different. He had programmed his laptop with a simple PowerPoint presentation. All Tiffany really had to do was press a button. He didn't think she would have a problem with that. He hoped not.

Tiffany could tell that she had charmed these new clients. She'd complimented the woman in a subtle manner, had managed to actually talk about the Giants without embarrassing herself with the man. Now, as she did her infamous picking up the check trick, she beamed at her reflection in the mirror behind the bar. This was something she'd learned back in college from a rich friend's mother. The woman had excused herself from the table, on the pretense of freshening up. She'd returned fairly quickly, and the party had sat around, finishing their deserts, drinking their coffee.

Ultimately, someone had asked for the check, only to be told that 'it had been taken care of'.

How? They all looked around, shocked. Caroline's mother had a wicked grin on her face, and Tiffany had understood then what true class was. There was no haggling, no dividing, no penny pinching on a college budget. This woman had paid for them all. Now, Tiffany employed the same trick. Clearly, her company was supposed to pay in a situation like this, but she enjoyed the benefit of having everything done surreptitiously. No need to see her figure out the tip. No need for any mucking about at all. She couldn't wait to tell Kurt how smoothly the whole thing had gone.

But when she got back to the office, she found that she had even more news to share.

'We've been hoping for something big like this for months now,' Kurt's boss said with a huge smile on her face. 'A big client like this could help the bureau in untold ways –' She spread her hands magnanimously. 'Well, you know what it means, Kurt. And it's why I feel so good about giving you this raise.'

Tiffany would have liked to have jumped or squealed or done something very Tiffany-esque at the moment. Or acted like one of the contestants on *The Price Is Right*. Instead, she shook Carly's hand warmly and thanked her.

'You know, there's something different about you, Kurt,' Carly said after a moment. 'And it's not just the beard, or the fact that you're on time. You seem much more driven lately. Much more focused.'

Tiffany took the compliment in her stride.

'I like this new you,' Carly continued, giving a definitive nod before leaving Kurt's office. Tiffany's fingers fumbled as she tried to get Kurt on the phone to tell him the awesome news. It took her three tries before she'd punched in the correct numbers.

'I got a raise!' she squealed.

'You what?'

'I got a raise!' She couldn't believe it when he responded by telling her to go fuck herself. 'What did you say?'

He repeated the expletive.

'Kurt, why are you acting like that? It's the raise. The one you've been dreaming about –'

She realized suddenly that she was talking to a dead line.
Tiffany didn't understand. She called Melissa in tears.

'Why is he so upset? I just got him the raise he's wanted for the past two years.'

'Clearly, that's why he's so upset, Tiffany.'

'I don't understand.'

'*You* got him the raise. You've been in his body for two weeks, right? He's been working his tail off for two fucking years.'

'Jesus, you sound just like him.'

'Put yourself in his shoes, Tiffany.'

'I AM in his shoes!' She glared down at the Engineer Boots she'd bought for Kurt. They were amazing shoes, if she did say so herself. They added an edge to every outfit, from jeans to a suit. She didn't know why Kurt wasn't more into fashion. There were so many cool things about being a guy – and these kick-ass black boots were one of them.

'Don't yell at me, Tiffany,' Melissa retorted. 'I'm not the one who told you to go fuck yourself.'

'I'm *in* his shoes,' she repeated, softer. 'And his navy-blue polka-dot silk boxers, and his gaberdine slacks, and his crisp white shirt, and his tie –'

'Tiffany, stop it. This isn't helping anything.'

'I'm in his life, Melissa. I thought I was doing a damn good job at it. At least, I did until now.'

There was a silence on the other end of the line. Then finally Melissa spoke. 'Perhaps you were doing too good a job.'

'What the hell is that supposed to mean?'

'Well, you know how you can get, Tiff. Like you're some kind of superhero. Superwoman, or in this case, Superman. You take over. Every event. Every task. If there's something that needs to be done, get Tiffany. She'll stay up all night putting the right colored candy almonds into little lace bags. She'll pull out the offending color of MnMs. She'll pluck a whole bushel of rose petals off to scatter on a newlyweds' mattress.'

Tiffany sat down heavily in Kurt's desk chair and put her feet up on the new leather desk blotter she'd bought for him. Her heel scuffed the leather, and she found that she didn't care.

'I'm right, Tiffany, and you know I am.'

'So I'm an over-achiever –'

'You're a bit more than that.'

Tiffany sighed. 'I don't know what to do. I thought I was doing everything to make this situation bearable. I cleaned up his act at work, got him on the road to being a non-smoker, dealt with his disaster of an apartment, organized his bills, landed the big deal.'

'How'd you land it?'

'Well, Kurt gave me all the information I needed, and then I did a PowerPoint presentation –'

'You learned PowerPoint?'

'No, he set it up on the computer for me.' She winced as she spoke, realization setting in. 'Actually, all I really had to do was press a button.'

'And you honestly don't know why he's upset?'

Tiffany was silent. She was starting to see where Kurt was coming from. After two years of toiling, he'd wanted to be in the office when Carly praised him. All Tiffany had really done was press a button and pay for a meal. She'd dressed him up nicely, but she always did that, advising him before big events. She loved laying out his clothes, playing with the colors in the sweaters or the ties. Of course, he was upset. He felt as if she'd sashayed in and scooped up the prizes at the end, taking credit for the hard work he'd done over the past two years. Suddenly, she felt lower than ever.

'I have to go,' she told Melissa. 'I need to call Kurt.'

'And a florist.'

'What do you mean?'

'If ever there was a time to send flowers, dozens and dozens of flowers –'

Tiffany didn't even bother saying goodbye. She simply disconnected the line, but when she dialed her own cell-phone number, the automatic recording told her that the individual she was calling was currently unavailable, and would she care to leave a message.

No, she thought, standing up. This was something she needed to do in person.

This turned out to be more difficult than she would have thought.

'He's not taking my calls,' she told Melissa over drinks.

'I know. He's really upset. He doesn't want to talk to you right now. He's afraid of what he might do.'

'How would *you* know?'

'He called me. We had dinner together.' At Tiffany's hurt expression, Melissa said, 'Look, Tiff. He's my friend, too,' and Tiffany nodded. Melissa had been the one to introduce them in the first place, warning both of them that if they ever split up she would not take sides. But was she more involved than that? Would she make a play for Kurt – turn lesbian if she had to? No, Melissa would never do something like that to Tiffany.

'So what did he say?'

'Well, it's more how he looked.'

'Crushed, right?' Oh, Tiffany could just imagine it. Kurt, wearing one of her sloppiest outfits, his hair all messy, his face totally make-up free. She hoped he hadn't run into too many people that they knew. What would people think of her when they finally were able to switch their bodies back?

Melissa shook her head. 'Not crushed, exactly.'

'Angry? Furious?' She could easily visualize this, too. Kurt, incensed, teeth clenched, pounding the table in fury. He had a temper.

'God, Tiff. I hate to be the one to tell you this.'

'Just say it.'

'He's gone sort of goth.'

'Goth?' Tiffany winced.

'Yeah, goth, kid. Tight, tight clothes. Those funky striped tights. Lace-up boots – blue patent-leather docs. Cool for a fourteen year old. A bit much for someone in her thirties.'

Tiffany hissed through her teeth. Goth? She hated that look. It was only appropriate for teenagers who listened to The Cure or The Smiths. And they were practically golden oldies now.

'He was really pleased with how he got his hair cut.'

This wasn't at all what Tiffany had expected to hear. 'You mean *my* hair!' she spluttered indignantly.

'Well, whoever's hair. Before he dyed it, he cut it and –'

Tiffany was stalled at 'cut it'. He cut her hair. A dye job was no big deal. She could fix a color she didn't like. But to actually cut her hair when she'd worked so hard to finally get it to a length that she liked. Suddenly, she realized that Melissa had said 'and'. 'And what?' Tiffany demanded, feeling as if she were standing on the edge of a high dive. Her stomach clenched, her hands were shaking.

'He's got a tattoo.'

Tiffany looked at Melissa, devastated. There were no words to describe the feelings coursing through her. How dare he? How could he treat her body like that? She didn't *want* a tattoo. She drained the glass of white wine in front of her, and then realized that she needed something more than this stupid girly drink to numb the sensations coursing through her body.

Melissa stared at her sympathetically, but Tiffany didn't want sympathy. She wanted information. 'Where?'

There was a slight hesitation, but Tiffany wouldn't let Melissa get away with silence.

'Where?' she demanded louder.

'On your – oh, I'm sorry, Tiffany. On your ass.'

'Oh, Jesus.' Tiffany shook her head, shocked. 'How did you see it?'

'He took me into the ladies' room and did a reveal. It's pretty detailed work, kiddo,' Melissa said, clearly looking for the bright side of the situation. 'I mean, you're definitely going to be impressed. Especially since you said he had a hard time managing the pain of that wax job.'

'I don't care how much it hurt! How could he do that?'

'Don't be like that,' Melissa started. 'How could you do *this*?' She spread her hands out to indicate Tiffany's whole self. She hadn't done that much to Kurt, had she? A better haircut. A nicer set of clothes. A more expensive shoe. A signature cologne. Prescription contact lenses. She swore less. She didn't smoke. She ate better. Her weight was down, as was her blood pressure. What could he possibly complain about?

'You've turned him into a female you.'

Tiffany still didn't see the problem.

'It's like you chose a gift for someone that you wanted for yourself. Kurt didn't ask for any of this. And he was a good sport at first, playing along, trying to make the best of a bad situation, but you've taken things too far.'

'I don't see what the problem is. I got his truck detailed. I started wearing the Nicorette patch . . .'

'Don't be dense, kid. He wanted to date you, Tiffany. Not *be* you.'

'I know that.'

'I don't think you do. You've made him obsolete. You can be you and you can be him. You don't need him at all. Men like to feel useful, Tiffany.'

'He *is* useful. I never said that he wasn't.'

'You've got to give Kurt a bit of Kurt back. Otherwise, he's never going to come around and you'll be stuck. I mean, I don't have any idea how this magic works, but my guess is that if you two split up, you're going to stay Kurt forever.'

Tiffany shook her head, trying to understand. She saw her reflection in the mirror over the bar and couldn't help give herself the once-over. In her opinion, she looked damn good. From the reaction of women on the street, and at work, and at Kurt's gym, she felt vindicated for the choices she'd made. 'I thought I was helping.' And then, when Melissa didn't respond, she said, 'What color?'

Melissa stared at her.

'For my hair. What color?'

'It's not so easy to describe.'

'Red? Black? Or like Blondie? Blonde with black tips?' Tiffany gazed around the bar, trying to think of other hair colors. 'Oh, like that bartender he always tips so well. The one with the noticeable highlights.'

'More like punk – black with blue and violet ribbons.'

'Oh, fuck,' Tiffany said, her head in her hands. She'd never have done that. Not even back in her experimental stage in college.

'There, that's it. That sounds like the Kurt I know!'

'Melissa, what am I going to do?'

Chapter Twenty-four

This was more like it. Kurt enjoyed the whole dress-up scenario much more now that he'd given Tiffany's look a bit of a rock 'n' roll edge. Forgoing the malls with the cookie-cutter outfits he was sick to death of, he went shopping in the Haight, heading to a store Tiffany had always claimed that strippers favored. And she'd said it as if that were a bad thing! Whenever they'd been to this region of San Francisco, Kurt had wanted to go inside. He'd felt quietly disappointed each time that Tiffany insisted on shopping at Antoinette, the high-end Victorian-esque store on the left.

'Pasties just won't pass for work,' she'd told him.

'What about play?' he'd always wanted to reply, but never dared, not interested in starting an argument. Tiffany in pasties was a look he hadn't seen before. No time like the present, he thought to himself.

The 'stripper store', as Kurt always mentally called it, was adorned above the entrance by a pair of three-dimensional stocking-clad legs. That was one of the things that Kurt had found the most alluring. Now, that he was finally inside, the place reminded Kurt of photos he'd seen of a foreign bazaar, fabrics and stockings and sequins spilling out from every display case. Simply looking around was overwhelming at first. This place was far more cramped than Star Baby Lingerie, and that store had seemed like a fantasy come true. But finally Kurt chose several pairs of multi-colored fishnets before heading to the shoe store next door on the right to buy another pair of lace-up docs. He liked this look. Always had. A female Robert Smith. A bit of the lady from Garbage. A touch Gwen Stefani. He chose black patent-leather docs and ones covered all over with tiny skulls, and then hit Wasteland and Aaardvarks for some thrift-store attire.

Tiffany always claimed he didn't know how to put a look

together properly. She hadn't said the words meanly, he conceded now, she'd simply acted as an observer. 'Why would you put that tie with that shirt?' and Kurt had felt hopelessly over his head every time.

But he knew what he liked. And it was easier, somehow, showing his creativity now that he was dressing as a woman. This was his second day of shopping the way he wanted to, and he appreciated the looks he got in these places. When a man in a leather jacket with zippers all over gave him the once-over, Kurt couldn't help but wink back at him. Yes, he looked good, and he knew it.

Yet when he walked back to Tiffany's noticeable car, he grimaced. He hated this car. Why she'd insisted on having the fluorescent-pink paint job was seriously beyond him. Every time he climbed inside it, he felt as if he were entering a little candy heart. Maybe that was the point. The fact that she kept fresh flowers in the little vase on the dashboard was simply too cute even to comment on. The blooms had died, but he hadn't replaced him. The curled fallen petals on the dash suited his mood.

He decided he needed to change his mode of transportation. And fast. He understood that she couldn't be seen as him in this car, so there was no question about doing a switch. He'd made too much of a stink to all of their friends that he'd rather be dead than caught driving it. Did any of that really matter now? Staring at the thing parked by the curb made him want to actually key it down the side. But it wasn't the car he was mad at, was it? No.

God, he was pissed at Tiffany. Every time he thought about Carly walking into his office and promoting Tiffany instead of him he wanted to punch something. In fact, he'd taken Tiffany's body out earlier in the day for a killer workout. Not at her favorite gym, with her sweetheart Rolf, but at his, signing her up for a trial membership, kicking ass in the boxing ring against some dyke who thought she was going to wail on him. Not so fast, sweetheart, he'd wanted to tell her. Just 'cause I look pretty in pink doesn't mean I'm a pushover.

He shivered all over, thinking of the pleasure he had during the fist-to-fist combat.

But this shopping spree had worked to take the edge off

a bit further. His next stop was the drugstore. He wanted to get a few white Hanes undershirts. There was a wet T-shirt contest at one of the local bars, and he had every intention of winning.

'Where are we going?'
  'You'll see.'
  'You hate bars in this area. You always say they're for the Yuppy crowd.'
  'Forget about that, Tiffany.' Melissa seemed to have regained a bit of her joie de vivre now that Tiffany and Kurt were on the outs. She was acting as if she'd gotten two girlfriends now, shopping and doing girly things with Kurt, hanging out boys-style with Tiffany.
  In one respect, Tiffany was happy to see Melissa rebounding so well. But on the other hand, her friend's gleeful reports as to what Kurt was doing to her body seemed a bit heavy-handed.
  'I don't even feel like going out.' This was true. Although she'd been forced to celebrate the night of her promotion with her coworkers, she hadn't gone out even once since then.
  'You have to see this.'
  They'd reached the bar. Melissa showed her ID and Tiffany followed suit.
  'You don't look anything like your picture,' Melissa said, glancing over Tiffany's arm at Kurt's California driver's license. Kurt's hair was longer in the photo, he was clean shaven, and he had on a brightly colored Hawaiian-print shirt.
  'He thought it would be cool to look so tropical,' Tiffany explained. 'Then every time he flashed his license, he'd think about being on vacation. If he could have, he would have worn his favorite pair of shades.'
  'What did you do about the glasses?'
  'I couldn't get used to having to keep track of them. So I got contacts. They were easy after the first few tries.'
  Melissa eyed Tiffany's current get-up. 'Even without the glasses, you look much more conservative than the old Kurt.'
  Tiffany shrugged. 'So I like a guy in a suit. Sue me.'

'That's what Kurt wanted to do.'

'What?'

'Sue you. He actually brought that up over brunch –'

Tiffany held up a hand. 'Kurt hates brunch.'

'Yeah, well, he's more into it now. He didn't realize you could have a Bloody Mary. He thought it was all bellinis, mimosas, that sort of girly thing. Anyway, it would have been the first lawsuit like that of its kind.' Melissa said this with relish. 'You're damn lucky I talked him out of it.'

'Oh, my God,' Tiffany couldn't believe what she was hearing. She was so focused on what Melissa was saying, that she didn't immediately take in the décor of the bar. But when they'd found seats at a round table near the stage, she suddenly noticed the sign overhead. 'Amateur night. This isn't some Karaoke contest, is it? I despise Karaoke.'

As she spoke, a college-aged MC took the stage. 'Hey, out there. You guys are in for one hell of a treat tonight. The sign may say "amateurs", but from what I've seen backstage, these girls are pure pros. Pros at looking hot, that is.'

Tiffany glanced around. The bar seemed to be filled almost exclusively with men. When their buxom blonde waitress came by to take their orders, she bent toward Melissa and said, 'Why aren't you up there, hon? You've got a beautiful figure.'

'What's she talking about?' Tiffany asked, as the first pretty girl walked on stage. *Oh, holy shit*, she thought in a very Kurt-like manner. 'You're not thinking of doing that, are you? That's not why we're here, is it?' She couldn't believe that Melissa would want to get up on stage. Was that how she planned to get over Rick? The first girl out was wearing a totally sheer white T-shirt that grew even more sheer as an attractive female helper doused her with a bottle of water. Was Melissa going through some sort of exhibitionist phase now that Rick was out of the picture? If so, Tiffany was going to do everything in her power to talk her friend out of joining the competition.

'Are you kidding me? This dress cost more than the grand prize.' Melissa looked indignant.

'Then why in God's name are we here?'

A redhead was up next. She had one of those power-water guns which she handed to the MC with a flirtatious wink. He took delight in spraying her down, and the crowd roared their approval.

'You'll see,' Melissa said mysteriously as a hot chick in a V-neck T-shirt strode onto the stage.

'What makes women do stuff like that?' Tiffany wondered aloud as she stared at the new contestant. The girl was wearing magenta high heels and as she poured a bottle of water over her head, the hot pink thong beneath her T-shirt became instantly visible. Her breasts were beautiful. They were perky.

They were Tiffany's.

'Fuck me,' Tiffany murmured, feeling dazed. Kurt had cut her hair shoulder-length. The blackness of it was startling against her pale skin, but the ribbons of color added an unexpected spice. If she hadn't been staring at a version of herself, Tiffany would have understood that the contestant on stage was the prettiest one they'd seen yet. But she couldn't get over the fact that the body beneath the lights was her own, and that Kurt had definitely been practicing at walking in heels. He pivoted with style.

'Why is he doing this?' Tiffany asked under her breath as Kurt pirouetted on stage, and then exited to the right. He had the moves down.

'Because he can,' Melissa replied. 'And because you never would.'

'Why would any woman want to?'

'I don't know.' Melissa sighed. 'For fun? You've heard of fun, Tiffany, haven't you?'

'I know how to have fun,' Tiffany snorted. 'I'm plenty of fun.'

Melissa said nothing. But while Tiffany watched, shell-shocked, Melissa stood and went to speak to the MC. He nodded and motioned her back stage. Tiffany couldn't believe what was going on.

Tiffany wanted to leave. She even started to stand up. But the waitress arrived at that moment with their drinks, saying, 'Oh, good. I'm so glad your girlfriend's joining in. The winner gets five hundred dollars, you know. And usually the contestants are all ringers. They come from the clubs around the block. I love it when we have true amateurs up there.'

Horrified, Tiffany watched her friend take the stage in a borrowed T-shirt with the name of the bar imprinted over her clearly bare breasts. Melissa was nervous, and it showed. Tiffany cheered her on, though, loyalty winning out over mortification. Who knew her friend had this sort of exhibitionist streak running through her? Who knew her boyfriend had one of his own?

When Melissa was crowned second runner-up, Tiffany bought her a bottle of champagne. Melissa seemed giddy with delight at what she'd just accomplished.

'You wouldn't believe it,' she told Tiffany. 'I mean, to have everyone watching like that.'

Tiffany smiled, trying to understand. Is that why Kurt had done it? Or was he punishing her for being so uptight? She couldn't figure it out. Without him talking to her, she was forced to work out all the problems on her own. She waited, hoping that Kurt might emerge from backstage and join them. But after half an hour, she had to come to terms with the fact that he wasn't interested in making up.

As the women headed to Melissa's car, Tiffany held up a finger. She slid behind the vehicle and faced the brick wall at the back of the bar.

'What are you doing?'

'Peeing outside,' Tiffany said without looking over her shoulder.

The only thing that would have made the end to the evening better was if Kurt hadn't left out the side door, disappearing into the night.

Kurt was pleased with the $500. He was more pleased as he got onto his Harley Sportster, garnering an appreciative look from the bouncer in front of the club. No more little pink putt-putt car for him. Kurt had an M-1 license of his own, knew how to drive a motorcycle, and with Tiffany's figure decked out in leather, felt as if he could seriously conquer the world. Although he knew that if he were pulled over, he'd get a ticket. Tiffany didn't have the required license to operate motorcycles. He'd have to make a DMV appointment.

He wasn't entirely sure what was next on his plans. All he knew was that taking charge had made him feel better than he had since the change had first taken place. He had a camera in his bag and was considering heading out to the Golden Gate Bridge to take some shots of the bridge at night. Just because he was a woman didn't mean he'd lost his eye.

Chapter Twenty-five

When her cell phone rang, Tiffany reached for it hopefully. Maybe Kurt was ready to talk. Instead, she saw a number on the LED screen that she didn't recognize. Thinking it might be a client, she answered, even though she had no desire to enter work mode.

'Mr Fielding?'

'Speaking.'

'Hi there, this is Trish down at the Delia's Costumes. The item you ordered is in.'

Costumes? This was December, not October. What was a costume shop calling Kurt for?

'Thanks,' Tiffany said quickly. 'Can you remind me of your address?'

Trish gave Tiffany all the details, and Tiffany shook her head, thinking, You never really knew anyone. Not truly. What was Kurt renting? Something secret, as he'd not let her in on the plan. She didn't want to call him again – he still wasn't talking to her – so she headed down to the store.

'And what was it?' Melissa asked, curious.

'You have to guess.'

Melissa shook her head. 'It couldn't have been too bad, because you don't sound mad.'

She wasn't mad. She was touched. 'Just one guess.'

'Give me a hint.'

'It's bright red.'

'Something sexy for you –'

'That I'd have to return?' The thought revolted her. 'No, it's a Santa suit.'

Melissa laughed. 'Who would ever have thought?'

'What do you mean?' Sometimes Tiffany couldn't figure Melissa out. Even after all these years as being friends.

'It's just that there's a fetish I'd never have pegged on Kurt.'

'Fetish –' Melissa clearly believed she understood something that Tiffany didn't.

'Come on, kid. He wants to dress as Santa and have you confess all your naughty little misdeeds. I would have believed him to be much more into "coach and cheerleader" or "doctor and nurse". I mean, at least from the occasional stories you've shared with me.'

Tiffany flushed. Perhaps there was such a thing as too much information. Even between best friends. 'He puts on the suit and wears it at the children's hospital,' she explained before Melissa could embarrass her any further. 'He really never told you about it?'

There was silence, and then Melissa said plainly, 'You're kidding me.'

'I'm not. Apparently, he's played Santa there for the past three years. Delia's donates the fee for the costume as part of the charity. The woman there practically had her panties off for me in total admiration of my humble act of goodness.'

Melissa was quiet, and Tiffany realized that for once she'd shocked her buddy. 'I'd never have guessed. Why don't you think he told you? Or me, for that matter. Or anyone.'

'Because it's not something he needed to share.'

'So what are you going to do?'

'What do you think?' Tiffany asked her quietly. 'I'm going to find a soft, round pillow for my belly and go play Santa.'

When Tiffany had finished performing for the children, she found herself filled with conflicting emotions. She walked slowly to Kurt's truck, holding the red felt Santa hat in one hand, the empty sack in the other. Upon her arrival, the hospital had filled the sack with a multitude of donated presents, and all Tiffany'd had to do was hold each child in her lap and hand out a gift. But there had been more to it than that. She tried to remember what Kurt said he was doing right before Christmas during the previous years. They didn't live together. There were plenty of times they didn't see each other. But why hadn't he ever clued her into this side of him? She would have been thrilled to help – to wrap the presents, to pick up his suit, to organize a milk and cookie table.

Maybe he was tired of her running the show every time. Melissa had hinted at that. More than hinted.

She climbed into the truck, still trying to sort out her feelings toward Kurt. She loved him, because he did things like this. And the more she thought about him, the more she realized how many things like this that he did do.

She'd seen him pay the toll for the people in the car behind them on the bridge, total strangers, hoping to lift someone's spirits for the day. She'd seen him put change in parking meters that had expired, saving someone from getting a ticket. He never did these deeds with any sort of fanfare – never called attention to himself.

Feeling tearful, she dialed him up, but he still wouldn't take her call. There was the sound of her own voice, reverberating in her head. 'Hey, this is Tiff. I'm out and about. Leave it at the beep.'

God, she'd never leave a message like that on her cell phone. And what was the music playing in the background? She tried to place it: Southern Culture on the Skids. That was it. She winced, thinking of her friends calling and hearing 'Dirt Track Date' rather than something more appropriate, or more festive. And just as quickly, she was back to hating him.

Look what he was putting her through!

He'd trashed her wardrobe, appeared nearly naked in public, and had been spotted by several of their mutual friends astride his Harley, something that Tiffany had told many people she'd never be caught dead doing. Just think how dangerous it was! He'd left her to her own devices at work, where she still scrambled each day to make sure nobody caught on to how clueless she was.

She was driving through traffic now, although she didn't have any idea where she was going. Tears sparkled in her eyes as she glanced at the holiday decorations on many of the buildings. She and Kurt generally walked through their neighborhoods together during the season, commenting on their favorite displays of holiday spirit. The twinkling lights blurred before her eyes, and she pulled over to the curb, worried she might get into an accident.

She loved him. She hated him. She loved him. Just like that fucking flower back in New Orleans.

He was obviously a softy at heart. The nurses at the hospital had thanked her profusely for her continued generosity, and some of the older kids – the ones who realized that there was an imposter behind the beard, but not an imposter in the suit – seemed to know Kurt on a personal level, which meant that he visited more than once a year, didn't it?

Tiffany, seated in the front seat of Kurt's truck, looked around. The cab of the vehicle remained immaculate and smelled fresh and clean. But so fucking what? She'd spent several years wanting to change Kurt.

Was *she* the one who truly needed to change?

Chapter Twenty-six

'I don't know if this is such a good idea, Tiffany,' Melissa said, gazing at the array of interesting paraphernalia spread out before her on the glass coffee table. She noted silently that the table had been Windexed to within inches of its life. She'd never seen Kurt's apartment so clean, his belongings so pristine. It was like walking into a furniture showroom. No, that wasn't right. It was like walking into Tiffany's apartment.

Of course, Melissa had been in Tiffany's apartment lately, visiting Kurt, and the place looked as if it had been through a tornado. Kurt had returned to his standard style of living. Shoes were everywhere, stockings strewn about, magazines opened on all the counter tops. As a woman, Kurt was even messier than he'd been as a man. He had more items to spread around – cosmetics, jewelry, purses.

'Look,' Tiffany explained, 'I've never done it before.'

'Yeah, and that's your only reason? You've never had unsafe sex with a rodeo cowboy, either, but I don't see you rushing out to the circus. You've never eaten the delicious yet deadly puffer fish. You've never dived out of an airplane, although I think Kurt might be planning on trying that –'

Tiffany held up one hand. She didn't want to hear about her boyfriend's plans. 'Apparently, Kurt found the stuff very pleasurable. I'm ready to learn to relax a little. You all seem to think that kicking back is something I'm not so good at.'

'So this is how you're going to unwind? You're going to get high?'

'I'm going to try.'

'It's not like brain surgery or anything.' Melissa laughed as Tiffany tried to light the joint without inhaling. 'But you are going to have to breathe in if you want that thing to stay lit.'

Tiffany worked a little harder. The purple lighter shook

slightly in her hand. This was something she'd refused to do for so long. Not that Kurt had ever pressured her into trying. He'd simply offered her a hit every once in a while, on the rare occasions when he chose to get stoned in front of her. And it wasn't as if he were a major pot head. He smoked marijuana the way some people – like Tiffany's friends – drank champagne, as a once-in-a-while celebratory event.

'You game?' Tiffany asked, her hand still shaking.

'Give me that,' Melissa snorted. 'You're hopeless.'

She lifted the joint from Tiffany's fingers and expertly lit the thing. Tiffany was amazed as Melissa inhaled deeply, and with obvious pleasure, then held the smoke for several seconds. In a graceful motion, Melissa tilted her head back and exhaled gently. The fragrant smoke filled the air. Melissa settled back into the sofa cushions, a pleased look on her face, her cheeks flushed and eyes gleaming. Tiffany had no idea that her friend was such an expert, but before she could query Melissa about this, it was Tiffany's turn to try.

With the image of Melissa in her mind, she tried to mimic what she'd seen her best friend do, but she wound up coughing so hard she thought she was going to pass out. Her face turned red and her eyes stung. So far, she was less than impressed with the wonders of marijuana. And here was a prime example of Kurt's body not helping her. She would have thought there was some imprinted memory on how to do this sort of thing. Like riding a bicycle.

Melissa started giggling. 'You really *are* hopeless,' she said, taking another hit, then leaning forward and attempting to press her mouth to Tiffany's.

'Hey –' Tiffany backed away.

'Let me help.' Melissa grinned at her, clearly enjoying the situation. 'You'll have less trouble this way.' Tiffany struggled within herself for a moment, and then gave in. Melissa exhaled the fragrant smoke between her lips and Tiffany felt as if she could actually see the smoke entering her body. In her mind, the pot was colored, a deep blue smoke that swirled throughout her lungs in intricate designs. She shut her eyes, trying to place the sensation, but failing. She'd never gotten so much as a contact high before. Now, she waited for the effect of the drug to take place. Was she expecting too much? She still felt like herself.

'You didn't smoke enough,' Melissa insisted. 'If you really want to get stoned, you have to make more of an effort.' When Melissa handed her the joint a second time, Tiffany found that inhaling was much easier. She understood now. Ah, here was the memory imprint that she had been expecting. Kurt's body rose to the challenge, holding in the smoke and keeping it in. She exhaled, took another hit. Then another.

'Slow down,' Melissa said. 'It's like drinking for the first time. You have to pace yourself. Remember that time you had five beers in an hour?'

'You're not supposed to talk about that – I was nineteen. We had a pact.'

'Yeah, well, don't do that again.'

Tiffany lay back on the sofa, breathing deeply.

'You like it?' Melissa asked curiously.

She didn't know. She felt tired, but not as if she wanted to go to sleep. Her limbs were heavy. Her head was heavy. Melissa watched her apprehensively. 'You okay?'

'I feel different,' Tiffany said, trying to find the right word. But after several seconds of searching her brain for it, she took another hit instead.

'You're supposed to feel different,' Melissa said after what felt like a long silence. 'You're supposed to feel stoned,' and now she started to giggle again. 'Or maybe that's how I'm supposed to feel. And I'm doing a damn good job at it, I have to say.'

'What's the best thing to do when you're stoned?'

'Eat.'

'Naw, I don't want to eat.'

'Really, you will. You'll want to eat all sorts of fun things. Like Mother's brand cookies. Those iced animal ones. Or Cheeze Whiz right out of a can.'

'I'd never eat that sort of thing.'

'You'd never have thought you'd have a cock, either, would you?'

Tiffany laughed. Suddenly, everything was funny. The thought of eating Cheeze Whiz. The fact that she had a cock. She laughed harder, and Melissa started to laugh with her. So *this* was why Kurt liked weed so much. Laughing felt unbelievable. As good as working out. As good as sex. She sprawled out on the sofa and just let her body shake with the laughter. When she finally recovered, she looked over at her friend. 'I know what I've got to do,' she told Melissa.

'Eat raw cookie dough until you get sick?'

Tiffany shook her head. 'I've got to show Kurt that I understand him. That I don't want to fix him.'

Melissa grinned at her. 'You've already fixed him, Tiffany. You got him fucking spayed.'

'I mean, that surface things don't matter. That what I love about him is what's on the inside.'

'Fine,' Melissa nodded. 'But first you have to get him to talk to you again.'

Tiffany shook her head. 'No, first I have to try Cheeze Whiz out of a can,' and both girls – or girl and boy – collapsed into giggles again.

'So what would you do if you were me?'

'What do you mean?' Tiffany asked. She was settled down deep in Kurt's leather sofa, enjoying the hazy way her brain felt. 'What would I do about Rick?'

'No, I know you think I did the right thing. I mean, if you'd switched bodies with me instead of with Kurt. How would you fix me?'

'There's nothing wrong with you.'

'Spoken like a true best friend,' Melissa told her. 'But I'm serious. If you were in my body, how would you live my life differently?'

'Don't get me started, Melissa. I've learned my lesson. I don't need any more trouble.' Tiffany put her head in her hands.

'You've been doing a kick-ass job until recently,' Melissa said. 'Seriously. Most people would have cracked if they'd found themselves in this situation. But not you. You've taken the task to heart and done your very best. It's why you're so good as a party planner. You're extremely focused and very well organized.'

'I have to be.'

'Well, do the once-over on me. It's not the same as wishing you were Kurt so you could fix him. I'm *asking* you for help.'

'I'm not one of the Queer Eye guys, Melissa. I don't do makeovers.'

'Sure you do. Just look at you. Carson Kressley couldn't have done nearly as well with Kurt's raw material as you have. You're so handsome now, it's almost unbearable. And you did that divine thing with Kurt's photography, bringing it to the curator in the Mission.'

'It's only a tiny little show.'

'But you did it. You took the initiative.'

'Yeah, but the photos were all Kurt's. His talent is what the lady noticed.'

'And your drive got his pictures on the walls of that gallery.'

'He doesn't even know,' Tiffany said sadly. 'He won't talk to me.'

'But I will,' Melissa said. 'So go for it.'

Tiffany looked at her friend through her fingers. 'You're serious?'

'Hit me with your best shot.'

'Lose the bob.' Tiffany said it almost before she'd decided whether or not she would do what Melissa was asking. Maybe that part of it was the marijuana. Loosening her tongue over the better judgment of her brain.

Melissa touched her hair. 'What do you mean?'

'You've worn that style since college. Very coquette, which is what you were back then. But now you're a high-powered lawyer. A *partner*, for Christsake, as of Monday. You need something a little sharper. A little more cutting edge.'

'Like?'

'Go ultra short. Razor cut it. Don't mess with the color at all, just the style. You'll look amazing, and your eyes will seem absolutely huge. They already are, of course. But they'll take up your whole face.'

Melissa leaned up on one arm and gazed into the mirror over the mantle. She was thoughtful for several moments.

Tiffany watched her thinking, and then she said, 'Now me.'

'Now you what?'

'How would you change me, if I ever get back to being me again.'

It was as if Melissa had been dying for this question. 'You need a new signature lipstick. A drop-dead red. Not the wimpy pale mauve color you always use.'

'It's my lucky color.'

'Why? Because some guy asked you out in high school while you were wearing it? L'Oréal retired that color for a reason. The fact that you've hoarded it ever since, having those specialists re-create it, ought to tell you something.'

'All right,' Tiffany said, settling herself against the pillows. 'Point taken.'

'Your turn,' Melissa said.

Now that she'd gotten started, Tiffany found that she was having a difficult time holding back. 'Okay, but you're not going to like this.'

'Go on –'

'Stop buying people so many gifts. Stop paying for lunches. Stop purchasing rounds.'

'What are you talking about?'

'You want people to like you, and they do. But when you're always the one paying, some of your friends feel as if you have to be top dog wherever we go. And when you pay, you call the shots, so you're always in charge. People will like you even if you don't pick the restaurant, and even if you don't snag the check.'

Melissa didn't say anything. The doorbell rang and she didn't move.

'Did I go too far?'

Melissa shook her head. 'No. But that's the take-out guy, and I'm going to let you pay for that.'

After Melissa left, Tiffany stumbled to Kurt's bedroom. She was full. More than full. And she felt boneless, as if she could slide all the way down the hall to his room. It wasn't such a bad idea, was it? She walked slowly, looking at the art work on the walls. Kurt was right. Sometimes if you saw something every day, you stopped paying attention to it. Now, she noticed the quality of his photographs, and she missed him.

But the fact that he hadn't insisted on moving back home was a good thing, wasn't it? If they were really breaking up for good, he would have wanted to move back, to get his stuff, to kick her out.

At least, that's what she told herself.

Chapter Twenty-seven

Even after the pot wore off, Tiffany's realization didn't fade. To win Kurt back, she had to show him that she valued him. That she appreciated him. That she loved him for who he was – whether he was himself or whether he was her. She felt sad that she'd never understood this before, that she'd never shown him this with her actions when she was in her own body.

But maybe she was being too hard on herself. Perhaps she hadn't said that she appreciated him as often as she should have, but this was no Willy Nelson song. Kurt was more than 'always on her mind'. He had to know that she loved him. That she needed him. She relied on him to be her partner at every dance. She expected him to attend every charity ball, to work the party circuit with her. And much more than that, she needed him in bed next to her, needed to see him first thing in the morning when she woke up.

Still, she wasn't sure whether or not she should go to the game. In one respect, her teammates were counting on her. They had a right to believe that she'd be there, even if they were still smarting over the vicious loss they'd suffered at the previous game. No, it hadn't all been her fault. But she had let them down nonetheless. Kurt was known for his three-point shots, and she'd choked at the moment of truth.

She'd been watching basketball religiously ever since, viewing the miles of videotape Kurt had kept of his favorite teams, and she had gone on her own early every morning to practice by herself. Kurt's body was willing to move however she told it, but the graceful quality that generally inhabited him was missing. Over and over, she'd attempted shots from the foul line, from all around the court, and from the three-point region.

She looked at Kurt's uniform and, without thinking, pressed her face into his shirt and inhaled deeply. She'd washed the uniform already, washed all of his clothes that she'd worn, so this one didn't have any scent left of Kurt. And she could just smell herself if she wanted to breathe him in, couldn't she? But there was a difference. She rifled through his shirt drawer until she found one of his favorite T-shirts. Bringing this one up to her face, she breathed in again. There. That was it. The shirt smelled divine.

Did she dare go to the game?

Melissa called Kurt on his cell phone and told him to head to the YMCA.

'I don't want to.'

'You have to go.'

'Tell me why –'

'You just have to be there.'

He tried to ignore her, but he couldn't help showing up in the end, even if he didn't go into the gym to see the actual final score. Instead, he walked around in the lobby, and when his teammates began to exit, he asked what had happened.

'Kurt was excellent, Tiff,' Axel told Kurt. 'You should have been there.'

'Yeah, where were you?' Malcolm asked curiously. 'You never miss a game, Tiffany. We always look forward to seeing you up there in the bleachers, getting confused by the plays.'

Kurt looked at them. Were they fucking with him? 'Are you serious? Did she –' He shook his head. 'Did he score?'

'Did he score?' Axel was beaming. 'Only made the winning shot. Your man deserves a celebration tonight.'

Kurt was incredulous. How had Tiffany managed to do that? And they were right. Tiffany never did miss a game. Not ever. Not even when she was in the midst of planning a giant party. She always came to the games and sat, cheering, in the front row.

'What's up with you two, anyway?' Axel asked. 'Rick mentioned something about the two of you splitting. It's not catching, is it? Like a break-up bug or something.'

Kurt shrugged. He wasn't willing to go into those sorts of details with Axel.

'Well, you look great,' Mike told him, nodding approvingly at the short skirt Kurt had on. 'Very classy.'

Kurt's mind raced. Was Mike coming on to him? Did all of his friends secretly – or not so secretly in the case of Rick – want to fuck Tiffany? He sighed. No, that wasn't the truth. When he complimented one of Tiffany's friends, it was never with ulterior motives. And he knew that she hadn't had ulterior motives when she got his raise. She hadn't done it to piss him off. Of course, she hadn't. She was only trying to help. Only being Tiffany. That's what Melissa had told him.

He had to trust her.

He had to.

Chapter Twenty-eight

Melissa, radiant in her multi-hued gown, stood on the top of the stairs looking down at her best friends in the world. At the bottom, her bridesmaids, who had equally punked out their dresses in a medley of different manners – splashes of dye, torn hems, safety pins holding the seams together – waited impatiently. There was friendly jostling amongst them until Eleanor said, 'Really, now, does anyone even want to get married after what Melissa's gone through?'

'What a shmuck he was,' one of the girls whispered.

'Come on.' Jocelyn nudged her. 'That's not what this is about. It's all in good fun. A tradition even when traditions have been stomped on.'

That put a pause in the chaos, and at precisely that moment, Melissa tossed the flowers. Kurt hadn't been paying attention to the gaggle of girls, but he effortlessly caught the bouquet anyway.

'Oooh, Tiffany,' one of the maids shrieked. 'It'll be you next.'

Kurt gave her a sideways look. 'Me what?'

'You to get married.'

Kurt dropped the flowers as if they were on fire. 'Even if I caught the break-up bouquet?'

'That's not what it was. Those flowers still have magic to them.'

Kurt wondered whether this was true. He knew a thing or two more about magic than these girls did. But he kept quiet and went off in search of Tiffany. He wanted to find her before she took Melissa's garter off.

Tiffany looked at Kurt. She couldn't believe that he'd gotten dressed like this for her. Because from the first glance at his attire, she knew that it was all for her. The goth look had completely disappeared, and Kurt's stance made it look as if he'd never worn a pair of torn fishnets or patent-leather docs in his life.

He was clad in a perfect black velvet dress. *The* perfect black dress. The hem hit in classic form just above the knee and pinched in smoothly at the waist. The velvet bodice showed just enough cleavage to be sexy without slutty. Kurt had chosen a pair of high-heeled orchid pumps that Tiffany had never seen before. They weren't her shoes, and they weren't something borrowed from Melissa. She'd recognize heels like that.

Kurt had brought her hair back to its normal shade. He'd done good. The question was: would he even talk to her? Or was he only here to support Melissa? After all, she was his friend, too.

When Kurt took his place at her side, Tiffany felt her body stiffen.

Was he going to tell her off? Was he still as angry at her as he had been?

She drew in a breath and smelled the scent of her favorite perfume – Coco Chanel. He didn't have on Poison anymore, and there wasn't even the faintest whiff of cigarette smoke. Tiffany turned her head to drink in every part of the look close up. Kurt had bought new earrings. Chandelier types, they sparkled against Tiffany's platinum hair. His make-up was immaculate. Tiffany was unbelievably impressed.

'Hey,' she said, her voice constrained.

'Hey,' Kurt said back. 'You look good.'

Tiffany would have flushed, had she been a girl. Instead, in Kurt's body, she felt her chest expand. She *did* look good, and she knew it. But she was pleased that he approved. Finally, she'd gone to a barbershop for a shave, getting rid of the beard and returning Kurt to his clean-shaven self.

The tux was to die for, a classic that she felt was worth the expense. She'd spent hours choosing the right one, knowing that if Kurt had been at her side, he wouldn't have been able to tell one from another. But because this was Kurt, she'd added a bit of zest to the outfit. The cummerbund had tiny skulls and bones embroidered in white on the black silk, and she'd worn the tux with a pair of shit-kicking Doc Martens. The watch, when he got a look at it, would undoubtedly bring a smile to his face. It was a Lucien Pelat-Finet. She hadn't been able to decide at first between a grinning skull or the marijuana leaf on the face, but had ultimately chosen the pot – planning on revealing to Kurt her day of bliss with Melissa at a future date.

She could tell from the look in Kurt's eyes that he liked what he saw. She wasn't going to admit to him how much she spent on the gold-skull cufflinks, no matter how many times he asked.

'Melissa told me that you played Santa.'

Tiffany nodded.

'Thanks for that.'

'Why didn't you tell me?'

He was quiet for a minute. Then, 'I didn't tell anyone. Didn't want the guys ribbing me about it. You know how they can get. They would never have let up on me.'

'That's not true,' Tiffany said softly. 'They would have been impressed.'

'Maybe deep inside, but on the surface they'd have been pissed at me for showing them up. I'm telling you, they'd have been calling me Santa year in and year out.'

'But me?' She tried not to sound hurt. 'I wouldn't have teased you at all.'

'It wasn't about you,' he said, and she nodded, understanding. 'Why didn't *you* tell me about getting a ticket?' he asked, shooting it back at her.

She grinned. 'Didn't want you ribbing me.'

'So instead you snuck off to traffic school as if you were some truant teenager hiding a secret from her mean old Daddy. What's that about, Tiffany? Why do you always want people to think you're perfect?'

Tiffany shrugged.

'You don't have to be, you know. Not for me. God, Tiffany, you should have been able to realize that by looking around my apartment.'

'I know,' she said. 'I mean, I'm learning that.'

'You know, this place is amazing,' Kurt told her. 'The wedding would have been truly lovely, but it's terrific even for the break-up party.'

'Yeah,' she said, nodding. 'Thanks. We scoured the city before landing on this one. I probably should have spent more time listening to Melissa talk about her issues with Rick than worrying about whether or not the ice sculpture was going to be pristine and perfect.'

'You did forget one thing.'

Tiffany looked surprised. Quickly, she gazed around the room, seeing the twinkling white lights, the sparkling tower of champagne glasses, the band in their retro forties suits. Hadn't Kurt just finished telling her that she didn't have to be perfect, so how had she failed?

'You forgot this –' Kurt pulled out a tiny sprig of mistletoe from his antique beaded bag, and now Tiffany did feel her cheeks flush. In the light, she was sure nobody else noticed. On tiptoe, Kurt held the mistletoe up in the air. Even in heels, he wasn't tall enough to hold the little sprig over their heads. Tiffany grabbed the holiday cutting from him and held it high, and the two kissed. Warmth spread through Tiffany's entire body. She pulled Kurt to her and held on tight. His tongue met hers, and she felt relief wash over her. Kissing him was as good as it always had been.

When their lips parted, Kurt reached once more into his darling little purse and pulled out a small pale-blue box.

'I didn't expect things to be like this,' he said in a gruff voice. 'I mean, when I originally bought this ring for you.' He saw her eyebrows raise, and he said, 'And I *did* buy the ring before, Tiffany, you should know that. But I've never doubted this moment would happen – with you as a man or as a woman.' He shook his head. 'Christ, that sounds crazy, doesn't it?'

Tiffany put her arms around him and said, 'No, it doesn't at all.' She couldn't believe he was doing this. Here. Now. In the very midst of an 'I Don't' party. Ah, but then he *had* caught the bouquet, hadn't he?

Swiftly, Kurt handed the box over to Tiffany, and she lifted the tiny blue lid. Her heart soared when she saw the diamond inside. The ring was flawless. Exactly what she'd always dreamed of. A simple platinum band with a tasteful stone set in the center. So he *did* know her, know who she really was inside. She began to lift the ring out of the box, and then hesitated as she realized that the gem would never fit her finger. Not the way it was now. Besides that, it would look extremely girlish on her manly hand.

'I'll get you another,' Kurt promised, as he saw the sadness in her eyes. 'One for *you* to wear.'

Tiffany shook her head, her own eyes tearing up as Kurt started to go down on one knee in the classic pose. A pose that looked out of place as Kurt was in the sleek velvet dress. Generally, it wasn't the woman on bended knee, was it?

But Tiffany met him there on the floor, so that they were facing each other. She didn't care that people were looking, didn't care what people thought. With grace, she plucked the ring out of the box and placed it on Kurt's finger. As she did, she saw tears well in Kurt's own eyes. When he ducked his head, so she wouldn't catch him crying, she saw that he'd kept one cobalt streak in her hair.

He'd brought a little of Kurt to her body, she'd brought a lot of Tiffany to his. But it didn't matter to her anymore. The important thing was that they were together.

Forever.

Chapter Twenty-nine

Kurt lit candles, and the dreamy scent of vanilla filled the room. The curtains were almost completely closed, but soft light filtered in from the street lamps outside. A fire in the rarely used fireplace created warmth and sparks of red and gold shadows. Christmas decorations gleamed hypnotically on the mantle. Kurt had taken down her treasured box of family ornaments and hung them from evergreen boughs. She couldn't have done a better job herself, Tiffany thought, surprised. The glistening baubles caught the light of the fire and seemed to twinkle on their own.

Tiffany turned around and around, taking in the entire scene. The flowers on the coffee table hadn't been there before. They were her favorite flowers, a bouquet of purple hyacinths in a vase made of an old milk bottle – God, where on earth had he found these springtime blooms at this time of year? And had he actually remembered that they were her favorites, or had Melissa cued him in?

That didn't matter, Tiffany knew. Nothing like that mattered now.

Music – what had he chosen? Was it Sade? – played from the stereo, just loud enough to create a soft, background noise, but nothing too strong. For once, he wasn't playing something he felt she should like, but something that she actually did like. She looked around the room. The place was clean. Not Tiffany-spotless, perhaps, but neat. She'd heard from Melissa what the apartment had looked like. She knew what it had taken for him to put the whirlwind of chaos back in order.

As she gazed around, she saw that Kurt had rewired her stereo and saw that he'd added flat speakers in the walls. The fact that Kurt had taken the time to do all of these things made Tiffany want to cry.

No, that wasn't exactly true. It made her want to make love.

And finally, she was ready. Tiffany had gained control of this unpredictable body – See? she thought to herself – all that jerking off has come in handy!

She was going to show Kurt exactly how exquisite it could be for a girl. She was going to bring him to new heights, take him to places he'd never been before, as a man or as a woman –

'We'll start like this,' she told him, sitting down on the sofa and pulling Kurt astride her. She'd always liked to be face to face when fucking and, in this position, Kurt could lean forward and gain the contact she knew he'd need to get off. 'And then you lift up your dress in the front.' She could see the entire scene in her head, every step of the way.

'Why don't I just take the dress off?' Kurt asked, 'so the velvet won't get crushed.'

'Who cares if it gets crushed?' Tiffany asked, surprised at herself. It was an extremely un-Tiffany-like thing to say. Although Kurt would have generally voiced that opinion in a heartbeat.

'You won't believe what this cost –' Kurt started and then he began to laugh. They definitely *had* changed places. That was for sure. He was channeling the true Tiffany at this moment. 'There was a knock-off, but I wanted the real thing.'

'Just this once,' Tiffany said, 'let's skip all that. Let's just not care about what things cost or how they might rumple.'

Kurt grinned, obviously embarrassed, and did what Tiffany said. Slowly, he raised the dress and she rocked him back and forth against her, so that he could feel how hard she was. Although she had to suck in her breath and the connection between them, she had no fear that she was going to lose her concentration. She still had on the tuxedo pants, and she had no plans of disrobing just yet. Tonight was all about Kurt. Later, she'd tell him that the tux wasn't a rental. That she'd bought it, and his own personal Santa suit, and that both would hang forever in his closet.

When she saw him close his eyes, she upped the ante, slipping his pearly white panties aside. His nakedness against her clothed member took her to an even higher plane. But for the first time, she felt as if she were truly getting off on how much Kurt was enjoying the situation. She was in his body, and yet she was also somehow in her own, seeing things from Kurt's point of view, discovering new pleasures with him. This is what it meant to care about the person you were with. This was a place she'd always hoped to reach someday.

Gently, she moved him, spreading him out on the sofa. Kurt was wearing garters and stockings and she left these on, but she pulled his panties off, tossing them somewhere in the dark corners of the room. Perhaps they landed on the ottoman, or maybe on one of the barstools. She didn't give a hang.

With every motion of her body, she made sure Kurt was receiving the pleasure she knew she was capable of giving. She recalled from years of experience what it took to make her come. Now, she put those years of knowledge into practical use.

Tiffany split the fly on her pants and then turned Kurt around. She faced him so that he could see the fire, and lifted his velvet dress in the back. She noticed, almost as if from a great distance, that there was no tattoo on his rear end. Had Melissa made that up to tweak her? She shoved the thought from her mind as she entered him; she could query him about tattoos and hair dyes at a different time. Now, she strummed her fingers along his clit.

'Oh, my God!' Kurt cried out.

'Let yourself go,' Tiffany urged, her voice husky, her fingers making spirals, diamonds, intricate designs up and over, around and around. She touched him the way she'd always touched herself when she was alone. She stroked him, matching the rhythm with the thrusts of her cock inside of him. With every ounce of strength, she held back on her own pleasure, stomping down on it, refusing even to acknowledge how excited she felt.

'Oh, sweet Jesus –' Kurt moaned, tossing his head so that his hair fell forward over his eyes.

Tiffany waited. Now the plan was getting more difficult for her, because Kurt was gripping onto her, squeezing her, and with each tightening of his body on hers, her own pleasure ratcheted up another level. This is the part that had made her come each time before. When he contracted on her, she lost her head. The sounds he was making were turning her on as well. She was as hard as she'd ever been, but she did what Kurt had told her to do. She thought of baseball. She thought of tax returns. She thought of any non-sexual thing she could.

Muni buses.

Traffic stops.

Bungee-jumping.

But the magic of that trick wore off quickly. Being connected to Kurt in this way was ultimately too powerful. She hoped that he was as excited as she was, hoped that she'd given him all the time he needed, hoped that he was close as she was.

He looked over his shoulder at her with those wide eyes that she was so used to seeing in her own reflection – in the bathroom mirror, in her compact, in the windows she walked past on the way to the gym. It was disconcerting, but she tried to push through, to see Kurt behind those eyes. He was in there. She knew it.

'Kurt, I'm going to –'

But before she could finish the words, he beat her to them. 'Come, Tiffany. I'm gonna come, too –'

And they reached it together, with her thrusting in time to the rhythm of his climax, taking him through it, taking him beyond. She felt how powerful his orgasm was, and she dove off and into that sweet sea of pleasure herself, thoughts fading, melting, until the two were merged together – forgetting where one stopped and the other began.

This time, the sex was right. More than right. It was perfect.

Epilogue

'And the tattoo?' Tiffany asked, confused. 'Melissa swore to me that she actually saw it. You did a whole sexy reveal in the ladies' room for her.'

'Just a decal I bought at a party store.' He stared at her seriously. 'You don't think I'd really have done that to you, do you?'

She didn't reply. The answer wasn't as simple as 'yes' or 'no'.

'I mean, without your permission,' Kurt continued. 'Truthfully, I think you'd look awesome with a tattoo. I've said that before. Something small,' he said quickly, 'something that you like, you know.'

She tilted her head, considering. Maybe he was right –

'But I can't believe you thought I'd marked you for life without giving you a chance to offer your input. Or at least go with me to the tattoo parlor and hold my hand.'

'Well –' She was unsure of how to continue. 'I did put you through all this. I thought maybe you'd want to get back at me someway.'

'By getting a tattoo of a tiger on your ass? That's the sort of guy you think I am?'

She shrugged, helpless to explain how she felt.

'Look, Tiffany, I was upset. You can understand that, can't you? But I know that you didn't mean to make this happen. You had no intention of actually switching our bodies, did you?'

She shook her head.

'Of course, you didn't. Nobody would have expected a wish to come true in that store. If you had believed in the magic, I'm sure you would have wished for something very different.'

'Yeah, like, world peace.' She was only half-sarcastic.

'Right, if you were trying for the Miss America crown. But

247

that's not what normal people would wish for. A million dollars, or a new car, or a dream job, or three more wishes, or –' now he looked down and spoke softer, '– a dream man rather than a fixer-upper.'

'I love you,' she told him simply, cradling his face in her hands and making him look at her. 'Just you.'

'I was upset,' he told her. 'That's all. I wanted to get the promotion myself. I wanted to show you that I had it in me to be the man you've always wanted.'

'You are, Kurt.'

He beamed at her. 'And you know, you've done some neat tricks so far with my body.'

'What do you mean?'

'Kicking smoking? I've been wanting to break that habit for seven years. And you've finally put me on a real road to recovery. You didn't do that to be obnoxious or bossy, or whatever. You did it because you care about me.'

She nodded. Finally, he understood that.

'And the gallery show. That's fucking awesome. I've always wanted to have my work displayed, and I've been too chickenshit to put my pictures out there.'

'Well, I knew the lady. We've done a few parties for them in the past for openings and fundraisers. But it was your talent, you know. All I did was gather up your pictures into a neat portfolio and show them off at a few different places. It's not like I took the photos myself or anything. That was all you, Kurt.'

'But you got it done. I can't really thank you enough for all that –'

Tiffany blushed, happily embarrassed by his praise. 'But I have a few more questions for you.'

'Go ahead.'

'All of the hairstyles were wigs?' This hadn't even occurred to her during their separation. She wondered why she'd been so quick to think he would demolish her appearance. Perhaps because she'd been so willing to transform his.

'All but the last one. I wouldn't hack off your hair, Tiffany. In spite of my lack of obvious interest in your various styles, I do love your hair. But I did enjoy trying out my various fantasies – you as a redhead, as a brunette, as a sexy goth chick. Trish at the costume store was more than happy to help me out. And I kept the wigs, so you know we can play that way again.'

Now he looked at her appraisingly. 'The contacts were a good way to go. That's an interesting difference. I never really considered *not* wearing glasses.'

'Same goes for the colors,' she told him. 'I always wore black. I didn't even think of branching out into the other colors. I felt safe in wearing the same thing all the time. You showed me a whole new range of looks.'

At that moment, the Elvis impersonator who was to officiate their marriage appeared in front of them. He must have come from behind the deep purple velvet curtain at the rear of the room, but Tiffany hadn't seen him enter, hadn't seen the fabric rustle or heard him walk to the podium. It was as if he had just magically appeared.

Where had Tiffany seen curtains like that before?

Her mind worked at a startling speed. She'd spied them at the Witches' Shoppe in the New Orleans' French Quarter. Quizzically, she gazed at the officiator. He made an ideal Elvis – a perfect young Elvis, that was – with a hard body, dark pompadour, sexy sneer in place. Yet his eyes were all wrong. Deep bottle green, they seemed to shine even when the light wasn't focused on them. Tiffany felt her heart race as she and Kurt walked down the red-carpeted aisle together, hand in hand, to the tune of 'Love Me Tender'.

The ceremony was a quick one. Other customers waited impatiently out in the lobby for their turn down the aisle. But when Elvis told Kurt to kiss his 'sweet little bride', Tiffany took her time. They kissed gently, delicately, and after several seconds Kurt made as if to pull away. But Tiffany felt compelled to continue. She couldn't explain why. She simply knew somehow that she was supposed to kiss him, to meld with him.

Her heart pounding, she pulled Kurt into an embrace for a deeper, longer kiss, and as the passion beat through them, she felt something else. A strange wash of emotions. An understanding of what Kurt's heart was made of, and who he was as a man. A thankfulness and a gratefulness that he loved her.

'I won't ever –' She started when she finally moved her

lips from his. 'Ever,' she repeated, and was surprised to hear her voice – her *own* voice – sound in her head. For the first time in a month, she was speaking as a girl. She didn't have to look down to know that she was back in her own body, didn't have to touch her white lace dress, or run her fingers through her glossy shoulder-length hair to know.

'Sh –'

'I won't ever try to fix you again,' she assured him, tears streaking down her face. As she spoke, she saw the realization dawn on Kurt's face. He was himself again. He started laughing with relief, and then he lifted her into the air – lifted her, so that her feet actually left the ground. She was herself again. She was his and he was hers, and both knew this fact to be true.

In her head, she suddenly heard a soft, southern drawl: 'What do you want, hon? Money? Fame . . .?'

What did she wish for? That was simple:

Love. And she already had it.

Oh, did she ever.

And understanding this, she knew that she would never let it go.